Unwritten

By Helena Harte

2024

Butterworth Books is a different breed of publishing house. It's a home for Indies, for independent authors who take great pride in their work and produce top quality books for readers who deserve the best. Professional editing, professional cover design, professional proof reading, professional book production—you get the idea. As Individual as the Indie authors we're proud to work with, we're Butterworths and we're *different*.

Authors currently publishing with us:

E.V. Bancroft
Valden Bush
Addison M Conley
Jo Fletcher
Helena Harte
Lee Haven
Karen Klyne
AJ Mason
Ally McGuire
James Merrick
JP Preston
Robyn Nyx
Simon Smalley
Brey Willows

For more information visit www.butterworthbooks.co.uk

This trade paperback is published by Butterworth Books, UK

CATALOGING INFORMATION
ISBN: 978-1-915009-74-6
CREDITS
Editor: Victoria Villaseñor
Cover Design: Nicci Robinson
Photo credit (model): Olga Yefimova
Production Design: Global Wordsmiths

Acknowledgements

Who knew that working on a series could be so much fun? It's kind of like a game of chess; I need to think several books ahead to ensure that my characters have the right strategies in place to navigate their relationships.

Anyhoo, a huge thanks to my beautiful and talented wife, my editor and cheerleader, for helping me through this book. For understanding that I have to squirrel myself away instead of adventuring with you. For loving me the way you do. For being my everything.

A huge and heartfelt thank you to my sensitivity readers, who made sure Shay didn't read like a white woman failing to write a Black woman.

As always, thank you to Margaret Burris for your patience with my Britishisms. Thanks to the amazing people who make up my ARC team—I can't tell you how grateful I am to you for taking the time to read and review my stories.

And finally, thank you to the reader with my latest book in their hands. I hope you're enjoying the Windy City Romance series as much as I'm enjoying writing it!

Dedication

To my wife,
I don't know what I would've done if your
love hadn't been written into my future.
I do know my life's jigsaw would've been
incomplete without my puzzle piece.

(Imagine TV announcer voice!)

"Previously in the Windy City, ex-soldier
Gabe came to Chicago to fulfil her dream
of owning a vehicle repair shop with her old
Army buddies, Shay, Woody, RB, and Solo.

"While Gabe was busy getting her heart
in a twist with Lori, owner of the Sanctuary,
Gabe's best friend, Shay, and Lori's best
friend, Rosie, were beginning to explore a
friends with benefits situationship..."

Chapter One

It was obvious Gabe's plan to play it cool was flawed from the moment Rosie and Lori walked in wearing their high-femme outfits of tight pencil skirts, silk blouses, and killer heels. And the way Gabe's jaw practically hit the ground the moment she laid eyes on Lori was comical. Shay had expected nothing less, and honestly, she couldn't blame Gabe. The two best friends were stunning. Almost everyone in the bar had clocked their arrival, either with a full-on stare or a surreptitious sideways glance. And more than a few women had pulled their partners' gazes away from the door as Rosie and Lori entered. And yes, Shay appreciated them too. Why wouldn't she? While she'd never go anywhere near Lori even though Gabe was adamant she couldn't go beyond friend status, pursuing Rosie was a distinct possibility. Rosie had seemed pretty interested last Saturday when she and Lori had dropped into the garage to make a TikTok video.

Right now though, Shay was still reeling from Gabe's confession that she'd been terrified to come out of the Army. After twenty years of being best friends, Shay thought she'd become an expert in reading her. How could she not have known? But Gabe had promised she was okay, *and* she was already locked into an animated conversation with Lori as they played pool. Shay glanced over at Rosie as she returned from the bar with a couple of beers. She *was* exactly what Shay had been looking for tonight.

"Hey, you." Rosie placed her hand on Shay's hip and nodded toward Gabe and Lori. "I guess that leaves you stranded with me."

"Unless you want to play doubles?"

Rosie shook her head. "I don't really like games that involve more than two people."

Shay smiled, appreciating Rosie's directness. "One on one is my preference too. You can really get to know who you're playing with then." She motioned to a nearby booth. "There's nothing wrong with watching though, right?"

"Sometimes," Rosie whispered and dropped her hand from Shay's hip.

Shay sat facing the pool tables, enabling her to monitor Gabe, but Rosie slid elegantly into the booth beside her, putting the game out of view. She figured that'd be okay. Gabe seemed happy enough, and Rosie had obviously decided they had their own game to play.

"I like what you're wearing." Rosie slipped her hand onto Shay's thigh. "I didn't think I liked trouser suits on a woman, but you look fabulous."

Shay tugged on her vest then shifted the loose tie she was wearing with no shirt. "I enjoy playing with conventions."

"What else do you enjoy playing with?"

Shay ran her tongue over her top lip. "All sorts of things." Her breath caught when Rosie inched her hand all the way to Shay's crotch.

"What's wrong?" Rosie pressed a little harder. "Are you used to being the one in control?"

Shay nodded slowly. "That's usually how it works out, but I'm not fixed on anything. I can be incredibly flexible."

"It certainly looks like it." Rosie dragged her nails along Shay's arm, following the gentle lines of her muscles. "Yoga?"

"Among other things, yeah." She hadn't expected Rosie to go all-in so quickly, but she was more than prepared to go with the flow. "Is this a good idea?" She hoped that Rosie didn't back up, but she had to ask once.

"Why wouldn't it be?" Rosie pressed the heel of her hand between Shay's legs. "Am I going too fast for you? I got the impression you weren't really interested in small talk."

Shay relaxed back against the plush velvet material of the bench. "What other impressions did you get?"

"I think you enjoy short-term fun and aren't looking for anything serious."

"And you're good with that? The U-Haul stereotype really isn't for me."

Rosie bit her bottom lip and moved in closer. "I think I'm good to take whatever you're offering. Is that what you're worried about?"

She brushed her lips against Shay's neck, making it hard to concentrate on conversation, though her body was talking up a storm in response to Rosie's touch. Shay waved her finger in the general direction of Gabe and Lori. "It might get complicated."

"I don't think so," Rosie murmured into her neck and kissed her collarbone. She tugged Shay's tie gently. "We're all adults. Your friend has promised me she won't hurt Lori, but I don't need the same assurances. I know what I'm getting myself into."

"That's refreshing," Shay whispered.

"So you should kiss me and see if there's any real chemistry worth following up on."

Rosie eased up, and the air conditioning cooled Shay's skin where Rosie had pressed her hot, wet lips.

"Is that how it works?" Shay placed her hand over Rosie's, which was still pressed hard against her crotch. "Because this already feels like real chemistry."

Rosie shook her head slightly. "It's always in the kiss, Shay. If there's nothing in the kiss, there's nothing worth pursuing."

"Some people don't kiss at all when they're fucking."

"I'm not 'some people.' The way a woman kisses tells me everything I need to know about how she fucks. I won't waste my time getting into bed with a woman who kisses like a horse."

Shay laughed at the gross image. She'd had her fair share of sloppy kissers, and now that she thought more deeply about it, Rosie was dead on. "Seems like a lot of pressure to put on a simple kiss."

Rosie traced the shape of Shay's lips with one of her perfectly manicured nails, and the sensation bolted straight to her core.

"Can't you handle a little pressure?" she asked and pushed her other hand harder between Shay's legs.

"I think I can handle *you*." Shay took Rosie's hand from between her legs. "But you only just got here, and I don't think Lori is anywhere near ready to leave." She moved slightly so that she could see the table Gabe was playing at. They definitely seemed to be having a good time, but Gabe probably wouldn't be impressed if Shay bailed on their evening this soon.

Rosie drew circles on Shay's bare shoulder. "If you're not taking me home yet, maybe we *should* play some pool with your friends."

"That might be a good idea." Shay nodded across to Gabe and Lori again. "Given that those two are fast friends, you should probably get to know the rest of us. My bet is that we'll be spending a lot of time together."

"I have a feeling I'm going to enjoy that." Rosie trailed her finger down Shay's arm all the way to her fingertips. "But I'm not going anywhere until the mystery's been solved."

"The kiss?"

Rosie nodded. "The kiss."

Shay shifted to face Rosie fully. She tucked a long wave of Rosie's hair behind her ear and wrapped her hand around her neck. "Your skin's so soft."

"So is your touch," Rosie whispered. "I thought your hands might be rougher."

"I wear gloves, remember?" But she could forgive Rosie for not really noticing at the garage when they first met; they'd both been too busy looking each other up and down. She leaned in almost close enough for their lips to touch but stopped just short.

"Tease."

"If you really want this, you—" Shay didn't get the chance to finish the sentence before Rosie matched her hunger and crushed their lips together. She tasted of mint and sugar, and Shay gave the kiss her best shot. She pulled back slightly and ran her tongue over Rosie's bottom lip slowly. Rosie sucked Shay's tongue into her mouth, bringing their lips back together forcefully and taking Shay by surprise. She couldn't deny that she liked Rosie's take-charge approach.

Rosie slipped her hand under Shay's vest and dragged her nails across Shay's hip. Shay shuddered and jumped back slightly at the electricity of her touch. She pulled Rosie's head back slightly. "I thought you were just testing the kiss."

Rosie withdrew her hand. "Didn't you like it?"

"That's not the point." Shay tightened her grip in Rosie's hair, and Rosie let out a quiet gasp. "Didn't you like *that*?"

Rosie smiled wickedly. "You're saying I'm muddying the waters of the experiment with too many variables."

Shay raised her eyebrow. "Something like that, but sexier."

Rosie unwound Shay's hand from her hair and put some distance between them on the plush bench. Shay narrowed her eyes. She couldn't have failed the test...could she? No one had ever complained about her kissing prowess before, but then she'd never really stuck around long enough to ask. She stayed silent, unreasonably concerned that she was about to be rejected on the basis of a kiss that hadn't even lasted that long. *She'd* certainly enjoyed it.

Rosie edged out of the booth. "I vote we join Lori and Gabe. What do you say?"

Shay wasn't sure what to say. The longer the question over the kiss loomed, the more unsettled she became. She hadn't had a shake in confidence like this for a long time.

Rosie held out her hand, and once again, Shay admired her manicure, hoping that she'd still get the opportunity to feel those nails all over her skin.

"Are you coming?"

Shay shrugged. "I was hoping I would be, but now I don't know what's happening," she said.

Rosie laughed lightly. "You think I didn't feel something?"

"It was pretty short to tell you everything you need to know."

Rosie nodded. "You're right, but it was enough of a preview for me to want to find out the rest the old-fashioned way." She waved her outstretched hand. "Do you want to play or not?"

Shay took Rosie's hand and shimmied off the bench. "Oh, I want to play," she said and tugged Rosie closer. "I want to play all night."

Rosie put her hand on Shay's chest and pushed her away gently. "And we will. But first: pool."

She turned abruptly and sashayed across the club toward Gabe and Lori. Shay watched her with intense appreciation, then glanced at Gabe. She looked like she was about to sink to her knees to worship at Lori's feet, and Shay had her own desire for Rosie barely under control. *The Lord help us both.*

Chapter Two

"It's so good to see you, Karen." Rosie relaxed into Karen's warm embrace; she always gave the best hugs. Luckily, she'd passed that ability onto Lori.

Karen held her at arm's length. "You've lost some weight since I saw you last. What's going on?"

Rosie wrinkled her nose. "Lots of long days at work, and no time to eat, I guess." She settled onto the seat opposite Lori, who rolled her eyes and mouthed an apology.

Karen swatted Lori's shoulder before budging her along the bench. "I'm allowed to be worried about your best friend. She looks like she's wasting away to nothing."

"Lucky that she's joining us for lunch then," Lori said. "You can make sure she eats something healthy."

"*And* find out if there's more to it than time constraints." Karen waved for the waiter's attention, and they placed their order. "How's your new job going?" she asked when the server had gone.

Rosie smiled. Karen had almost as good a memory as Lori, and warmth spread through her chest at Karen's motherly concern, something she was entirely unfamiliar with. "It's good. I'm busier than I ever was with my private practice, and it's been a challenge getting used to having a boss again."

"I can only imagine," Karen said.

Lori chuckled. "That's because you've always been your own boss."

"That's what I'm saying." Karen gently nudged Lori's shoulder. "There's no way I could work under anyone else after running my own business for so long."

"I do miss my old workplace." Rosie sighed, remembering her bright, spacious office on the edge of Millenium Park.

"I miss our lunches at the roof garden restaurant. That was one of my favorite views of Lake Michigan," Lori said.

Rosie nodded, though they hadn't lunched at that office since Lori withdrew into herself following her divorce from Katherine. "And I miss the autonomy. Having someone else tell me what to do is taking some getting used to. Especially when they're fifteen years younger than me."

Karen frowned. "How can that be? They wouldn't be out of high school."

"She might be exaggerating slightly, Mom. Isn't your manager twenty-five?"

"Twenty-three," Rosie said then waited to continue until the waiter had placed their drinks on the table and left. "He's a millionaire whizz-kid who made his money in Silicon Valley on the latest social networking app the world can't do without. Now he wants to revolutionize the world of advertising."

Karen raised her eyebrow. "You're not convincing me that your career change has been all that successful."

Rosie emptied two packets of sweetener into her latte and stirred it slowly, contemplating the question. "It's only been six months. I think I just need more time to adjust."

"When Lori told me about it, I have to admit I was baffled, and she didn't really explain what prompted the move." Karen tapped her biscotti on her saucer. "I'm always intrigued by the motivation behind job shifts."

"Mom," Lori said, "not everyone has a calling like you did. Lots of people have lots of jobs. Change can be good; it stops the rot."

Rosie shrugged. "I thought being a therapist was my calling... until I didn't."

"Did something happen?" Karen asked.

"Are you sure you want to talk about this? I want to hear all about Hank's veteran project, and your daughter is desperate to grill me about my weekend."

Lori wiggled her eyebrows. "It's only fair. You already know the nonsense I got up to, but my night finished a lot earlier than yours."

Karen gave Lori a sideways glance. "I thought you didn't like gossip."

"That isn't gossip; it's BFF talk."

Lori's enthusiasm made Rosie smile. It felt like it had been way longer than a year since she'd seen her best friend smile like that. She cursed the ex-wife for the millionth time for hurting Lori so badly.

"You can save that until I leave. Hank will be finished talking to your team at the garage soon enough, and I promised we could go to see the Bean—again. I swear I don't know why he's so fascinated with that thing."

"He says that it gives him new perspectives on whatever's going on in his mind," Lori said. "There's probably some piece of his new project that doesn't fit, and he wants to contemplate it in the park. You know that, Mom."

Karen huffed. "How am I supposed to remember that? We haven't been here together for four years." She took a sip of her coffee and murmured appreciatively. "Remind me to buy some of this Bonnie's Beans to take home."

"Sure, Mom."

"And yes, Rosie, I do want to talk about you. I only see you once a year, so you've got to fill me in on everything you've been up to, especially your new job," Karen tapped Rosie's hand gently, "*if* you don't mind talking about it, that is. I don't want to push if you're not comfortable, but I do remember you telling my daughter that it was healthy to talk things through."

"I did say that." Rosie shrugged. "But I said a lot of things that people generally seemed to ignore, so you probably shouldn't quote me."

Karen put her arm around Lori's shoulder and pulled her closer. "I disagree. Lori only started to heal once she began seeing your colleague. And now she's back to her old self."

Rosie chuckled. "I think that might be more down to a certain six-foot super-soldier than little old Rae."

Lori kicked her under the table. "That's not accurate. Rae helped me get to the place where I'm able to entertain the thought of a 'six-foot super-soldier.'"

"You did more than entertain the thought of Gabe on Saturday," Rosie said and shifted quickly to avoid another tap on the shins.

"*Anyway*," Karen said, "you were saying…"

The waiter returned with their food, and Rosie swirled her latte around in its glass before setting it down, aware it was avoidance when there was no reason for it. "It's pretty simple, really. The same people were coming to me, session after session, and they weren't changing. They weren't getting better. It made me question my worth as a therapist and then as a person." She shrugged. "I don't need that; I had enough of it as a kid. So I took action before it dragged me to depths I might not have been able to climb out from. And if this doesn't work for me, I'll try something else. I'm using my psychology degree too, so it's not like my education has been a waste of time." Though convincing people they couldn't live without certain products wasn't exactly what she'd had in mind when she fought her way through college. "And it's paying those debts."

Karen munched on some garlic bread and nodded. "Mm, that's important, but it's nice if you can do something you enjoy at the same time."

Lori huffed. "Ninety-five percent of the population work to live, Mom, not the other way around like you and Dad."

"I know that. It's just that Rosie seemed to love her work like we do. And now," Karen patted Rosie's hand, "that doesn't seem to be the case."

"Maybe I'll learn to love it," she said, more in hope than belief, and twirled spaghetti on her fork.

"Why did you go into therapy, Rosie?" Karen tilted her head to one side.

"Mom! You wanted to catch up, not therapize her."

Rosie smiled and waved Lori's protestations away. "It's okay, Lori. Honestly, it's good to talk about it, and even nicer to have someone interested enough to ask questions that make me think."

Lori glanced away briefly and sighed. "I haven't asked those questions. I've been too involved with my own problems to see yours."

Rosie shook her head and took Lori's hand in hers. "Hey now, that's not what I meant. Please don't go guilt-tripping yourself." She squeezed gently. "That's my job."

Lori smiled. "Still. I wasn't there when you needed me."

"You're here now," Rosie said. "And whether it's Rae's miraculous therapy or Gabe's amazing abs that have brought you back to me, I don't care. I'm just glad you're starting to feel like yourself again."

Karen side-shuffled out of the booth. "I need the restroom. You two should hug it out while I'm gone, and then Rosie can answer my probing question." She walked away before either of them could respond.

"Your mom missed her vocation. She would've made a killer therapist."

Lori got up and sat beside Rosie before pulling her into a warm embrace. "I've already said that I was sorry for disappearing on you and freezing you out when you tried to help, but I'm really sorry I've been such a poor friend."

"Honestly, it's fine." Rosie closed her eyes and relaxed in Lori's arms. She *had* missed her terribly, and she *had* needed Lori as her sounding board, and it *wasn't* fine. In Lori's absence, Rosie had made a life-changing decision, and she had to deal with the consequences. "Worst-case scenario, I could always come and help you at the Sanctuary, right?"

Lori chuckled and pulled away from the hug. "Yeah, right. I can see you donning some coveralls to muck out the stables. I'm not sure Prada has a workwear line."

"Fine. I'm sure there's plenty of admin work I could help with then."

"Absolutely," Lori said. "Or we could build you a special office to give therapy to the horses and hounds."

Rosie arched her eyebrow. "Now you're taking it too far."

"What? Why?"

Lori's attempt at a serious expression only made Rosie laugh. "You know why."

"Animals are very complicated beings. They get depressed too."

"I'm sure they do, but I don't think they'd respond to Jung."

"That's what I like to see: my two favorite women smiling and laughing." Karen slid back into the booth opposite Rosie and Lori. "Are you ready to tell me why you got into therapy?"

"I'll give you the Cliff notes version after I've eaten this Bolognese. I can't eat it cold." Or rather, she wouldn't. Too many frozen meals not properly warmed had fostered a serious antipathy for lukewarm food.

Lori and her mom filled in the gaps with talk about the upcoming auction. "Sounds like it's going to be a wonderful event," Rosie said after listening to dress-code details and menu choices.

Karen smiled widely. "It will be the charity event of the season. Chicago has seen nothing like it before, and never will again."

"Until we host another auction?" Lori asked, amusement clear in her eyes.

"Until we host another event, yes." She raised her eyebrow at Lori then turned her gaze to Rosie. "Will you be bringing someone?"

"Maybe," Rosie said.

"Ooh, great segue, Mom." Lori nudged Rosie. "Will you be going with Shay?"

Rosie narrowed her eyes. "Who said anything about Shay?"

Lori chased some sauce around her dish with a dough ball before scooping it into her mouth. "Gabe may have let something slip in a text about Shay not coming home until Sunday evening.

Tell all."

Rosie gave Lori the side-eye. "Maybe not *all*," she whispered.

Lori grinned. "Oh, sorry. Save the finer details until Mom's gone."

Rosie hadn't seen this playful side of Lori for years. She'd almost forgotten how embarrassing she and her mom could be with the way they shared almost everything. "We got to talking while you and Gabe were playing pool, and we hit it off. She came to my place after we dropped you at home."

"So will you be bringing Shay to the auction with you or not?" Lori asked.

Rosie placed her fork in the pasta dish and pushed it away. Her stomach was already protesting at the amount of food she'd eaten. No doubt, she'd be bloated like a puffer fish for the rest of the day. "I don't think so."

"Oh."

The way Lori said that single word broadcast her wider understanding of Rosie's "love" life. Lori knew better than anyone that Rosie hadn't had any luck in finding her Princess Charming. And they were well aware that Shay was quite the prolific player who had zero intention of settling down. "I haven't spoken to her since she left my place on Sunday."

"She hasn't texted you?" Karen asked.

Karen arched her eyebrow in that protective momma bear manner that Rosie so appreciated, even though it'd taken a while to get used to. "It's no big deal, Karen. I wasn't expecting a repeat performance. To be honest, I wasn't expecting her to be into me at all. Shay's kind of a goddess; imagine a late-thirties Angela Bassett. She's got those same perfectly full Cupid's bow lips and high cheekbones. She could easily be her daughter—maybe she is." It wasn't like they'd spent any time talking about anything of significance. Their pre-sex conversation had been all about the flirting and foreplay, which had been fine. But post-sex had been perfunctory and shallow, and there'd been no promise of extended communication, let alone round two.

"Do you *want* to see her again?"

Rosie smiled at Karen's concerned expression. "I don't have much say in that." She glanced at Lori, who pressed her lips together and looked rueful. "Gabe is Lori's friend, and Shay is Gabe's friend. The math means that I'm Shay's friend by default, and that's okay. There's no need for it to be awkward. I knew what I was getting myself into, and I did it anyway." And God, the sex had definitely been worth it.

"Hey, lovely people."

Rosie looked up to see Lori's dad. "Hey, Hank."

Lori's love for him was clear in her adoring expression. "Hi, Dad."

"You're done already?" Karen looked at her watch. "Oh, time flies, doesn't it?"

Hank leaned down and kissed her then he scooped up the last piece of garlic bread. "Best join you," he said and popped the chunk into his mouth.

Rosie smiled at the picture-perfect couple and tried to stave off the thought that she might never find that kind of love. Being single wasn't so bad. She only got lonely when she was home alone, and the new job was keeping her out of her apartment enough that melancholy didn't have time to settle in.

"Is it time for your traditional pilgrimage to the Bean?" Rosie smiled at Karen's dramatic eye roll.

"For sure. I have plenty to think about after my chat with your soldier friends. They had a lot to say about my new veteran's project, especially RB. She's worked in non-profits before; I'd love to poach her as a consultant."

"I haven't been to the park for a while," Rosie said, "and a walk might stop me from exploding."

Lori pouted. "No dessert?"

"I'm stuffed, but you can grab something from Rink if you're hungry for something sweet." Rosie encouraged Lori out of the booth with a gentle shove.

Karen linked her arm through Rosie's. "This is wonderful. Now we get to talk more, and you can give me your 'Cliff notes version' of why you got into therapy, like you promised."

Rosie was vaguely hoping Karen had forgotten about that, but she also appreciated the chance to revisit what had been going through her head when she'd suddenly switched careers. Maybe it would help her escape the ennui of her current employment. And if nothing else, it was a beautiful summer's day for a walk with Lori and her family. Rosie always liked to soak up the loving energy the three of them exuded when they were together. Rather than allowing it to be a masochistic reminder of everything she'd never had, she took it as a blessed opportunity to be part of something positive. It gave her another memory to swap out with one from her childhood, and she'd never say no to that.

Chapter Three

"I NEED YOU TO come home and check out my car, Shanae. It's making a helluva racket. Sounds like the engine's about to fall out. I can't afford to be without my car, you know that. It's the only way I can get out of the house."

It *wasn't* the only way. Any one of her five brothers could take him wherever he wanted to go, but no, he'd only ever ask her now that she was out of the Army. Gabe scribbled something on the whiteboard then stepped away so Shay could read it.

DON'T DO IT!!!!

Shay pulled the eraser from the fridge and wiped the message away. I HAVE TO, she wrote then tossed the pen at Gabe and exited the kitchen, switching her phone from speaker for privacy. "I only just serviced it, Daddy. There's nothing wrong with it."

"That was weeks ago, girl. You're not here; you can't hear it. Come on over and listen to it. You'll see. What if when I'm driving down the freeway, something breaks, and I have an accident? Will you believe me then?"

"I believe you now, Daddy." She closed her bedroom door behind her and leaned against it heavily. "But we're in the middle of the Brewster restoration I told you about, and we need to get it finished so we can open the garage."

Her daddy scoffed. "We, we, we. Your Army friends have always been more important to you than your family, than your own blood. Your momma'd smack you upside the head if she was still here, the Lord rest her soul."

Shay ran her hand over her box braids and sighed. Her momma had never raised her hand to her when she was alive, so Shay was pretty sure she wouldn't do it if she came down from heaven either. "That's not true, Daddy," she said. "They're important in a different way."

"I don't wanna talk about them, girl. Are you comin' or not?"

"Of course I'll come." She checked her watch. "I'll be there around noon."

"Can't you get here sooner than that? I'm playing dominoes with Joe and Sidney at two."

"It's just after eight a.m. The city's gridlocked with morning traffic. Noon is the best I can do." And since there'd probably be nothing wrong with the car at all, she was sure he'd still make his daily dominoes meet at the rec center to talk shit with his old work buddies, the same men she thought were more important to him than his family.

"Well, I guess I'll just sit here stranded until then," he said and hung up.

Shay closed her eyes and did some deep breathing, but even yoga was powerless against the inevitable and immediate tightening of every muscle and nerve in her body the moment he had called. And it never settled until she'd dealt with whatever false emergency he cooked up. Even then, only a meaningless encounter with a woman could fully release the stress.

Maybe Rosie would be free. She fired off a quick text and hit send before she really realized what she'd done. It had only been a few days since they'd hooked up. Any subsequent contact with her flings was usually by accident. But Rosie was different; she'd said she knew what to expect and what *not* to expect. Shay recognized a kindred spirit when she saw one, and it was clear that Rosie enjoyed casual just as much as Shay. She'd know not to read anything into the timing of the text.

The firm knock on her door rattled Shay's head.

"I'm driving in alone then," Gabe said.

Shay pushed away from the door and opened it. "What do you think?"

Gabe raised her eyebrow and put both hands on the door frame, almost filling the space. "What I think doesn't change every time this happens. I think that you should tell your dad to call one of his sons occasionally. They live a lot closer."

Shay rolled her eyes. "They don't come even when he does call. You know that."

"Yeah, and I also know that your dad thinks your time is less important because they're in relationships and you're not."

She shrugged. "I'm not about to change that situation anytime soon."

"So you're stuck playing the dutiful daughter, answering every time he cries wolf. It's not cool."

Gabe backed out of the door as Shay stepped forward, making it clear she needed to leave.

"I appreciate that you've got my back, Gabe, but he's family." Shay headed out of her room and down the stairs, while Gabe's heavy footsteps behind her were an assurance the conversation wasn't over. It never really was because this kind of thing just continued to happen.

"Do you want me to come with you?"

Shay snorted. "Yeah, that'd go down well." She poured coffee into her to-go mug then shooed Gabe away from the fridge to get milk. "And you need to be at the garage. The Brewster isn't going to restore itself."

"It's nearly finished. Solo's lacquering today, and there's not much else to do until the panels are dry enough to rehang." Gabe spun her truck keys around her finger like a fidget toy. "I'm pretty much a spare part today, so it really wouldn't be a problem to keep you company. I could drop you at your dad's house and wait at Cris' Café until you call. He doesn't even have to see me."

Shay laughed. "*Everyone* will see you." She waved her hand toward Gabe. "You're not exactly easy to miss." Her size, color, and presentation set Gabe apart in her dad's neighborhood. "Then Cris will report to Daddy, and I'll get earful about bringing my *other life* home."

Gabe shook her head. "Okay. I'll wait outside the county lines."

"Honestly, I'll be fine." She tapped the spreadsheet fixed to the fridge. "And this says you're supposed to be machining the valve seals today."

"I could just work late and do them tonight," Gabe said.

Shay punched Gabe's shoulder. "Take the hint, buddy. You're not wanted."

Gabe chuckled. "Fine. Be a martyr and go through your family drama alone."

Shay raised her coffee cup and nodded. "I will." She patted Gabe's arm as she left. "Thanks for the support, bro."

"Always."

The drive out of the city wasn't as horrific as she'd anticipated, and she pulled into her daddy's driveway just after eleven. The blinds at the living room window twitched, indicating he'd probably been watching for her since he'd hung up the phone.

The front door swung open, and her daddy hustled out of it, holding out his arm and tapping his watch. "Better hurry, Shanae. You're cuttin' it fine."

"Good morning to you too, Daddy." She closed her car door gently, though she'd wanted to slam it. Hard.

"Don't sass me. I told you I've got things to do. I don't have time to be hanging around waiting for you to remember what's important in life." He raised the garage door and tossed his car keys toward Shay. "Go ahead. Listen."

Shay caught the keys and clicked the fob to start the engine on the 2021 Ford she'd all but begged him not to choose. He didn't share her love of classic cars, and the dealer had clinched the sale with the remote start and heated seat functions. "Bet your Javelin doesn't heat your butt on wintery days," he'd said. "I *need* these for my arthritis." The arthritis he'd self-diagnosed that Shay suspected he didn't have. He was still plenty spritely when he thought she wasn't looking.

The engine came to life first time, sounding as lacking in personality as it had when he'd first driven it off the car lot. "It sounds fine, Daddy." She popped the hood, surveyed the array of plastic parts, and shuddered internally at its abject ugliness.

"You can't hear it now. You gotta drive it."

She leaned in closer. The characterless, generic whirr of the engine indicated there were no issues with it.

"Don't get your pawprints all over it."

Shay eased away from the garish chrome finish of the bumper—another thing to dislike—and got in the driver's side.

Her daddy stepped in front of the car just as she was about to pull out of the wide garage. "Where'd you think you're going without me? I'll drive. You ride shotgun."

She clenched her jaw, swung her legs over the central console, and slid into the passenger seat.

"You better not've scuffed my interior with your dirty boots," he said as he got in. "And your jeans better be clean too. Why you can't wear a skirt like a lady, I'll never know. Your momma always looked so beautiful and feminine." He looked her up and down with unconcealed disdain. "Dressing and acting like a boy; you may as well've been another son."

When she got back to the garage where Gabe would insist on a blow-by-blow account of this, that comment would get a big laugh, for sure. "I wear skirts, Daddy," she said for maybe the thousandth time since she'd come out of the Army, "but they're not practical for work."

"Huh. *Work*. Tinkering with engines wasn't supposed to be work though, was it?"

Fantastic. He was running through his greatest hits. What she wouldn't give to have a real father-daughter chat instead of his constant jibes at how she lived her life. He hadn't been this mean before her momma had died, but then he hadn't been around that much to *be* mean.

"You were supposed to do something that mattered with your

life," he said, cutting into traffic. "I remember when you wanted to be an astronaut. Other girls your age had posters of Michael Jackson on their walls, but you had Mae Jemison. You remember that?"

"Yes, Daddy." Of course she did, but it wasn't just Dr. Mae's pioneering she admired. She had other reasons to have *that* beautiful Black woman on her wall. "But I did do something that mattered; I went to war."

"Huh. *War.* Because that was a good use of your 150 IQ– offering up your Black ass to be blown to bits by terrorists. You could've been engineering the bombs to blow *them* up from the safety of US soil."

Shay held onto the dash when he slammed on the brakes at a stop sign. "I wanted to do something on the ground, Daddy."

"You wanted to get away from your family, girl, that's what you wanted to do."

She swallowed hard against the temptation to scream out why she hadn't just wanted to get away, she'd *needed* to get away. Instead, she stayed silent because he was half right, and she'd been forced to sacrifice her relationship with her momma in the process. "I still don't hear anything. Is it worse at speed?"

He gave her a sideways glance and shook his head slowly, the way he did to show his all-round disappointment in her as a daughter. Its impact hadn't lessened as she'd grown older. If anything, it might've become even more powerful despite her best efforts.

"I guess it must've worked itself out," he said. "It sounds just fine now."

Of course it did, because it had probably never sounded anything other than fine. He'd just wanted another opportunity to mess with her life. "The charity auction for the Sanctuary is a week from Saturday. Have you decided if you can make it or not?" She heard the petulance in her voice and regretted it immediately. She didn't even know why she'd invited him. If he did come, he'd spend the whole evening looking down on her friends, and if he didn't come, he'd find some way to make that her fault.

"Charity begins at home is what your momma used to say. If you spent as much time with your real family as you do your Army *friends*, maybe you wouldn't be tempted to live the way you do. The Lord sees everything, girl."

Shay pressed her lips together and bit her tongue. She sure hoped God didn't see *everything* and that She gave her children some privacy. The thought of the Almighty watching her bedroom antics would cramp her style. Speaking of, she checked her phone to see if Rosie had responded yet. She couldn't help being a little amused when she discovered Rosie hadn't even opened her message, if the checks at the side were accurate. A woman *not* after her own heart. This could be a friends-with-benefits situation that could save her a lot of needless cruising time.

They continued in silence for a while until Shay realized he wasn't heading back to the house. "You missed the turn home."

"Home? Now you're calling it home again," he said and kissed his teeth.

Shay sighed and looked up through the panoramic sunroof he'd insisted on having. It had added even more to the build price and was only one of many add-ons and upgrades that meant she was still making vehicle payments. It was all a far cry from the old Pinto he'd driven into the ground. Still, the view of a clear bluebird sky calmed her a little, so maybe it was worth it.

She began to recognize the route he was taking and closed her eyes briefly. He had a nerve to talk about her abandoning the family when he spent more time with his friends, Sidney and Jo, than he ever did with them. "Do you need to make a stop for something before you drop me back at my car?" she asked, not ready to relinquish all hope.

He looked at her, his brow furrowed deep enough to drive a toy truck down it. "No use going all that way back just to turn around again." He gestured down the road to the rec center they were approaching. "A walk through town will be good for you. You might see some old friends. And I don't like to keep Joe and Sid waiting."

But he was okay making his daughter make the one-mile trip back. "I have to get back to the garage, Daddy."

He turned into the recreation center's parking lot and swung into a disabled space regardless of him not having a disability plate or placard. "Well, I hear we have one of those new-fangled non-taxi services around here now if you don't want to walk."

She got out, already checking her Lyft app for nearby cars.

"I'll call you if the car starts acting up again," he said over his shoulder as he headed toward the rec's entrance.

She watched him practically jog to meet up with his buddies, trying to ignore the stab to her heart when he didn't even look back to wave goodbye. Her phone pinged, and she switched over to WhatsApp.

Client being an asshole. Working late. I'll be home at midnight if you want to drop by for round two.

Shay grinned and took a deep, cleansing breath. She could be back at the garage before three, put in an eight-hour shift, and still have time to clean up before heading to Rosie's. She texted *I'll be there* then laughed out loud when a nail clipper emoji popped up in response. She extended her fingers to inspect her hands. They weren't exactly talons, but she hadn't manicured them for over a week, and they needed shortening a little. *You got it* she replied and returned to the Lyft app.

Finding a long-term friend-with-benefits had always eluded her—deeper emotions from the other side of the situationship inevitably got in the way—but Shay could see Rosie was different, and damn, she needed the tension relieved after this. There had been no real emergency, and her daddy had been next-level dismissive. Maybe Gabe was right about him crying wolf, but if she didn't come just one time, it could end up being something genuine. She'd been on the other side of the world the last time that had happened, and there wasn't a day that went by that she didn't regret not being able to make it home in time.

She looked up to the sky and blinked back the soft burn of tears. "I miss you, Momma."

Chapter Four

ROSIE HEARD THE THROATY roar of Shay's old muscle car and looked out the window in time to see her pull up and get out. God, she was stunning. Rosie couldn't believe she'd actually managed to seduce Shay into coming home with her once. She really didn't think she'd get a repeat performance, even it was a midnight booty call. She didn't know what had possessed her to be so sexually aggressive last Saturday—that *so* wasn't her style at all—but Lori had inspired her. Rosie had watched her masterfully marionette Gabe into a giant marshmallow soldier-puppet under her strings, and it'd been wonderful to see her friend happy again. If the catalyst for that was Gabe, so be it. She seemed harmless enough, and if her puppy dog eyes that night were anything to go by, Gabe would probably walk over a bed of nails rather than hurt Lori.

And Rosie had Gabe to thank for more than just helping Lori recover from her ex-wife, because Gabe came with Shay...

Shay looked up to the window, and Rosie's breathing quickened at the vision standing before her. She curled her finger to encourage Shay to come closer. Rosie had no idea if this was going to turn into a regular casual thing, so she was determined to make the most of it now. She'd been pretty drunk the first time, and she wanted to appreciate Shay fully sober. She shook off the tiredness of the day, invigorated by the thought of getting her hands on Shay again, and buzzed her in.

Rosie opened the door then closed it. She didn't want to seem too eager. But then, Shay had been the one to initiate this, so maybe eager was okay.

She opened the door again and leaned against the door jamb

before adjusting her satin nightshirt to reveal more cleavage. Rosie looked across the hallway. If her neighbor looked through his peephole, he'd get quite the show. She pushed away quickly and closed the door behind her.

What was the etiquette for these things? She'd had plenty of women who'd turned out to be one-night stands, but she'd never been a booty call before. Did they have drinks first? Should she have prepared some pre-sex nibbles for fuel? Would a cheese platter be sexy or stinky?

The light rap on the door interrupted her panic, and she opened it instantly, not stopping to think whether she should've made Shay wait or not. She chided herself. You didn't make a woman like Shay wait for *anything*. "Hi, beautiful," she said, willing the sexually aggressive version of herself back into her body.

Shay's eyebrows quirked as she swept her gaze over Rosie's body, making Rosie consider the reality of spontaneous human combustion.

"Hey." Shay came in without invitation and closed the door behind her. She put her hands on Rosie's hips and pushed her back against the wall. "Nice shirt," she whispered and kissed Rosie's neck.

"Are you hungry? I've got leftovers from last night."

"I'm not hungry for food," Shay said, her breath hot against Rosie's skin.

No food. No conversation. Noted. She gasped when Shay raked her nails up her thighs and hooked her finger into the waistband of her lace panties.

"I've been thinking about this all day." Shay slipped her hand into Rosie's hair and tugged gently before kissing her hard and hot.

Rosie had been thinking about it since they'd parted on Sunday afternoon but saying that out loud was bound to be too eager. Then the feel of Shay's full lips on hers melted any other thoughts away. And as Shay gently guided her down the hallway to her bedroom, Rosie didn't want to think at all.

She just wanted to feel.

***

Rosie tilted her head slightly to enjoy the rear view of Shay as she padded to the bathroom completely naked. She bit her bottom lip and sighed contentedly. Aside from grasping the initial etiquette, booty calls were surprisingly simple. Rosie's only concern now was how she could make them a regular occurrence. She slipped her hand under the covers to touch herself; she was deliciously sore—in a good way and not from overly long nails, which Shay had been quick to point out that she'd attended to—and she wanted more of that. Much more. Shay had stamina the likes of which Rosie had never come across. This time though, Shay hadn't been interested in receiving, so Rosie had to call time out after she'd hit double figures in the orgasm department.

The toilet flushed, and Shay emerged from the bathroom to treat Rosie to a full-frontal delight.

"That was unexpected...and wild," Rosie said, hiding her disappointment at Shay retrieving her discarded clothes and beginning to redress.

"In a good way?"

From the way she asked, it was clear Shay didn't expect a negative response. Why would she? If their two encounters were indicative of Shay's prowess, she'd probably *never* had a negative response. "In a *very* good way."

Shay shimmied into her skinny jeans and sat on the side of the bed. Rosie glanced at her phone; a photo of Shay half-naked would be perfect stimulation for future nights alone.

Shay grinned as if she'd read her thoughts. "Looking for a memento?"

"I'll own that." Rosie tugged at the back of Shay's waistband. "I promise it'd just be for my own purposes."

Shay scooted onto the bed and straddled her. "I take it you

wouldn't mind me coming back again?"

Rosie shrugged, affecting a nonchalance that her instant excitement threatened to bubble up and drown. "What are you thinking?"

"I'm thinking this might work for both of us." Shay sucked Rosie's nipple between her teeth and nibbled lightly. "When we hooked up, you said you weren't worried about it getting complicated."

Rosie cupped Shay's breasts in her hands and squeezed firmly. "I'm not. There's nothing complicated about two adults wanting sex with each other, is there?"

Shay's lips parted, and she moaned. "Not until the lesbian cliché kicks in, no."

Rosie squeezed harder, and Shay pressed against her, making a guttural sound that drove Rosie wild. "I'm pretty sure my Mercedes doesn't have a tow hitch. You don't have to worry about that particular stereotype with me, I promise."

Shay eased up and out of Rosie's reach. "You're not looking for forever?"

Rosie huffed. "From what I've seen, it doesn't exist." She stroked Shay's thighs, enjoying the texture of the soft denim on her hands. If they were going to do this, she guessed honesty would be the best way forward, and if talking kept Shay straddled over her, half-naked, she was prepared to talk up a storm. "I won't lie; I've been looking for my Princess Charming for a while, but I've kind of given up. Lori seemed happy enough for six years, and then the lawyer broke her heart. Ellery is in a toxic on-off relationship with a gold-digging—"

"Who's Ellery?"

"Another friend. She's Lori's vet. Well, she's not her vet, obviously. She's the vet for the Sanctuary. Anyway, it's not important. My point is, I don't think happily ever after exists, so I'm interested in happy for now. No pressure. No expectations."

Shay grinned. "That sounds exactly right. Happy in the moment works for me."

"And I'm just finding my feet in a new job, working crazy hours and dealing with even crazier clients." She ran her finger along the crotch seam of Shay's jeans. "*This* was perfect. I needed to flush the day from my system, and a few orgasms have done exactly that."

Shay raised her eyebrow. "A few?"

"What do you need? Validation?"

"I got that from your string of expletives and the way your eyes half-lidded in clear ecstasy *thirteen* times."

"You were counting?"

"I was making sure you got what you needed."

"And what about you? Did you get what you needed?" Rosie wasn't going to point it out, but there were times during the sex when it felt like Shay wasn't really there, and that Rosie could've been anyone. But that was the nature of casual sex, wasn't it? With no complicating emotions involved, it was simply about the pleasure.

"Yeah, I did."

Shay climbed off Rosie and went back around to her pile of clothes, but not before Rosie had seen a flicker of something like sadness in her eyes. The playfulness was gone, and her tone was flat. Rosie scrambled to decipher what she might've said that had killed the mood. Her phone buzzed on her bedside table. She rejected the call, wanting to keep her focus on Shay. Had she fucked up the casual situationship without even trying? Christ, she couldn't even do booty calls right. No wonder she was always alone.

"Was that one of your crazy clients?"

Shay fixed the clasp on her lace bra and pulled her sheer sweater on. Rosie was impressed it was still in one piece given the way she'd torn it off. "Maybe. The international ones sometimes forget the time difference, but I work in advertising; I'm not a first responder. They can email me." She didn't want to think about the only other person who might call regardless of the time.

Shay tied the laces on the Converse Chuck 70 De Luxe heel

satin sneakers Rosie had briefly admired before they'd been thrown aside in their desperation to get into bed. The same shoes were in her Converse basket waiting for checkout, but if she got them now, she'd have to check with Shay anytime they went out, so they didn't end up wearing matching shoes. That was a stereotype borne from reality, just like the U-Haul.

Rosie's phone buzzed again and this time, she checked to see if she recognized the number before rejecting it. Her heart pounded when she registered the California area code.

"Looks like they don't share your view on what constitutes an emergency." Shay stood and retrieved her purse from the chair in the corner.

"They'll learn. Are we good?" Rosie asked, still slightly confused by the sudden shift in Shay's mood.

Shay paused at the end of Rosie's bed and nodded. "We're more than good," she said.

Her wicked grin eased the tension in Rosie's shoulders. She hadn't blown it with the hottest woman who'd ever graced her bed. Yay for her. "Before you go... I can text you for this too, right?"

"Sure. It has to go both ways."

"And there's no expectation of exclusivity?"

Shay laughed. "Don't worry, that word isn't even in my dictionary."

"Okay then." Her phone began to buzz again, tempting Rosie to throw it out the window.

"Maybe you should turn that off when you're home," Shay said as she opened the bedroom door.

"Then how would we organize these hookups?" Rosie kicked the covers off and parted her legs slightly. If she could tempt Shay back into bed, she could ignore her phone a little longer.

Shay smirked and shook her head. "You asked me to stop, remember?"

"That doesn't mean you can't get on your back."

"Next time." Shay winked and closed the door behind her.

Rosie pouted until she heard her front door click shut then she grabbed her phone and checked the missed calls. When the phone buzzed again seconds later, she answered it. "Yes," she said, waiting for the inevitable outpouring of yet another sad story.

"Hey, Rosarita, whatcha doing?"

"I'm not sleeping, thanks to you." It wasn't like the guilt trip would work, but she couldn't stop herself. Her mom sounded high or drunk, possibly both. "And please don't call me that; it's culturally insensitive. My name is Rosie."

Her mom snorted. "All that college time has killed your sense of humor. I know what your name is—I chose it for ya. Took me a long time to decide on it too."

That wasn't true at all, but she didn't have the energy to argue. She wanted to end the conversation, sleep, and have sweet, sweet dreams about the sex she'd just enjoyed. "What do you want, Mom? It's four a.m., and I'm tired." And Thanksgiving, the next time she'd be forced to spend time with her mom in yet another "new" cruddy apartment or trailer, was three months away, so what the hell was this call about?

"I just wanted to let you know I'm going on a little trip."

"And you couldn't text me the details? Or call in the morning?" Her irritation outweighed the need for patience, and she was so sick of her mom's never-ending drama.

"I was going to call tomorrow, but Keith wants to get an early start, and I don't know if my phone'll work on the road."

"You're not going to the moon, Mom."

"No, I'm going to Mexico."

Rosie screwed her eyes shut and pinched the bridge of her nose. Even the afterglow of phenomenal sex wasn't strong enough to temper the hysteria of her mom's theatrics. "They have cell towers in Mexico, Mom."

"Aren't you going to ask why I'm going to Mexico?"

I don't want to know. "That's your business, Mom." And she was sure her mom's reasons would be completely logical and not at all knee-jerk reactionary to whatever situation she'd gotten herself into. And it was probably all Keith's idea, whoever the hell Keith was.

"I need special medication, and it's cheaper over the border. I'll be back in a week."

Rosie shook her head. "Unless you're arrested for smuggling."

"We'll be fine. Keith does this a lot."

Of course he does. "Then why does he need you?" Damn it. Her mom had hooked her in.

"He doesn't need me. I need the meds in my system urgently."

That sent a shiver through her body, and Rosie pulled the comforter up to her neck. Surely her mom was just being her usual melodramatic self, and there was nothing serious going on. "What's wrong, Mom?"

"Chronic kidney failure. I need—"

"Come on, Bren. I'm not waiting no more," a man shouted in the background.

"I've got to go, Rosarita. Love ya. I'll call you when I get back."

"Wait! I don't have—" But she'd already gone. "I don't have your new address." She flicked to received calls and tried her mom, but it went to a recorded message. She tried four more times with the same result. This was her usual behavior: drop a bomb and cut all communication so that Rosie stewed in the uncertainty of limited knowledge.

So, it was researching kidney disease and no sleep then. She rose from her bed and headed to the kitchen to brew some coffee. Lori's birthday party was tonight, and she didn't want to be a zombie for it, so she'd just have to load up on caffeine. She was looking forward to the evening and the feeling of it being a date with Shay without the associated pressure. And she'd enjoy spending Lori's birthday with her, of course.

Shay's scent was still strong in the hallway, and she smiled at the memory of the last few hours. Her smile grew wider at the thought of more to come. But she had to park that pleasure for now while she tried to figure out what the hell was going on with her mom. Again.

Chapter Five

Shay poured more of the super strong, leaded coffee into Gabe's cup, and sat back down beside her. She'd found Gabe hunched over the kitchen table with her head in her hands three hours ago, and she'd barely moved since, except to empty mug after mug of the black stuff. At eleven a.m., that was preferable to the double-digit shots they'd downed after they'd gotten back from Lori's disastrous birthday dinner. Shay had a high alcohol tolerance, but even she was feeling the after-effects of the full bottle of Jose Cuervo they'd finished at five a.m. When she'd managed to put Gabe to bed shortly after, Shay had thought she'd be unconscious until noon at least, but the rattling cups and coffee pot bubbling had started just a few hours later.

If this was love, it was another good reason for her to stay clear of it. And she had to concede that if Lori didn't forgive Gabe for not being fully truthful about her past, Shay's newly found situationship with Rosie would probably be over too. It was selfish to be thinking about that right now, but she'd run out of platitudes and promising prophesies for Gabe and Lori's future two or three cups ago, and the tension from last night's confrontation had initiated an itch that only one thing could scratch.

Which was why she was thinking about Rosie...and all the positions they'd gotten into on Thursday night. There'd been no awkwardness about any of it until Rosie had asked if she'd gotten what she needed. No one had ever asked her that question before and given that she was essentially using Rosie's body to work out all the residual conflict from contact with her father, it wasn't a question she wanted to answer. She didn't *want* to use Rosie that way. She was going to be different from all the transient trysts of Shay's past because they had an explicit understanding of what they were going to be together. Casual. No strings. No messy emotions. It was going to be perfect.

Or at least it had promised to be. Until Solo had opened her big mouth last night and revealed the elements of Gabe's past she'd been keeping from Lori, Shay and Rosie had been heading to night number three, and Shay had been looking forward to laying back on Rosie's bed and letting her loose with her body. Rosie had hinted at restraints, which had been something Shay always wanted to try but hadn't been able to give that kind of control over to any of the women she'd had short encounters with. Maybe now she could build that kind of trust with Rosie.

"No improvement?"

Shay looked up at Woody's question and shook her head. "Not cured by coffee, tequila, or sleep." She nodded toward the counter when Woody sniffed the air. "I just brewed a fresh pot. Have at it."

Gabe emerged from the fortress of her forearms and leaned back in her chair. "Love isn't a disease that needs curing."

Woody stopped pouring her coffee and raised her eyebrows. "So it's officially love? How the hell did you let that happen?"

Gabe shook her head slowly. "I have no idea... Maybe it isn't love, but whatever it is, it doesn't feel good right now." She took a long slug of coffee and glanced at her watch. "Do you think she'll be there to let me see Max?"

Shay shrugged. "I think someone will be there, but I wouldn't count on it being Lori. She was angry in a way that takes a while to settle down."

Gabe motioned to Shay's phone on the table. "Still no word from Rosie?"

"No," Shay said. And there probably wouldn't be since she hadn't texted her like Gabe had asked her to. Gabe had told Shay about Rosie's "threat" with regard to not hurting Lori when they'd visited the garage together a couple of weeks ago; there was no way she'd be interested in hearing about how bad Gabe felt right now. More like she was already creating a voodoo likeness for Lori to torture.

Gabe reached for her own phone, and Shay pushed it out of the way. "Don't do it. You've sent one text. Don't be the asshole that doesn't give a woman the space to process her feelings."

"For someone without them, you sure know a lot about feelings," Woody said.

She sat in a chair opposite them and stared at Gabe with the kind of bemused and bereft expression reserved for children discovering their parents weren't superhuman after all.

"That's what looking after five brothers'll do for you." Shay gripped Gabe's shoulder. "Okay, it's time to move. You stink of sweat and regret, and you'll blow Max's nose away. Take a shower and get ready to go see him."

Gabe pushed away from the table and got up. "You think she's still going to let me see him?"

"You've got one way to find out," Shay said and waved her out of the kitchen just as RB got to the doorway.

"Morning, fam." RB sidestepped Gabe, who grumbled something inaudible before heading upstairs. She thumbed in Gabe's direction. "Is this about last night?"

"Of course it is." Shay stood up and began to gather the ingredients for a smoothie bowl.

"First Solo and now Gabe." RB rubbed at the back of her head. "It makes me glad I'm a confirmed bachelor."

Shay glanced over her shoulder. "That's not what you are. You just haven't found anyone reckless enough to take you on yet."

"What about you? Are you next? You and Rosie seemed awful cozy last night. Until, you know, everything went to hell." RB nudged Woody as she sat beside her. "We thought you were about to go at it right there at the table."

Shay scoffed. "We're just fuck buddies. And I don't have time to fall in love, even if I wanted to. Which I don't."

Woody cocked her head. "On that note, have you heard any more from your pops about the menacing knock on his car?"

"No."

"So did he want something else from you?" Woody asked.

Shay ran through the conversation quickly before switching on the smoothie machine.

"I don't get it," RB said. "If there was nothing wrong with the car, and he didn't need help with anything else, what did he really want?"

Shay poured the smoothie mix into the bowl alongside the granola then carefully laid pineapple pieces between the two. "I wish I knew. It's like he just wanted to remind me how much I disappoint him. He doesn't approve of my career, my lifestyle, the way I dress. This time, he even accused me of acting like a boy."

Woody clamped her hand over her mouth, and her shoulders shook with the obvious effort not to dissolve into laughter.

RB shoved Woody so hard, she had to stop herself falling off the chair. "What would he make of us then?" RB asked.

"We'll probably never find out. I invited him to the auction, but I'm pretty sure he won't be coming."

"Why not?"

"He'll be too busy playing dominoes and talking trash with his best friends at the rec center. I swear he's spent most of his life with his work buddies."

"Are any of your brothers coming?" Woody asked.

Shay shook her head. "If I invited them and their families, there wouldn't be room for the people interested in actually buying the Brewster. And black tie events aren't really their thing."

"They're not my thing either, but Gabe insisted on taking me to get a new suit," RB said.

"A *new* suit?" Woody laughed. "You mean your *first* suit."

"Whatever." RB got up and stuck a bagel in the toaster. "I'm not on sale. I don't see why I can't just wear my sweats."

Shay shook her head and took RB's seat. "Because you're

representing our business, so you have to *look* the business."

"What're you wearing, pretty boy?" Woody asked.

Shay rapped Woody's knuckles with her spoon. "A very elegant evening dress and four-inch heels. Why? You want to try it on for size?"

Woody laughed and rubbed her hand. "Obviously, I'd love to. I look like a bad drag queen in a dress, although I do have amazing calves."

"But you walk like a farmer with a sack of potatoes on his back, and you'd break your neck in heels." RB chuckled. "Though I'd pay to see you try."

A heavy thundering of feet downstairs announced Gabe's imminent arrival.

"That was fast, even for you," Shay said. "Are you sure you've buttoned up your shirt straight?"

Gabe tugged on the hem of her plaid shirt and inspected herself. "Looks like it."

"*Looks* like you're dressing to impress. I don't think Max cares if you wear Ralph Lauren as long as you bring him treats."

"No, but Lori's got a soft spot for this style."

Shay smiled. She wasn't used to seeing this vulnerable, slightly desperate side of Gabe and wasn't quite sure what to make of it. She'd just have to be around enough to support Gabe when she needed it. But she couldn't help thinking that it was another indication that love wasn't for her. And maybe it wasn't for Gabe either, at least, not with Lori. "Good luck. Text me when you're on your way back; we'll get something to eat."

"Sounds good. See you later, guys," Gabe said and left to a chorus of goodbyes from RB and Woody.

"If they don't fix things, do you think it'd still be okay to stay in touch with Hank?" RB dropped into a chair and took a huge bite of the cream cheese bagel she'd prepared.

Shay frowned. "Why would you want to do that?"

"He was interested in what I had to say about his veterans'

project, so I told him that I'd write down some ideas and send them to him."

Woody snatched the other half of RB's bagel and licked the top of it before RB could reclaim it. "That'd be okay as long as that was the end of it. If Lori cuts Gabe out of her life completely, I'm pretty sure she won't want you talking about Lori's dad all the time."

"Do you think she'll do that?" RB asked.

Woody shrugged. "She was damn angry last night. Gabe's been spending a lot of time with her, and she had plenty of opportunities to come clean about Cynthia Nelson. Lori might not be able to forgive that kind of betrayal after what she's been through."

"It's not a betrayal." Shay dropped her spoon into her bowl and pushed it away, the sudden acidic burn in her stomach destroying her appetite. "We all know why Gabe fucked Cynthia, and it was nothing like someone cheating on their wife for fun."

Woody held up her hands. "Hey, I'm sorry, Shay. I shouldn't have said anything."

Shay released her death-grip on the kitchen table and got up to empty her breakfast into the trash. She sighed and leaned against the countertop. "And she's paid a heavy price for it already."

Woody nodded. "That wasn't your fault, Shay. Gabe doesn't blame you, you know that."

Shay studied her feet and directed her focus on the need for a pedicure. The polish had chipped off on her big toe when she'd caught it on Rosie's bed in her haste to get Rosie naked. Thinking about that was preferable to revisiting her guilt over what Nelson had done to Gabe.

"Shay..."

She looked up finally and tried to smile.

"Nelson had to go, and Gabe made it happen," RB said. "She'd do that and more for you, for any of us, in a heartbeat."

"I know that. But she shouldn't still be paying for it. She's really opened up to Lori. If this doesn't turn out the way it should, it'll break Gabe's heart." *And mine.* Anything that hurt Gabe hurt her twice over. She might never entertain the romantic version of love, but she loved Gabe as much as she'd loved anyone.

"If that happens, we'll be here for her like she's always been there for us," Woody said. "It'll make a change for us to look after the alpha, right?"

Shay smiled easily this time. Their chosen family could be as dysfunctional as a blood family, but their bonds had been forged in the heat of war and were unbreakable. If Lori was stupid enough not to listen to Gabe's explanation, if she was too short-sighted to give Gabe a chance, and if she did break Gabe's heart, Shay and the rest of their little family would circle the wagons and hold her safe until she recovered.

After everything Gabe had been through, she deserved her happily ever after. Shay hoped that Lori was just as smitten with Gabe. Everything would work itself out. It had to.

Chapter Six

THE TROUBLE WITH HAVING a best friend was that they often knew you better than you knew yourself. Rosie had told Lori she was slammed this week and too busy to have lunch, but Lori had launched a text offensive to rival a celebrity stalker, and Rosie had eventually caved. She was happy that Lori and Gabe had made up after the disaster that had been Lori's party, but with that over with, she had plenty of time to think about the chaos in her own life.

"I'm sorry I spent the whole time waxing lyrical about Gabe." Lori hugged her and squeezed even tighter than usual.

The Turner family hugs could be a national treasure or an ancient curse; today, it was the latter. Rosie was one excessively long Turner hug away from dissolving into a flood of tears, and she had to pull away, not wanting to create a spectacle in view of people she knew. Lori had booked a table at the eighteenth-floor garden restaurant of her ex-office building for "old times' sake." Lori was moving on with her life, and Rosie was supposed to be doing the same with her new job, so Lori had postulated that it'd be nice to eat at one of their old haunts. The logic was flawed, but the view of Lake Michigan wasn't, so Rosie had reluctantly acquiesced.

Worry flashed across Lori's expression at her withdrawal, and she took her seat without taking her gaze off Rosie. The waiter who'd seated them confirmed their usual order, while Rosie adjusted the cutlery on her place setting to avoid eye contact.

"What's wrong?" Lori asked.

"What makes you think something's wrong? I told you I was busy this week. I haven't been avoiding you."

Lori arched her eyebrow and took Rosie's hand. "I know when

you're not okay, just like you do with me. What was it you said last month? 'The good thing about someone knowing you so well is that you can barely do anything without someone caring about it.' And my BFF radar tells me you're avoiding me, but I can't figure out why. So talk to me."

The waiter interrupted with two glasses of white wine, and Rosie took a much-needed sip.

"It's Mom," she said, knowing that Lori wouldn't give this up now that she had a sense something wasn't right.

Lori rolled her eyes then frowned. "Isn't she a couple of months too early to begin her usual Thanksgiving drama?"

"That's what I thought...at four a.m. on Thursday morning."

"Four a.m.? That's a new low, isn't it?" Lori picked up her glass then put it back without drinking. "Wait. That was a week ago, and you're only just telling me now."

Rosie tsked. "I'm only telling you now because you're forcing it out of me."

"That's a good thing too, because apparently, you don't share your troubles with your best friend anymore. What's up with that?"

Rosie smiled at the waiter after he placed their starter platter on the table and waited until he left before she answered. "I wasn't sharing because I love you, and you don't need this. You're just re-emerging from over a year in hiding after a particularly vicious end to your marriage, and you're only a few days into a brand-new relationship with a woman whom you may well have manifested into existence from your dreams. You should be riding the rainbow on your pink unicorn, not sharing in the atomic bomb disaster that is my mom." She chose a warmed tigelle and placed a piece of ham on top before taking a bite. She let out a contented sigh, grateful that her mom's latest drama hadn't affected her appetite...yet.

"No. Just no." Lori popped a cherry tomato in her mouth and shook her head. "I've disappeared on you enough. I wasn't there when you were coping with your career change, and that was bad enough. I won't let any new relationship get in the way of being there for you, especially when you're dealing with your craz—with your mom."

Rosie chuckled. Having someone in her corner as loving and supportive as Lori had taken some getting used to after spending her life practically alone, but that unconditional compassion was also why she'd struggled so much when Lori had retreated into herself after her divorce. "It would be nice to talk to you about it." She filled Lori in on the early morning conversation and reeled off the cocktail of chemicals her mom might need to manage the condition, as well as the astronomical cost to get the drugs in this country. "With the basic insurance she's got, she can't afford it."

Lori bit her bottom lip and shook her head. "She'd need to win the Powerball lotto to afford that. I hate to say it, but it seems like Mexico was her only choice."

Rosie nodded and chewed on another piece of melt-in-the-mouth tigelle. "And I understand that, I do. But why the early morning phone call and then nothing?"

Lori's expression made it clear that Rosie knew the answer to her own question. "That's how she operates, isn't it? That's been your whole life. She has no motivation to change that behavior."

Rosie tried to spear a tomato with her fork, but it skidded off the plate and onto the floor, before rolling under another table. She and Lori pretended not to notice. "Her behavior is the whole reason I got into counseling. I thought I might be able to help her change."

"It was her job to help mold you to cope with the world, not the other way around," Lori said and waved her fork at Rosie. "You told my mom that you left therapy because the people you were helping weren't changing. Was it that? Or was it more about your mom never changing?"

"I thought *I* was supposed to be the therapist." Rosie chuckled, but Lori's question sowed a seed she knew she'd have to cultivate eventually since it was something she hadn't thought of. "I can't deal with that right now. Mom disappearing has me suspended in limbo."

"Which is exactly the way your mom likes her audience—waiting with bated breath for the next act. Enter Brenda Morgan, stage left."

Lori was right. After all the experiences Rosie had recounted to her, she didn't need a degree in therapy to make that judgment. "Meanwhile, I'm scurrying around trying to figure out how to come to the rescue. Again. I can't cover her on my insurance unless she's considered dependent on me, which would mean having her move in and—"

"You can't do that." Lori practically slammed her fork down and looked at Rosie, her expression serious. "It took you too long to extricate yourself from that situation to go back now... You're not considering it, are you?"

Rosie rubbed her forehead and blew out a long breath. "I don't know. I don't know what to do. She and Aunt Sheila are the only family I have left. I can't just wash my hands of her." She paused, unsure whether she could say what she was really thinking. But if she couldn't tell Lori, she couldn't tell anyone. "You probably can't begin to understand, but I sometimes wish that I could do exactly that and forget she even exists. What kind of a callous monster does that make me?"

Lori placed her hand over Rosie's and squeezed gently. "You're not a monster for thinking that. You're human. That woman has done nothing for you except give you life, and she only did that because she wanted to escape her own mother." She smiled. "And they're not the only family you have; my mom and dad adopted you years ago. I've had a great childhood, yeah, but that doesn't mean I can't empathize with what you're feeling. I think that if I'd had the same experience as you, I would've cut my mom out of my life long ago. Perhaps that's easy for me to say *because* I've got great parents. But I do understand, and please don't ever think that you should censor or dilute your feelings for me. I'm your best friend, Rosie. I won't ever judge you."

Rosie inhaled deeply and nodded slowly. If she tried to speak now, the words would never make it out before her tears fell. And the building's main receptionist had just come out onto the terrace and was heading toward them.

"Rosie! It's so good to see you," Sarah said.

She held out her arms as she walked, clearly expecting a reunion hug, which was strange since they'd shared the briefest of conversations and zero physical contact during Rosie's three years in this building. Rosie rose reluctantly and managed to keep the embrace short and distant. She introduced Lori and retook her seat without extending an invitation to join them.

"Take care, Rosie. It was lovely to meet you, Lori," Sarah said and left to join a male companion whom she greeted with an X-rated kiss.

"She seemed nice," Lori said.

"She's a terrible gossip. Before lunch is over, everyone in this building will have been told I'm having a secret affair with a married woman."

Lori laughed. "Why would she think I'm married?"

Rosie tapped Lori's naked ring finger. "Tan line."

"Ah..." Lori clasped her right hand over her left to cover it. "I'll be more discreet and wear makeup next time," she said and winked. "Anyway, back to family stuff. Has your mom been in touch with her sister?"

"Aunt Sheila said she hasn't heard from Mom since Thursday, like me, though her phone call was at a more reasonable time of day, and Mom didn't say anything about kidney disease or medication."

"What *did* she tell her?"

"That she was going to Mexico to get married to Keith."

"Isn't she still married to the last guy?" Lori asked.

"That's what Aunt Sheila asked too. Mom said that one didn't count because it was in Canada."

Lori spluttered her wine back into her glass. "Does she really believe that?"

"God knows, but—"

"Now you don't know which story is true."

Rosie tapped her nose. "Exactly. With my mom, it could be both, and I can't ask to find out because her phone is switched off and goes directly to a recorded message."

"Then all you can do is wait. Which is exactly what she wants you to do so she can make a grand re-entrance... I'm so sorry, Rosie."

She wrinkled her nose and shrugged. "That's why I'm keeping as busy as possible to fill the hours. This way, I have less time to spin my wheels and worry about her. So let's talk about something else."

"No problem." Lori wiggled her eyebrows. "Are you filling your hours with Shay too?"

"Mm, I'm sorry to disappoint you, but no. I haven't seen her since the debacle on Saturday."

"Haven't you spoken to her at all?"

Rosie narrowed her eyes. "Why do you look so disappointed?"

Lori scooped a piece of poached egg onto her fork and grinned. "I might have a romantic notion of two best friends getting their happily-ever-afters with two *other* best friends."

"I'd be okay with happy-for-now, but wow, you're five days in, and you already know it's forever?" Rosie laughed. "That's impressive. Is the U-Haul rental imminent?"

Lori waved the notion away and ate her food. "Definitely not. Shay said the same thing to Gabe, and I think it freaked her out. We're taking it slow."

"And how are you feeling about tomorrow and finally getting rid of that car?"

"I'm excited to have that piece of *the lawyer* out of my life. Woody is convinced bidding will blow the reserve price out of the water. She even thinks some celebrities are quietly interested in it. We'll see. I'm just happy that the sale of that car will close the chapter of my life."

"And on that sour note," Rosie motioned in the direction of Lori's hip, "how's your new tattoo feeling?"

Lori sucked in her breath. "Sore. I'd forgotten how painful the original one was, and that was just an initial. With all the line work and detailing of the heather and the wings of the butterfly..." She gave an exaggerated shudder. "It was two hours of pain and tears I won't forget."

"You won't be in a hurry to get matching tattoos with Gabe then? If she's got any virgin skin left." She held up her hand when Lori's eyes lit up. "I don't want to know."

"Would you want to know about Shay's tattoo?"

Rosie raised her eyebrows, remembering every inch of Shay's beautiful skin, untouched by an artist's needles but severely scarred on her left shoulder from the lightning strike she barely survived. "Why would she get one now?"

"Relax. Gabe said she changed her mind." Lori wiggled her eyebrows. "Skillful avoidance of my question, by the way, but it's not like I'm going to forget I asked, is it?"

"Of course you won't... Fine. I haven't seen Shay, but I got a text from her yesterday asking about my plans for the auction."

Lori gave a low whistle. "Ooh, she asked you on a date."

"Nothing that formal," Rosie said. "More of an inquiry as to my availability to celebrate with her when the auction is over. She did say she'd pick me up if I didn't want to play third wheel to you and Gabe."

"Romantic," Lori said, deadpan.

"I accepted. You two are sickeningly sweet and simultaneously exploding with hormones. It can be a bit much in a small space like the inside of a car."

Lori tapped Rosie's arm and grinned. "I'm not apologizing for finally discovering the joys of love and sex."

"And you should know that I would never ask you to. I just don't need to be exposed to it."

"You make it sound like a virus."

"That's what Shay thinks it is. I get the impression that their little circle of friends expected to live their years out bachelor-style, and none of them want to get caught up in a long-term relationship."

"Does that work for you with Shay?"

Rosie held out her hands. "She's a stunning woman. I'll take whatever she's prepared to give for as long as I can get it. We've agreed to be friends with benefits, and that's fine with me right now."

Lori didn't look convinced. "Will it be fine with you in a few weeks or months?"

"Honestly, I don't know. But I'm not sabotaging the chance to have fabulous sex with a gorgeous goddess like Shay on the off chance that my feelings might get involved where they're not wanted." She glanced at her phone and tapped the screen with her fingernail. "I'm sorry, I have to go. I pushed a meeting back thirty minutes to come for lunch on the proviso that I'd meet him at his office instead of our HQ, and his building is across town." She began to pull her wallet from her purse.

"I'll get this. I dragged you out here. The least I can do is pay."

They got up, and Lori enveloped Rosie in another glorious hug. What she would have given to have had these as a child. But she had them now, so she soaked it in and embraced Lori hard.

"Call me anytime, okay?" Lori said when they finally parted. "I'm here for you."

"I will." Rosie walked away with Lori's last words adding to the comfort of her hug. They were words she'd never heard from her mom's mouth, and she probably never would. She hit the button for the elevator and did a little shake, as if that might loosen her mom's grip on her thoughts right now. She scoffed at herself. It had never worked before; why would it work now? Instead, she'd continue to do what she'd told Lori she was doing: filling her hours with work. She flicked through her messages to find a new one had come in from Shay during lunch.

Do you want a late-night visitor?

Rosie responded with the knotted rope emoji and a question

mark. Since she'd broached the possibility of tying Shay to her bed, she'd had some wicked fantasy dreams and was eager to turn them into reality.

She stared at her screen impatiently as *typing...* appeared beneath Shay's name. When her message finally popped up, Rosie took Shay's returning grinning devil emoji to be the green light. If anything could take her mind off her concern for her mom, it was a few hours with Shay under her hands.

Chapter Seven

GABE PULLED UP OUTSIDE Bonnie's Brew, and Woody jumped out of the truck. "Don't forget I want coconut milk now," she shouted after her.

Woody waved over her shoulder, and Gabe rolled back into traffic.

"Remind me why you've changed milks?" Shay poked Gabe's bicep. "It's not like cows haven't done their fair share to build this body."

"I'm just trying something different."

Shay arched her eyebrow and twisted to talk to RB in the back. "Doesn't Lori like coconut milk?"

RB's expression indicated she had no idea, but she grinned. "Yeah, I reckon she does. She works quick. Didn't take her long to get you under control, did it?"

"What're you talking about? It's just milk." Gabe took the right into the alley alongside their garage.

Shay shook her head slowly. "It always starts with the milk, doesn't it, RB? Then it's the meals, and 'Honey, are you sure you want that second helping of pie?' Before you know it, she'll be sending you to work with a to-go cup of green tea and no money for coffee."

"What the hell have you two been binge-watching now? No lesbians have done that ever in the history of the world."

Shay laughed. "Probably not. But you've been drinking a half gallon of milk every day since I've known you. So what's up with the coconut?" She didn't actually believe that Lori had any designs to change Gabe at all, but it was fun making her squirm.

"Jesus. If you really need to know, I picked up the wrong coffee at Bonnie's the other day, and I liked it." Gabe gave Shay a sideways glare. "So no, Lori doesn't like coconut milk, and she likes my body just fine so I can eat all the pie I—"

"What's this joker doing here?" Shay gestured to the huge black SUV with tinted windows parked sideways in front of the gated entrance to their garage lot.

Gabe pulled to a stop twenty yards short of the vehicle but didn't cut the engine. "Nobody recognizes it?"

RB shuffled to the center console and stuck her head between their shoulders. "Nope. And there's nothing on the books for a Yukon today or for the rest of the week."

Shay looked at RB. "You memorize what we've got coming in?"

RB shrugged. "It's a habit."

"Huh." Shay turned back to look at the mystery vehicle, but no one had emerged from within it yet. "Maybe it's been abandoned," she said and reached for the door handle.

Gabe grabbed her shoulder and pulled her back. "Wait. You don't know who's in there."

Shay chuckled. "Who do you think it is? Some covert government operatives who want our old Army skills for some undercover operation? This isn't an episode of the A-Team, Gabe."

"What's the A-Team?" RB asked.

"How can she not—"

"She's younger than us; we'll fix it later," Shay said and opened her door. "Let's go see who our clandestine clients are." By the time she'd gotten out and was at the hood of the truck, Gabe and RB were beside her.

"Should I get a tire iron?" RB asked.

Shay smirked. "We've got Gabe. If their intentions are nefarious, the only reason you might need a tire iron will be to unknot them after she's finished with them."

Gabe cracked her knuckles and grinned. "It's been a minute since we had a fight together."

"You sound hopeful," Shay said.

Before Gabe could answer, all four doors of the SUV sprang open. Two tall women got out of the front. From the look of their buzzcuts and the almost-matching outfits of dark trousers with shirts and ties, maybe Gabe wasn't that far from the truth. One of the passengers in the rear of the vehicle emerged, and Shay couldn't help but twitch a little. The woman wore a battered brown leather jacket and faded jeans stuck inside work boots, but she also had long brown hair that only softened the seriousness of her expression only slightly. The twitch switched gear into something else when Shay got a glimpse of the hardware she was packing. "Gun," she whispered and felt Gabe and RB's answering tension like a brick wall pressing against her chest. She couldn't see the final passenger until she walked around one of the buzzcut women.

"Sergeant Gabe Jackson and Corporals Shanae Washington and Felicity 'RB' Thomas. It's a pleasure to meet you all." She saluted and walked toward them.

Shay recognized the voice before its owner came fully into focus. "Elodie Fontaine?"

Elodie nodded and came around the front of the Yukon. "I'm sorry we didn't call ahead. I have to be careful who knows my schedule." She shook hands with Gabe then Shay and RB.

Elodie's long-haired friend stood by her side, though her approach had been stealthier, like she'd *appeared* rather than walked, and offered her hand too. "You should apologize for those two. I told her she didn't need 'em, but her agent insisted."

"Paige is just being extra careful after what happened to CJ in Utah," Elodie said. "And she didn't know *you* were coming with me."

Shay's interest piqued; that inferred Elodie's friend was more capable than her two hefty bodyguards combined. She assumed they were here to pick up the Brewster; maybe they were staying in the city and would be at a loose end. Shay had a hookup arranged with Rosie tonight, but she'd bet Rosie would be happy to entertain

Elodie's friend together. The friend's lips quirked slightly, clearly registering Shay's interest.

Elodie's friend motioned to Gabe. "Twenty bucks," she said to Elodie and held out her hand. "Pay up."

Elodie rolled her eyes. "Subtle, Ice."

She smiled at them, and Shay bit her lip. Elodie was a touch too hard and her hair too short for Shay's usual taste, but there was still something undeniably magnetic about her that made Shay swoon. She looked again at the friend Elodie had called Ice. Melting her seemed more achievable than a night with Elodie now that the infamous player had taken herself off the market to play happy families with a celebrated investigative journalist.

Elodie pulled her wallet from the inside pocket of her jacket and opened it. "We had a bet about how big you were compared to my friend Dak," she said and handed a crisp twenty-dollar bill to Ice. "She won."

Shay could almost feel Gabe preen beside her as she stood a little straighter and puffed out her considerable chest.

"Am I bigger or smaller than your friend?" Gabe asked.

Elodie's smile grew wider, clearly recognizing Gabe's fragile ego. "Bigger, like Ice said you were. I didn't think regular women came much bigger than Dak."

Shay heard "Oh my God" at about the same time as the sound of a tray of coffee hitting the ground echoed down the alley.

"It's really you," Woody said.

Shay turned to see Woody pulling her phone from her pants pocket. She shook her head and motioned for her to stow it.

"It's okay," Elodie said. "I'm happy for you to take photos, but maybe we could go inside." She gestured toward the passing pedestrian traffic at the top of the passageway.

"Absolutely." Gabe opened the side door.

The bodyguards entered first then everyone filed in except Woody, who stooped to pick up the wasted coffee. Putting a little more Shay into her sashay, she made sure to precede Ice, who came in last.

Ice caught hold of her wrist. "I appreciate the show, but we're heading straight out of town."

Shay groaned lightly. Had they been *anywhere* else but work, she would've suggested they connect in the backseat of the SUV. "That's disappointing," she said, though she'd been more interested in a hard-body sandwich with Rosie than taking on the dark and dangerous stranger alone. She waited for Woody to come in with the soggy remains of their coffee cups and closed the door behind her, while Ice sauntered away in Elodie's direction.

"I can't believe Elodie Fontaine is in our garage," Woody said. "I wish she'd brought her wife though; she's beautiful. I love a curvy woman."

Shay nodded. "I think we all do." She followed Woody into the back where they'd been storing the Brewster since the auction.

"You're driving her all the way to LA?" Gabe asked.

"Yep." Elodie ran her hand over the Brewster's grill. "That won't be a problem, will it?"

"No." Shay opened the digital lock box on the wall to retrieve the Brewster's keys. "You'll need to keep her at around three thousand rpm for the first five hundred miles, then you can increase to four thousand. After a thousand miles, take her up slow and steady. We've customized a V-8 engine to fit, and we've switched out the sliding mesh three-speed to a constant-mesh six-speed gearbox, so you won't be lacking power." She handed the keys to Elodie. "A two-k mile drive is going to be a great way for you to get used to her."

"Erm..." Woody cleared her throat.

Shay looked across at her. "Did I forget something?"

"God, no, of course not." Woody held up one of the digital SLRs she kept at the garage to document their restorations. "It'd just be great to get a team photo of us handing Ms. Fontaine the keys."

"Of course," Elodie said. "Take whatever you need. Where do you want me?"

Anywhere and everywhere would be great. Shay suppressed a smirk and didn't look at Gabe for fear of them both laughing like teenagers.

"What about Solo?" RB asked. "She won't be happy she's missing out."

Shay checked her watch. "She's normally here by now. The triplets must be acting up."

"Now or never," Ice said. "We can't wait around."

"I can add her in post-production," Woody set up a tripod and directed the impromptu photo shoot until she was satisfied she'd gotten the moment suitably immortalized, while the bodyguards stayed mute and hovered in the background on high alert.

"Is it okay to ask what made you go straight in at $1.5 million?" Gabe asked.

"History." Elodie opened the driver's side door and slid into the leather seat.

Shay couldn't help thinking that Elodie ran her hands over the steering wheel with the same reverence she probably used to touch her wife.

"Marie Zimmerman was an amazing artist, and she was one of us," Elodie said. "I want to help preserve the memory of as many butch women as I can."

"That's awesome." Gabe handed Elodie the original vehicle title, sheathed in protective plastic. "She used to live in Gramercy Park. Nice neighborhood."

Elodie tilted her head. "I actually own that property too. It came on the market just after I released *Night Deeds*—"

"Your first Oscar," RB said as if Elodie and the rest of them didn't already know that.

Elodie nodded and had the grace not to look irritated by the interruption. "I almost bankrupted myself buying it, but it's still one of my favorite properties."

That was high praise, considering that her extensive portfolio included a private island, if the article in *People* magazine was accurate. Shay looked over the car roof at Gabe and raised her eyebrows. What would it be like to have that kind of money? They'd scraped, bartered, and put everything they had—and everything they *didn't* have—to get their dream garage off the ground.

Elodie climbed out of the car and grinned. "Any chance we can get her out of here so I can get on the road?"

"Sure thing." Gabe motioned to RB, who then went to the wide rear doors that opened onto their parking lot.

The bodyguards quickly joined her and surveyed the area before they gave Elodie a thumbs-up.

Elodie pulled something from her back pocket and gave it to Gabe. "If you ever need any help with the garage, give me a call. It's so good to see veterans succeeding... Too many of us don't fare so well."

Gabe slipped the card into her pocket and nodded. "Thank you. That means a lot." She leaned into the car and released the parking brake, then the four of them pushed the Brewster out onto the tarmac.

"The paperwork!" RB ran back into the garage and returned with the relevant documents to sign ownership over to Elodie.

Ice put her hand on Shay's hip. "I'll drop in the next time I'm here."

"I have a feeling I'd like that."

"You'd more than *like* it," Ice said and squeezed Shay's hip firmly before joining Elodie outside.

Shay sighed quietly. When she told Rosie about this tonight, she had a feeling she'd be as disappointed as Shay was.

Gabe opened the side gates, then she and one of the bodyguards shifted their vehicles to clear the alley.

"Will Lori Turner be at the Sanctuary?" Elodie asked as she slid back into the driver's seat, while Ice sat beside her.

"That's where I left her this morning." Gabe's eyebrow quirked slightly.

Elodie grinned. "Ah, you're together. Nice." She nodded

approvingly.

Ice leaned out of the window. "Don't text or call to tell her Dee's dropping by."

Elodie shook her head. "She meant to say please, obviously."

"I did?" Ice wound the window back up without another word.

Elodie started the engine and pulled away, closely followed by the dark SUV.

Before they were out of sight, Solo pulled up in the lot. She jumped out of her car and slammed the door. "Tell me I didn't just miss Elodie Fontaine and Madison Ford picking up the Brewster in person."

Shay shook her head. "You didn't just miss Elodie Fontaine and Madison Ford picking up the Brewster in person..." She waited until Solo sighed with relief. "You *did* miss Elodie Fontaine and her friend picking up the Brewster in person." She laughed, and everyone but Solo joined in.

"Fuckity fuck fuck." Solo kicked the door panel of her car and left a dent. "Double fuck," she said, inspecting it.

"New cars get damaged so easily," RB said.

"Old cars don't fit three baby seats." Solo sneered then looked back out to the alley as if that might inspire Elodie Fontaine to throw the car in reverse. "I don't believe it." She spun back around. "Did you know she was coming?"

"No. They were here when we showed up a few minutes ago."

"We've got photos," Woody said.

Shay shoved her; it was clear there was more to Solo's outburst than mere angst at missing out on meeting a lesbian icon.

Woody grinned, not ready to give it up just yet. "I can superimpose you onto them."

"Gee, thanks." Solo gave her car another kick and stomped past them into the shop.

"Looks like there's still trouble in paradise," RB said. "Further proof that being a bachelor is far less complicated."

Gabe clapped RB on the back. "Less complicated but less

fulfilling," she said and followed Solo inside.

RB looked at Shay. "What do you think?"

Shay's watch buzzed with a message before she could answer, and she tapped the screen when she saw it was from Rosie.

Still on for tonight?

"I think you can be plenty fulfilled with no complications." Her situation with Rosie was proving to be exactly that. "Come on, let's go put Solo's world to rights." She motioned for RB to go before her and fired off a quick text back to Rosie. *Already thinking about it. I'll be there*. Recalling their last encounter, she rubbed her wrists and smiled, then she sent Rosie another text with the rope emoji and the words, *Your turn*.

Yeah, she was plenty fulfilled without complications. And nothing was going to change that.

Chapter Eight

Rosie stared out of her twenty-first-floor window and looked down at the Chicago River. It didn't give her the same joy as her previous office view of Lake Michigan, but it was a good enough competitor. She needed the water to calm her more now than she ever had as a therapist, because though her clients had often been challenging, her new boss, Billy Franklin, was in a whole other league.

Her phone alarm sounded, indicating she should begin the trek across the enormous building and up fifty-three floors to his office for a meeting marked as "super killer important" in the subject line. She didn't know if he or his PA written the email—their combined age was only a little older than her—but either way, it wasn't the professional approach she'd expected when she came to work here. She supposed she should be grateful that he wasn't a stuffed suit with a power complex, but couldn't there be a middle ground between that and millionaire frat boy?

Rosie scooped up her iPad and phone from her desk and headed out of her office. She saw the back of Mindy Fletcher entering the kitchen and hurried past; if she got waylaid with Mindy and her many tales of office gossip, she didn't stand a chance of making her meeting on time.

"Rosie Morgan! Just the person I wanted to see."

Damn it. Mindy had a nose like a sniffer hound and had probably gotten the scent of Rosie's perfume before she even left her office. She turned and smiled. "Mindy, hi. I can't talk; I'm on my way to see Mr. Franklin."

Mindy's plastered-on smile dropped, and her eyes widened,

making her look like a Tim Burton illustration. "You're on your way to see Mr. Franklin?"

Rosie nodded and took a step back. "Something 'super killer important' and very last-minute." *As usual.* She kept the opinion to herself, knowing it would be exaggerated ten-fold and repeated twenty times before she returned from Franklin's office.

"Last-minute? Oh, dear."

Rosie pressed her lips together and tamped down the irritation that always rose when talking to Mindy. She still hadn't gotten used to Mindy's predilection to repeat all, or at least part, of everything people said. Now that she was no longer a therapist, she didn't have to be quite so patient with people. "Yeah. I don't want to keep him waiting, so if it's nothing important..." She took another step and half-turned, but Mindy rushed forward and caught her arm.

"I was going to tell you that Rob and Tica got fired last night. Mr. Franklin is having another house-cleaning."

"House-cleaning?" Crap, now she was doing it too. "What does that mean?"

Mindy moved in even closer and glanced around the open-office layout before looking at Rosie with a serious expression. "Every six months, he fires a few people and replaces them with new blood, usually people with no marketing experience."

Now Mindy had her attention. Rosie had been there six months and was likely the new blood from Franklin's last 'house-cleaning,' and Tica had started the same week as her. "Exactly how many people does Mr. Franklin usually replace?"

Mindy squeezed her arm then finally let go. "Oops, sorry," she said, looking at the red fingernails marks she'd left on Rosie's skin. Then she frowned and touched the light bruising around her wrist. "Ouch, what happened there?"

Rosie pulled her arm away and pushed the sleeve of her sweater down, masking the evidence of the fun she'd had with Shay two nights ago. "Just a bracelet I wore too tight," she said, bending the truth only slightly. "How extensive is the clear out?"

"Always in threes," Mindy said.

And now Rosie understood why Mindy's initial glee had turned flat when she said she had a meeting with Franklin. It wasn't as if she loved her job just yet, but being fired after six months wasn't on her to-do list. That wasn't even long enough to get a decent letter of recommendation. It hadn't been sufficient time to prove her worth. What she lacked in marketing experience, she made up for with her understanding of the psychology of sales. That's how she'd gotten the position in the first place. "Has anyone ever talked their way out of being fired?"

Mindy shook her head. "Once Mr. Franklin has made up his mind, he won't be deterred. Steph Zawinski begged to keep her job—she has two kids and a husband with MS to support—but he had her escorted from the building like a criminal."

Rosie twisted a strand of her hair and sighed. She'd heard a different version of that story, one where Steph had been involved in corporate espionage. But that was the problem with office gossip: unless you were involved in the situation, it was impossible to know the truth. "You're telling me that my 'super killer important' meeting is actually me being fired?" She supposed the subject line made more sense if that turned out to be the case. He was killing her career in marketing before she'd had the chance to succeed.

Mindy shrugged and held out her hands. "I'm not telling you that, no."

"But three people get fired every six months, two people were canned last night, and I'm the only one with a meeting with Mr. Franklin this morning." She turned and headed toward the elevator. "In case I'm thrown straight out onto the street, it's been a trip getting to know you, Mindy. Take care," she said over her shoulder then ignored the multiple looks of both pity and relief from everyone else that she passed. It seemed that everyone knew her fate before she did.

In the elevator that she was thankfully the single occupant of, Rosie flicked through her messages. She sent Lori a text bemoaning her plight and asking if they could meet for drinks over the weekend, which would be completely free once she was relieved of her workload. Then she came to the stream of missives between her and Shay. Was this the kind of thing they could share? Or did it overstep the boundaries they'd been careful to implement? Rosie lowered her phone and followed the light on the wall panel as it ran inexorably upward through the floor numbers and toward her imminent termination. She shouldn't talk to Shay about this, no. That's what Lori was for. Shay was just for sex and fun, and there was nothing fun about being newly unemployed... except that it freed her time for more sex and fun with Shay.

The light stopped at seventy-four, and the doors opened slowly. Rosie caught herself being maudlin and took a deep breath. She exited the elevator before the doors were fully opened; if this was the end of her chapter here, there was no point delaying it. Her student loans, mortgage, and car loan wouldn't pay themselves. She'd have to regroup. And fast. She refused to go back to the life she'd lived as a kid, the life her mom was still living...wherever the heck she was right now, which was definitely something she could do without having to worry over on top of what was about to happen.

Franklin's executive assistant, Anna, greeted her with a genuine-looking smile. How she coped with Franklin constantly and in such close proximity, Rosie couldn't begin to fathom, but she never appeared harassed or overwhelmed.

"Billy's waiting for you in the purple room," Anna said. "Would you like an herbal tea? Chamomile?"

"No, thanks." So Mindy was right. Franklin occupied the whole top floor; half of it was allocated to his office, but the remaining space had been separated into rooms of various sizes and colors, painted to match emotions and/or the emotional state he wanted staff to be in. Purple was designed to calm and soothe—perfect for a parting of the ways that had the potential to be difficult. The offer of chamomile tea felt like too much though.

Rosie wandered along the hallway, taking the time to appreciate the wall art in a way she hadn't done before because she was usually hurrying to another urgent meeting. Since this was the last time she'd be making this journey, she figured she should make the most of the opportunity to be among millions of dollars' worth of the stuff.

The door to the purple room was open. Franklin was dressed in a fluorescent yellow tracksuit and neon-blue sneakers, both of which clashed terribly with the lilac wingback chair he lounged on, looking like he was chilling after an all-night party. A number of beanbags littered the floor. God, she hated those Styrofoam-filled excuses for furniture. She could never get in or out of them elegantly in a snug pencil skirt and three-inch heels, and she always had to ask someone to pull her up or end up rolling out of them in a very undignified manner. She looked around the room, praying for one sensible chair so that when she left, she could do it with panache.

Of course there was nothing. Okay, this meeting wouldn't take long; she'd just stand.

"Good morning, Mr. Franklin," Rosie said as politely as she could manage. If she was going to have any chance of getting a decent recommendation, she'd have to play nice.

"Roe-Roe, come in! Are you ever going to call me Billy?"

"Good morning, Billy." She entered the room and tried for a convincing smile even though his over-familiar pet name pressed its usual button. Was plain old Rosie too pedestrian? Even her mom couldn't manage it.

"I want you to clear your desk of every client you've got and hand them over to Jay-Jay."

Wow. No preamble or thanks, just straight into it. Did she want to know why he was firing her? It probably wouldn't be logical, and that might drive her more nuts than not knowing. Best just to accept his decision and get to moving on. If he wouldn't change his mind for a woman with a family and an ill husband to support, he certainly wouldn't care about for a single woman with no dependents, no matter how gigantic her student loans were. "Jason's a good choice. I like his work."

Jason was a terrible choice. How had Jason and his teenaged acne-face missed the house-cleaning to stay and take over her portfolio? She couldn't really accuse Franklin of discriminating against her on the basis of her age. He wouldn't have given her a job at all if that was his problem, so had one of her clients complained about the way she'd handled their account? Maybe it was about her sexuality. A couple of clients had hit on her, and she'd knocked them back. Franklin didn't seem like he was part of the old boys' network, but the threat of losing a multi-million-dollar account could make most people flexible with their morality.

"Exactly, right? Jay-Jay is amazing. I think he's going to be one of the GOATs in this business."

"Sure." The only way Jason might be the greatest of all time would be in using the greatest number of words to say nothing at all. His pitches were baffling, which she assumed was why he had such few clients.

"But Jay-Jay wasn't a good fit for this." He tapped his blue-painted fingernails on the bright pink folder on the table beside him. "But you're going to be *perfect*, like the missing piece of a jigsaw puzzle you find on the floor under the table. You'll slot into this project just like that."

She'd never been described as a dust-covered, discarded puzzle piece before, but he wasn't firing her, and Mindy was wrong. "What's the project?" she asked without missing a beat. No need to quiz him on the house-cleaning or make him aware of her self-doubt. It was every person for themselves in this place, and she got the feeling they'd all happily climb over each other's incapacitated bodies to get to the top.

He pushed the folder toward her. "Take a look. I don't have the words to do it justice. It's going to be ground-breaking though."

Rosie put her iPad on the table. She picked up the folder and flipped it open. "A new tool company?" Of course she'd be perfect for this: everything about her from her flawlessly manicured nails to her three-inch Manolo Blahnik slingback pumps screamed DIY and screw-y fix-y things. Pairing his marketing execs with items they'd likely never touched in their lives was a funny way to go about revolutionizing advertising. She'd have to spend a week researching which tools did what before she even began to think about how to sell them.

"Not just any tool company," Franklin said. "This one wants to focus on women and the LGBTQ community."

More interested now, she flicked through the glossy pages of shiny tools, sets, boxes, and bags that were available in every color of the rainbow, and then there were the exclusive hand-torched range where no two tools had the exact same finish. They were pretty, sure, but beyond the obvious, she still didn't see Franklin's logic in wanting her to lead the project. He insisted on his execs using every product he gave them to market for at least two weeks. She could think of some uses for the ones with the smooth long handles, but that would be a very different campaign to the one the tool company would be expecting.

Still, their budget was huge for a new account, and it might be just the challenge she needed to really kickstart a love for her new career.

"You can see why I thought of you, right?" He bounced up from his chair and offered his iPad.

Because a femme lesbian woman who's only interested in the kind of nails she has on the end of her fingers and toes would be perfect to convince other women just like her to buy the hammery things used for a totally different kind of nail. It was obvious why she'd gotten the account, yes.

But when she looked down at the screen, it did indeed become obvious why Franklin wanted her to handle this company, and her excitement stirred at the prospect. Staring up at her was a picture of herself, Lori, Shay, and the rest of her team standing in front of the vintage car Elodie Fontaine had just bought at auction for an eye-watering $1.5 million. How he'd gotten the photo, she couldn't imagine and didn't really want to know, but Shay's garage could be at the center of her campaign. Shay could be her poster girl because she was the kind of femme lesbian woman who *did* use all these tools and more, and she'd mentioned they were already getting a high proportion of gay male clients in there who were tired of their treatment at old-fashioned, toxic masculinity garages. Rosie's mind fast-forwarded to the photoshoot, and she sighed deeply. Happy times to come.

"I love it," she said and handed his iPad back to him. "What's the deadline for the proposal?"

"Yes! I knew you would! Fist bump!" he yelled.

She flashed her nails. "If I make a fist, I'll slice my palm open."

He opened his hand out. "High five then!"

She did that with a smile. Just a few minutes ago, she'd thought she was about to be canned. Now she was going to be paid to spend more time with Shay, *and* she'd get to dress her up for some sexy photo shoots. Rosie wasn't going anywhere. *Suck on that, Mindy Fletcher.*

Chapter Nine

SHAY FOLDED THE SILK scarf carefully and put it on Rosie's bedside table. "That has to be a record."

Rosie licked her lips and stretched luxuriously. The way her body went taut made Shay want to start all over again. Rosie had a way of making every time they got together just as sexy as the first.

"I can't get enough of the way you taste, and you come even harder after you've been tied up and teased—"

"For an *hour*," Shay said. "What did you expect?"

Rosie laughed. "I didn't expect to choke."

"You're complaining?"

Rosie shook her head. "Never. Like I said, you taste amazing... And you look amazing, by the way, which is one of the reasons I want you to help me sell wrenches and whatnot."

Shay sat up, not quite grasping what Rosie had just said or how she'd made the switch from sex to tools. "You want me to do what?"

"Make you the face of Unity Tools and build a whole marketing campaign based around your garage."

Shay propped herself up after fluffing her pillows, deciding to stay a while to see where this conversation led. "It's not my garage. There are five of us."

Rosie smiled. "I know that. And you all appeal to different markets—"

"You want to sell us?"

"No!" Rosie shifted to sit sideways and ran her fingers along Shay's arm. "I want to sell the tools, which your beautiful face will help me do. And you'll get as many sets of the tools as you need for the garage, plus image-rights fees. It's free advertising for you too;

you'll get a whole new customer group to boost your turnover."

Shay blew out a breath and rolled her eyes. "Isn't this just another company trading on our fears around inequality and profiting from it?"

"They're not like that," Rosie said, "although I had the exact same thought after I'd come down from the initial excitement of the idea of dressing you up in greasy overalls and shooting you with dark, moody lighting."

Shay grinned. That did sound like fun. "It's like you think I'm your walking, talking lesbian fantasy."

"I do, and you are. You can fuck me in your garage on the hood of your muscle car anytime you want." Rosie trailed her fingers over Shay's breast and circled her nipple with her nail. "But these photos would be for public consumption," she glanced at her phone and wiggled her eyebrows, "unlike the ones I've just taken."

"Which you'll never be tempted to use for revenge porn, right?" Shay's question wasn't serious. Rosie was crazy in bed, but she wasn't *that* kind of crazy.

"I wouldn't share those with anyone." Rosie arched her eyebrow. "A thing loses its value when too many people enjoy it. Anyway, the company is committed to donating ten percent of their net profit to LGBTQ charities and causes. It's written into their articles of formation. Plus, their whole management team is from our community. You can meet them if you like."

"And you'd be in charge of everything, would you?" Shay could get on board with the idea if she got to see Rosie in action, all ice queen and bossy femme.

Rosie tweaked her nipple, and Shay lifted her hips from the bed. Damn, she couldn't get enough of her touch.

"Like the sound of that, do you?" Rosie whispered before she shifted and took Shay's nipple into her mouth. She straddled Shay, pressing her pussy against Shay's stomach.

Shay put her hands on Rosie's hips, but Rosie grasped her wrists and pushed her arms above her head.

"Do you *want* me to be in charge of everything?" Rosie asked.

"Sometimes," Shay whispered and lifted her head to capture Rosie's breast in her mouth.

Rosie laughed lightly and pulled away. "So you'll talk to your boys about it?"

"My boys?"

"Boys with an i? Bros? Lori's my girl, but I don't think Gabe would take kindly to being called that."

"Let's not talk about Gabe right now." Shay moaned when Rosie tightened her grip and ground her hips down hard on Shay's stomach. She felt slick against Shay's skin, making Shay want to bury herself inside Rosie again.

"But you'll ask them?"

Shay nodded.

"I get the feeling you'd agree to anything right now as long as I don't stop doing what I'm doing."

Shay slipped out of Rosie's grasp and wrestled her onto her back. "I'll ask them, but I'm making no promises," she said and kissed Rosie hard before she could speak. The only promises Shay made were ones she was sure she could keep, like the one she made to herself about keeping this situation simple. What she and Rosie had was working well for both of them. She'd just have to make sure that if the rest of the team agreed to do this tool company thing, it wouldn't muddy the waters.

***

Solo swallowed the last of her beer and reached for another one from the cooler.

Shay pushed the box away from Solo's grasp with her foot. "If you have another, I take your keys. I'm pretty sure Gabe isn't ready to be a brom just yet."

Solo frowned, and everyone else looked just as confused.

"It's short for bro mom, like a masc parent who doesn't want to be called Mommy." Shay sighed. "Don't you guys know anything?"

"I don't *want* to know anything about parenting, thanks," RB said. "I don't want to be bound to another adult, let alone be responsible for a tiny human." She waved her hot dog in the air. "I don't *need* to know what a mini-me would call me."

Gabe clinked her bottle to Woody's. "Shay's right though, and I might never be ready to be a brom—though that's a great word."

"Lori is already talking children?" Woody asked.

Gabe held up her hand. "Weren't you supposed to be deciding whether you wanted another beer or not, Solo?"

Solo got up from her chair and popped the top on another bottle, then she dropped her car keys onto the table beside the BBQ. "I need this more than I need to drive. I'll get a Lyft home."

"Are you ready to tell us what's happening with you and Janie?" Shay asked.

"Yeah, spill, Solo," RB said. "It's been like working at a morgue this week. I could get more conversation out of a dead guy."

Gabe glared at RB, and Shay did the same when RB looked to her for backup.

"Come on, RB," Shay said. "This isn't a joke. It's Solo's marriage and family we're talking about."

"Okay, okay, I get it. I'm sorry. I'm just trying to lighten the mood."

"Sometimes the mood has to be what it is. Right, Solo?" Shay squeezed Solo's shoulder, and she nodded. "But we're your family, and you can talk to us about anything."

Solo took a long pull on her beer and dropped back into the soft lounge chair. "I've moved into the spare room. Janie doesn't want to share the same bed with me anymore."

Shay shared a worried glance with Gabe. If this was the end, Solo could go off the rails spectacularly; she'd never been good at handling bad situations, preferring to lose herself in the oblivion of alcohol than deal with them directly. Which was why no one could've been more surprised than Shay when Solo called to invite her to their wedding. She could never have imagined that Solo would settle down, let alone be the first one of them to do so.

In her peripheral vision, she saw RB almost bursting to make some amusing comment, so she shook her head. This wasn't the time for their usual banter.

"Has she told you any more about the person she's talking to?" Gabe asked.

"She won't tell me anything about him, other than he's a lawyer at her firm. And she says there's nothing going on between them. She says he's just a friend."

Talk about mic drop. Judging by the look on everyone else's faces, they'd assumed the same as she had: that the other person was another woman. Now that Shay thought about it, Solo hadn't mentioned gender when she said Janie was "talking" to someone. The bombshell opened up a whole heap of other questions.

"I thought... Is Janie..." Shay sighed. If she couldn't find the right questions, it was up to Gabe. She widened her eyes at Gabe, and her answering expression made it clear she didn't know what the hell to say to that either.

"She'd never been with a woman until me," Solo said finally. "Well, not since college, and she said they'd just made out."

Shit. This was beyond any of their little family's experience. What if Solo had just been a blip in Janie's otherwise gold-star heterosexuality? Solo could compete with another woman, but a man presented a whole different challenge, especially if that's who Janie had been used to in her bed.

"She's bisexual?" Gabe asked.

Solo took another slug of her beer. "I don't know, and I'm not sure Janie has a label for herself. It was a non-issue when we hooked up, and we didn't really discuss it because it didn't seem important. We were together, and the past was irrelevant because we were committing to each other."

"And now?" Shay picked at the edge of the beer label.

"Now she's *talking* to a guy and says she needs some space to work things out."

"Okay, that's what she wants." Shay looked at Solo. "What about what you want? Do you want to fight for your family or let her go?"

Solo frowned. "I don't want to let her go. And I'm definitely not letting my kids go. But I don't know how much control I've got over any of it."

Everyone was silent for a few minutes. They were used to fixing broken engines—relationships were a whole lot harder to put back together once the cracks started appearing.

But that had been Rosie's old job, hadn't it? "Would you go to counseling?" Shay asked.

Solo nodded. "I'll try anything. But I don't know if Janie would go with me."

"Maybe not, but she said that you've stopped seeing her since the kids came into your life. You could spend some time working on that issue and yourself. It would show Janie that you're serious about fighting for the relationship. About fighting for her."

Solo edged to the front of her chair, and some of the sadness in her eyes seemed to lift.

"That could work," Solo said, sounding hopeful. "Do you know someone?"

Shay shook her head. "Not personally, but Rosie used to be a therapist. I bet she'll have a recommendation." She motioned to the house. "Do you want me to call now?"

"You wouldn't mind?" Solo's eyes widened. "At least then I can feel like I'm doing something instead of floating in this weird limbo."

"You got it." Shay stood and headed to the doors leading into the dining room. It was clear that none of them could offer any useful help and just being supportive couldn't fix Solo's marriage. She retrieved her phone from where they'd all put their devices before coming out onto the patio. She liked Gabe's idea to shut out the rest of the world so they could focus on each other, just like they used to do when they were on base. But they needed some outside help right now.

"I wasn't expecting to hear from you tonight. I thought you were spending the night with your team," Rosie said when she answered on the third ring.

"I'm not calling for that. You sound out of breath. Are you okay?"

"Yeah. I was in the kitchen fixing dinner, and my cell was in the bedroom. What do you need?"

Shay grinned. She liked the idea of Rosie being in a hurry to answer her call, even when it wasn't for the usual reason. And she was low-key happy that she hadn't interrupted Rosie with another woman. "It's about Solo and Janie; they're having some marriage troubles, and I thought you might have an old colleague who could help."

"Oh... Sure. Give me a second."

While the line went quiet, Shay had a moment to consider whether she'd overstepped the boundaries of their situation. Did this stray into real friend territory? She supposed they were already there given their connection to Gabe and Lori.

"Hey, I'm back," Rosie said.

"Uh, is this okay?" Shay asked. Better to clear up the confusion than dwell in uncertainty.

"Is what okay? Calling me for something other than sex?"

Rosie's gentle chuckle made Shay smile. She could imagine the look on her face, and that made her smile wider, so she figured they *had* crossed from bed buddies into friends' territory. "Yeah, that."

"It's fine. I'm happy to help," Rosie said. "I'm sorry to hear they're having problems. Is that why Janie wasn't at the auction?"

"Yeah. She didn't want to be at the center of another scene with Solo after what happened at Lori's birthday dinner."

"Mm, totally get that. If they can't work it out, what happens with her share of the garage? Will you buy her out?"

Shit. "I can't say that I'd thought that far ahead. We're all hoping it's just a blip. Solo just needs to pay her wife more attention and stop being so obsessed with the babies—"

"God, the triplets... Things get even more complicated when

children are involved, don't they?"

Shay thought about the complications in her own family with her five brothers and their ever-growing brood of babies. "Being around things like this are a good reminder to stay simple."

"Like us."

"Exactly. You don't want to hear about the inanity of my troubled daddy relationship and knucklehead siblings."

Rosie laughed. "And you don't want to hear about my mom going missing in Mexico."

"Exact—wait, what?"

"I thought we weren't going to talk about complicated stuff?"

The lightness of Rosie's words wasn't matched by her tone. Talking about family stuff shouldn't affect their dynamic, and more than that, it sounded like Rosie *needed* to talk about it. "Maybe it would be okay since we're not in bed."

"Okay, I'll run with that, though I don't get your logic. But not tonight. I'm planning my pitch, and you're busy with your friends—who you're going to ask about my proposal, right?"

"I will, just as soon as we've scraped Solo off the floor and blown some life back into her."

"Of course. Right. Rae Trent is amazing with couples' therapy," Rosie said. "I'm sending you her card now. She often takes emergency appointments over the weekend, especially if there's any possibility of self-harm... Is Solo stable?"

Shay looked back out onto the yard, where the conversation seemed to have animated since she'd left it. "I'm pretty sure she's not about to do anything stupid, so I'd say she was stable, yeah."

"That's good. But look out for any changes in her behavior. Marriage troubles can trigger all kinds of past trauma, and it could also be those past traumas affecting the marriage in the first place. Do you know if Solo is holding onto anything or keeping anything buried? Sorry, don't answer that. I don't need to know. Rae will figure that out with Solo. Just keep a close eye on her, okay?"

"Will do." Shay looked out onto the yard again and saw Gabe

gesturing for her to come back out, but she wasn't quite ready to end the call yet, so she waved back and turned away. "I'll call you tomorrow. We can go for drinks and exchange sad stories about our families, but you're definitely going first."

Rosie laughed. "Okay, and we can talk about how you and your garage bois would love to be part of my pitch, yes?"

Shay laughed. "You're incorrigible. One of my *bois* is in emotional hell right now. I'm not sure she'll want to talk about fancy tools."

"Fine. I'll leave it with you, but I'll need an answer as soon as you can. Otherwise I'll have to find another bunch of hot lesbians to work with."

"I'm hanging up now—and you better not. You promised me sex on the hood of my Javelin after a dark and moody photo shoot."

"I remember talking about those two things but not making a promise to combine them. That said," she whispered hoarsely, "I'm more than happy to go with it, stud."

Rosie hung up, and Shay sighed deeply, enjoying the intense throbbing between her legs in response to the image of Rosie face down, legs spread on the hood of her car. She had finally met her match, and she couldn't be happier about it.

Chapter Ten

"You're out with Shay at a bar? That's progress, isn't it?" Lori asked.

Rosie shook her head at Lori's enthusiasm for her to get serious with Shay. "I don't need anything to progress. It's just for drinks. I let it slip about my mom, and she offered to talk about it."

Lori narrowed her eyes and peered closer at the screen. "Doesn't conversation about deeper things stray outside the boundaries of a casual relationship?"

"Not if you talk about it casually, it doesn't."

"And is it possible for you to talk about your mom that way? Especially under the current circumstances."

"I guess we'll see." Rosie looked up when the bar doors opened, but it was a couple of tall women with long hair and high heels. Usually that would be enough for her to end the call to Lori and proceed to catch their attention, but tonight, disappointment rather than anticipation of the chase flowed through her. Comparing those women to Shay was like comparing vinegar to a vintage wine.

"No one of interest?" Lori asked, pulling Rosie back to the phone.

"No one like Shay," she said.

Lori arched her eyebrow. "Have you agreed to be exclusive?"

Rosie shook her head. "I don't have the time or energy for anyone else, so it's a moot point."

"If you're not looking at anyone else, and things are just casual with Shay, does that mean you're still in the 'not looking for love' phase?"

"I have paused my search for Princess Charming, yes. But honestly, what I've got with Shay is better than anything that came before her. The friends with benefits thing is really working. We get to keep our personal space, and neither of us have to compromise on things that are important to us."

Lori frowned. "You can get all those things in a more serious relationship too, you know?"

"Everything is still going well with Gabe, I take it?" Rosie had never seen the kind of goofy grin that spread across Lori's expression in response to her question.

"Everything is *fantastic*. Taking it slow is harder than I thought it would be, and nights apart are no fun at all." She began to cough and didn't stop for a few moments.

"Are you okay?"

Lori sipped from a glass of water. "I think I'm coming down with something. I've had a pounding headache all day, and Advil hasn't touched it."

"Maybe you should get an early night and rest up instead of playing with Gabe." The doors opened again, and this time it *was* Shay. Rosie bit her bottom lip, and she swore there was a collective swooning sigh from a significant portion of the bar's occupants.

"I'll talk to you tomorrow then," Lori said. "And you should probably do something about that loved-up face thing you've got going on."

Rosie snapped back to her screen. "What loved-up face thing?" But Lori had already gone. She looked at the mirror behind the bar and checked her face. She wasn't loved-up. Sexed-up, definitely. Obviously they must look the same. She turned back to watch Shay cross the room to admiring looks. Her outfit of tailored trousers, high heels, and a soft-looking blouse open to her cleavage made Rosie want to skip the family conversation and head straight to bed. It wasn't like they could solve the mystery of where and why her mom had disappeared just by talking about it.

Shay slipped her hand around the back of Rosie's neck and

drew her in for a deep, hard kiss. She melted under Shay's touch and when they parted, she smiled at the looks of disappointment and jealousy around her.

"That's a nice way to say hello to a friend," Rosie said.

Shay sat beside her on a bar stool. "That's the benefits part."

Rosie nodded toward the rest of the bar. "And you don't mind people thinking we're together."

"We *are* together—right now," Shay said. "If I came in alone tomorrow, it'd be a different story."

Rosie didn't want to imagine that at all. Just because they weren't exclusive didn't mean that she wanted to know about all the other women.

Shay ordered white wine for them and picked up the glasses. "Shall we grab a table? Perching on these stools isn't all that comfortable."

"Sure." Rosie took her purse and followed Shay to a table in a quiet area.

She placed the glasses down and ran her gaze over Rosie. "You look hot tonight."

Shay's searing look was enough to scorch Rosie's clothes from her body right there, and it threw gasoline on her low-burning desire. "Do you want to ditch the conversation and head straight to my place?"

"As tempting as that is, I think we can focus on the friend part of our situation for a couple of hours, can't we?" Shay tapped her watch. "It's early, and I don't have to be at the garage tomorrow. Do you have to work?"

Rosie smiled, strangely pleased that Shay hadn't taken her offer, and now she got to have the best of both worlds. "That depends on whether or not you convinced your friends that your garage would be the perfect place to launch a brand-new tool company. If the answer is no, I have to spend my Sunday scouring the planet for another all-women run garage, preferably with a rainbow flavor."

"About that: I neglected to negotiate my personal fee for

brokering that deal with my team." Shay ran her finger around the rim of her wine glass and arched her eyebrow. "What's in it for me?"

"Are you looking for preferential treatment?" Rosie asked.

"I'm looking for *special* treatment, something just for me."

Rosie ran her nails along Shay's forearm. She liked that Shay wanted something extra from her, and it was a good sign that her friends had agreed to talk about the marketing opportunity. "Something you don't want to share with your team?"

Shay shuddered and wrinkled her nose. "Definitely *no* sharing, although you've made it clear that my *bois* aren't your type. Even if all of them would crawl over broken glass to get to a woman like you."

Heat rushed through Rosie's body. "Really?"

"Really."

"So that makes you their kind of woman too, doesn't it?"

"Yes, but no."

Rosie frowned. "What do you mean?"

"Yes, I'm their type, but no, I've never hooked up with any of them, because that was bound to be your next question."

"You got me." Rosie sipped her wine as relief coursed through her, grateful she didn't have any of Shay's butch friends to compete with. That might've made Lori's late summer party at the Sanctuary a little awkward, although if she'd imagined Shay with any of them, it would've been Gabe, and she was happily engrossed with Lori now. "Circling back to your original question of whether I'm working tomorrow, did you manage to convince your team that they'd be perfect for my marketing campaign?"

"I did, but maybe we could hold off on the work talk until Monday, and you can tell me all about the family drama of your mom missing in Mexico instead."

"Fine...but thank you. It means a lot to me."

"You're welcome." Shay gave her a wicked smile. "I've always thought I'd make a great calendar model."

Rosie chuckled. "You could model *anything*," she said and then told Shay the sketchy details she'd gathered from her mom, aunt, and the internet.

"You've never met this Keith guy that she's with?"

Rosie rolled her eyes. "I can never keep up with all the men. I see her on Thanksgiving and Christmas, and she always has someone different the next year. Sometimes, there's even a new guy between the two holidays."

Shay tilted her head slightly. "Sounds like she swaps guys out like I change the oil on my car. Has she always been that way?" she asked gently.

Rosie narrowed her eyes. "You want to talk family history and not just the here and now?"

Shay leaned back in her chair looking contemplative and didn't respond for a second or two. "It'll help provide context, won't it?"

"Sure, but it might also send you running out of the bar screaming for simple."

Shay shook her head. "Our lives being complicated doesn't mean that *we* have to be complicated, does it?"

"Only if you don't hold it against me," Rosie said. It wouldn't be the first time someone had run for the hills when they realized what they were getting into. "I promise you I'm nothing like my mom."

Shay's smile disappeared, and a sadness briefly blanketed her eyes. "I won't. It's why I keep my personal life so separate from my family life, and never the twain shall meet."

Rosie laughed. "'Never the twain?'"

"Rudyard Kipling. I took an English Lit class at Yale."

"You went to Yale?" Her opinion of Shay ratcheted up a couple more notches.

Shay straightened as if she was preparing to attack. "You're surprised because I'm—"

"Because you were a soldier, and now you're a mechanic. I didn't think you needed a degree for either of those professions, especially one from such a prestigious university."

Rosie frowned when Shay seemed to relax her shoulders. She tried to figure out what had just happened, and then the penny dropped. "Oh God, you thought I was surprised because you're Black, didn't you?"

"It wouldn't be the first time a woman—anyone—had that reaction."

Rosie couldn't be hurt that Shay had thought she was capable of coming to that conclusion. She couldn't imagine the number of times Shay had encountered that kind of racism, and Shay didn't know her well enough to assess her prejudices or lack of. There was nothing she could say that wouldn't sound patronizing or condescending, so instead she asked, "What did you study?"

"Applied mathematics, but we're straying off-topic." Shay tapped her nails on her wine glass. "Your mom. Her history with men."

Rosie fought the deep sense of shame she carried, which was currently trying to convince her to lie about her background. What if Shay did judge her? How could she not? Rosie was still judging herself even after all the years of therapy. She'd thought becoming a therapist would fix it all, but that hadn't happened either.

But this wasn't a first date where she was about to scare Shay off with way too much personal information, and Shay wasn't someone she was trying to impress or hang onto by being economical with the amount of crazy in her life. They'd been honest from the beginning. Why would she lie now?

"Rosie? You really don't have to censor anything. We're just two friends getting to know each other better; you're not preparing me for nightmare in-laws."

Rosie laughed to disguise the sting Shay didn't know she'd caused. Her mom had always been a source of shame in her intimate relationships. "I don't think there's any way to prepare someone for my mom. I've introduced three women to her, and they hated her within five minutes of them meeting."

"Three random women?"

Rosie frowned. "Of course not. They were vaguely serious. Or that's what I thought. I'm hanging on to the idea that Mom was the deciding factor in them fleeing, otherwise I have to consider than it might have been me." She wrinkled her nose. "And I don't want to go there."

"Nor should you... You've had three serious relationships?" Shay smirked. "That's three more than me."

"You've never been serious about anyone? I thought you might've gotten burned a couple of times before deciding you were a lifelong bachelorette."

Shay shook her head. "Nope. It's far less complicated than that. With my family, I just don't have the time or the emotional bandwidth for that kind of relationship."

Rosie rotated her glass by the stem, contemplating whether she truly wanted to know the answer to the question on her lips. She quickly decided she didn't want to know how many women Shay had been with, though she suspected there was no bedpost in the world big enough for the number of notches Shay could probably etch.

"We've somehow managed to digress again. I was trying to convince you that you didn't need to censor yourself."

Rosie rolled her eyes. "I already have a best friend with an insanely good memory. I'm not sure I can cope with another one." The way Shay looked at her made it clear she wasn't about to give up. "She's always been that way. So much so that I don't know who my real father is." She focused beyond Shay into the depths of the bar, unable to maintain eye contact. "Three candidates covered that period." And she hadn't met a single one of them because they were long gone by the time Rosie entered the world. Funny how her mom had no shortage of lovers, but none stuck around or came back. Maybe she was more like her mom than she wanted to admit.

"Has she done anything like this before?"

Rosie didn't answer immediately. She was busy processing

the complete lack of judgment in Shay's expression and words. Eventually, she nodded. "She disappeared on me a lot when I was a kid. She'd be gone for days, and I'd take myself to school, fix my meals, put myself to bed." She swallowed hard. She hadn't talked about this stuff since she'd shared it with Lori a long time ago, and her therapist well before that. These were things she hadn't even told the serious partners. "And she's gone dark on me a few times since I've been an adult. I didn't hear from her at all between 2020 and 2022. She had me thinking that she'd died of COVID. And then there was five months in 2017..." She shook her head, acknowledging the old realization that her mom was just repeating her usual patterns and that Rosie shouldn't waste her emotional energy worrying about her.

"So it's likely she'll reappear."

"You're probably right," Rosie said. "She's used health issues before, so this is nothing new. I just suppose that, regardless of what she's put me through, I can't fully close the door on her, on our relationship. For my own piece of mind, I want to know that I did everything I could every time there's a drama, because one day, it'll be real."

Shay blew out a breath and nodded slowly. "I know that feeling."

"You do?"

"Kind of, though it's nowhere near as difficult as you have it with your mom," Shay said after she'd taken a long drink of wine that emptied her glass. "I'll get another round."

Rosie watched Shay walk to the bar and saw the numerous women follow her progress too. She didn't blame them, and she also had no right to be jealous since she had no claim on Shay. And they could look all they wanted; Shay was coming home with her, at least for tonight. The butch bartender nearly fell over herself in her hurry to serve Shay before her colleague. When Shay left the bar with her drinks, she literally fanned herself with a bar towel, and Rosie didn't stifle her amusement.

"What're you laughing at?" Shay placed the glasses on the

table and retook her seat.

Rosie gestured toward the bartender, who was still staring unabashed. "You made quite an impression on her, and I think she's misreading the nature of our situationship."

Shay looked over her shoulder briefly. "Maybe she thinks she'd made a nice butch sandwich."

They hadn't talked about their preferences. Oh, no. That couldn't be where Shay's thought process was heading. She had to cut that off before it got any steam. "Not with this slice of bread," Rosie said. "She does nothing for me at all. I like my women... exactly like you, actually."

Shay laughed. "Don't worry. I'm not interested either. You're very much my perfect woman."

"That's one thing I've never been call—"

Shay leaned across the table and kissed Rosie with an intensity that made Rosie melt onto her chair. When Shay finally released her, she looked across at butchy bartender, winked, and mouthed, "Sorry," without meaning it even a little. The woman shrugged and focused on the next customer. *No sandwich for you.*

"You're perfect," Shay said as she sank back onto her seat. "Now you've been called it twice in one night."

Rosie grinned. "I can die a happy woman. Cheers." She raised her glass, and Shay clinked hers to it. They drank, and Rosie waited for Shay to pick up the conversation where she'd left it.

"My dad is a very complicated man," Shay said after a short period of silence. "He calls me to come over and fix everything. Sometimes things are broken, sometimes there's nothing wrong with them at all."

Rosie tried to keep the disbelieving frown from forming. She was complaining because her father wanted to spend time with her? Rosie had spent years of her childhood imagining what it'd be like to have a dad, to be his little girl, but she'd never had that chance. She cherished the time she got with Lori's father, Hank, but she'd missed out on so much already, it was impossible to make that up.

"Then he dismisses me like I'm an inconvenience." Shay sipped her wine. "I don't know what he wants from me."

That made more sense. "Have you always had that kind of relationship?"

Shay shook her head and looked rueful, and the same sadness Rosie had spotted earlier reappeared.

"No. Everything changed after my momma died."

Whoa. Rosie wasn't expecting that at all. "I'm sorry, Shay. Was that recently?"

"A little under six years ago," she whispered and rubbed her palm with her thumb before receding into silence.

Rosie placed her hand over Shay's but didn't say anything. If she'd learned anything from all her years as a therapist, it was simply to hold those silences and never try to fill them. She glanced around and observed other people while she waited for Shay to either continue or shut the conversation down and move on. She figured it would be the latter, though her suppressed therapist wanted to dig deeper. That surprised her. After nearly seven months away from it, she thought she'd fully lost interest in the intricacies of the human condition.

"It's still really hard," Shay said quietly.

The tears that edged her eyes made Shay's dark brown eyes even more beautiful, which Rosie had thought impossible. And the vulnerability that came with them clutched at Rosie's heart, almost causing her to shed her own tears in empathy. She kept her therapist-hat questions to herself and stayed silent.

"I think he blames me for Momma's death. I left for the Army right after I graduated, and I didn't get home as much as she would've liked." Shay's voice cracked slightly, and she took a long drink. "Would you mind if we didn't talk about it anymore? I didn't know it would be this difficult."

"Of course," Rosie said and removed her hand. "I've got to say that I'm surprised you're being so open. I didn't really think we'd be going that deep."

Shay raised her eyebrow. "Because simple should mean shallow?" she asked.

Her playfulness returned with impressive ease, and Rosie couldn't help being a little sad that their moment of deeper, intimate, personal connection had ended so abruptly. "That's been my experience."

Shay pushed away from the table and held out her hand. "Let's go back to your place, and I'll show you just how deep I can go."

Rosie stood, and Shay pulled her into an urgent kiss full of passion and promise, of need and sexual oblivion. "That's an offer I'll never refuse."

Chapter Eleven

Shay pulled into Aaron's driveway and cut the engine. The absence of her daddy's Ford gave her a little breathing room to enjoy at least a short time at the party. She got out of the car and popped the trunk to retrieve the homemade cake she'd cushioned between the gift for her brother and the soft blanket she kept in the car for impromptu drives with women. She hadn't gotten the chance to use it with Rosie yet; her apartment was so big and comfortable, there'd been no need. And Shay hadn't been required to pull out all the romantic stops to get her end goal; they'd just jumped right into bed with minimal preamble, exactly the way Shay liked it.

Aaron burst out of the front door and ran over to her as if he was escaping prison. "Shay Shay! Boy, am I glad to see—" He stopped a few feet short of her when he looked at the cake box in her hands. Sadness filled his eyes, and he covered the remaining distance between them slowly. "Is that what I think it is?"

"Depends. What do you think it is?" she asked, trying to keep the mood light. Birthdays were supposed to be a celebration; they weren't for mourning. But six years hadn't lessened the grief.

"Momma's German chocolate cake?" He lifted the cardboard lid and drew in a deep sniff. "Smells exactly like she used to make it."

He took it from her hands, put it back in the trunk, and enveloped her in a bone-crushing hug. They stayed like that for longer than she liked. Increased physical contact brought her emotions closer to the surface, and she wanted this to be a happy event.

"All right, you can let me go now." She pushed him away firmly, and her heart ached at his slight look of rejection. "Don't be like that, little bro."

He puffed up his chest. "Not so little anymore. I've been hitting the gym."

"Thirty-five or fifty-five: you'll always be my little brother."

Aaron poked the gift box. "Is that for me?"

"Nah, I'm dropping it off at the rec center for their annual toy drive." She pushed him and laughed when he curled up his lip in apparent disappointment. "Of course it's for you, knuckle head." She loved that he hadn't lost his enthusiasm for birthdays, even in his mid-thirties.

The space-age whirring of her father's car alerted her to his presence, and she sighed. She'd wanted just a little more time before things got strained. He pulled up beside them and got out.

"Shay," he said, gruff as usual, then he pulled Aaron into a hug and lifted him from the ground. "Hey there, birthday boy."

"Hey, Pops." Aaron offered Shay an apologetic look over their daddy's shoulder. "Shay baked Momma's special birthday cake," he said after their daddy had released him. He picked up the box from the trunk again.

Her daddy cleared his throat and looked away quickly, then he hooked his arm over Aaron's shoulder and started walking back toward the house. "Come on, son. Let's get ourselves a beer."

Shay watched them walk away, and the familiar pang of dread for the coming hours settled in her stomach. And worse, she couldn't drink to soften the edges. She pulled her phone from her purse then thought better of it. She had no idea when she'd be leaving, and she didn't want to make plans that she might break. It was Friday night, and Rosie deserved better than that. For all Shay knew, she was probably getting ready to go out. She wrinkled her nose at the thought of Rosie being unavailable but quickly pushed it aside. Simple included no rights to exclusivity.

So she pulled out the gift-wrapped, hand-torched Unity Tools set of weighted sledgehammers, slammed the trunk, and headed inside...

Where there was absolute bedlam.

"We've got guests arriving in less than an hour, Cyrus. What the hell?"

The sound of her daddy's all-too familiar disappointment set her teeth on edge, but it wasn't aimed at her right now, so that was something to be grateful for. She nudged her youngest brother, Matt, who was lounging on an armchair away from it all. "What's going on?"

Matt didn't lower his phone or stop tapping on the screen faster than spinning tires. "Cyrus didn't confirm the catering for the party, so we've got no food."

"And how long has everyone known this?" she asked, surveying the rest of her brothers, their significant others, and their children scattered throughout the open-plan lounge, dining room, and kitchen that Aaron and Elijah, her middle brother, had created. Every one of them seemed busy doing nothing but adding to the general chaos with loud opinions and no action.

Matt shrugged. "Couple of hours, I guess."

She didn't have to ask why no one had done anything about it. Bisa was too busy with the kids, and although Shay was running late and should've been there over an hour ago, they were clearly expecting her to rescue the situation, like always. She closed her eyes briefly, reminded once again why she'd abandoned the family to go in the Army. How her momma had expertly juggled the six men in her life, Shay would never know. She bit back the sting of tears, ever-present when she was around her family, and headed toward Eli and Luke.

"Hey, Corporal," Eli said, and he and Luke saluted.

She slapped their hands down. "Does Aaron still have the grill I bought him last year?"

Luke nodded. "He hasn't used it yet. Says he's waiting for the perfect occasion."

Shay tilted her head and sighed, keeping her irritation deep down for later meditation. "Good, we'll do a cookout. How many people are supposed to be coming?"

"Maybe fifty people."

"Including us?" she asked.

"Nah," Eli said. "Fifty plus the family."

"Kids?"

Eli nodded.

"Included in the fifty or on top?" If she was going to have to launch a rescue mission, she needed all the information.

"On top." Eli counted on his fingers and raised his eyes to the ceiling. "There's maybe ten kids," he said after a while.

So it was likely to be double that since Eli took zero notice of children and only had eyes for women. "Any vegetarians?"

Eli laughed. "I hope not," he said and made a crude sexual remark.

Luke shoved Eli's shoulder. "Yeah, there's some herbivans. Like, maybe ten."

Shay suppressed a grin and nodded. Luke had gotten the looks of the family, but Shay suspected she'd gotten his share of brains. She estimated sixty-five adults and twenty-six kids and did some quick math, then she pulled her credit card from her phone sleeve and handed it to Eli. She'd figure out the finances and who owed her what later. "Go down to Martin's meat market with Luke and get fifteen pounds of steak and the same in ground beef, and I need his giant bag of chicken wings and ribs. Give me your phone." When he'd unlocked it and handed it over, she typed in a list of ingredients she needed for veggie burgers plus salad, slaw, beans, and buns. "Then go to Clark's and get all of that." She handed his phone back. "Tell me someone handled drinks, or Daddy's going to work himself up to a heart attack."

Luke grinned and looked pleased with himself. "All sorted. Liquor, beer, wine, and sodas are stacked up in the basement and the fridge in the den."

"Great. Go!"

"Can we take your car?" Luke asked, just like he used to do

when he was fourteen.

"I don't want the smell of raw meat on my upholstery. Use your truck, Eli."

Luke rolled his eyes. "You're no fun."

Eli wiggled his eyebrows and bumped Luke's shoulder. "That's not what all the ladies say, is it, Corporal?"

She shoved them both toward the door and navigated her way back to Matt. She snatched his phone and slipped it into her purse away from his grasping hands. "Set up an outdoor bar under the veranda. The drinks are in the basement and the den." She hoped there was ice there too.

"Ah, come on. Do I have to?" He slumped back into the chair.

"Yeah, you have to. In case you haven't gotten your snoot out of your phone long enough to notice, it's your big brother's birthday. We're going to have near on a hundred people here, and we've got no food." She grabbed his arm and pulled him up. "If we don't have drinks set up either, we'll have a riot on our hands." She pushed him in the direction of the den, and he slouched away reluctantly, throwing her a look that she couldn't be bothered to categorize.

She turned to her father and Cyrus, who were still going at it, clearly resolving nothing. "Everything's under control," she said and relayed her plan before she grabbed Aaron and tugged him outside to uncover the grill.

Cyrus emerged from the back door holding hands with a beautiful woman with a complexion that reminded Shay of their momma. She had the same big, brown, kind eyes too. Shay smiled, thinking maybe that's what had drawn him to the woman, and from the grin on her brother's face, it looked like he'd finally found someone he might hang onto for more than a few weeks. She'd thought the last one, Kali, had a chance but obviously not. She pushed aside their similarities in their lack of ability to commit and ignored the small niggle that questioned why he hadn't told her about his new lady before today.

"I've brought you someone who can help with your plan, sis,"

Cyrus said. "Shay, meet Nia. She's a professional chef."

Her brothers exchanged an expectant look while Shay held out her hand. "It's great to meet you, Nia," Shay said then looked at Cyrus. "Where'd you meet this queen?"

"She's Bisa's best friend, and—"

"I moved in next door a few weeks ago," Nia said.

Shay nodded. "Perfect timing."

"Or fate," Nia said and continued to stare into Shay's eyes without letting go of her hand.

So she'd misinterpreted Cyrus' stupid grin, and this was a setup. Nia was exactly her type, but Shay believed in fate about as much as she believed a new car was better than a classic, *especially* when the word was bandied around in relation to potential bed partners. And then there was Rosie. They hadn't made plans, but Shay intended to text her when she could leave the party without too much hassle.

"If you'll excuse me, I have to show my little brother how to use his grill." Shay pulled her hand away gently and turned back to Aaron, who frowned at her like she was crazy not to be fawning all over Nia.

"No problem," she said, apparently undeterred. "I'll go familiarize myself with the kitchen."

"I'll show you where everything is," Cyrus said and glared at Shay before he left.

Despite her misgivings, Shay turned around to watch Nia walk away. She couldn't deny the woman was *fine*. Nia glanced over her shoulder, catching Shay appreciating the view, and she gave a small, knowing smile. She had full, kissable lips too.

"She saw your picture on the mantel when Bisa invited her over for dinner," Aaron said. "You shoulda seen her eyes light up when Bisa told her you were part of the alphabet mafia."

Shay put her palm on his forehead and pushed him away. "Your boo could just say lesbian." In truth, it was nice that her brothers had accepted that she was gay. She forgot that sometimes.

"Nah, she keeps up to date with all the lingo."

Shay shook her head and refocused on the task ahead. "Let's get this set up."

They uncovered the grill and got the coals ready.

"I can't believe you haven't used this," Shay said. "Luke said you were waiting for the right occasion."

"Something like that." He ripped open a box of firelighters and threw a couple on the charcoal.

"I didn't spend $400 on this so it could sit around waiting for perfect. Perfect is a myth." Shay repositioned them with a wooden skewer and looked at Aaron, waiting for a better explanation.

Aaron shrugged. "That's what Momma used to say," he said quietly.

Shay sighed as the reason dropped into place. "Is that why you haven't used the grill?"

He nodded. "Grilling was Momma's favorite... You remember all those times the whole family would come on over, and we'd sit in the yard until it got dark, 'till we were all sent to bed. But me and you would climb out on the roof just so we could smell the smoke?"

She swallowed hard and nodded. "I loved Daddy's ribs with Momma's special sauce," she said.

"I still have two bottles hiding in the back of the pantry, up high on a shelf so Bisa doesn't use it." He smiled, but the grief in his eyes was plain to see. "Pops hasn't used his grill since Momma died either, y'know?"

Shay clenched her jaw. "He doesn't need to; Mrs. Robinson's always feeding him up." It bothered her that the old woman was trying to take her momma's place.

Aaron shook his head. "It ain't about that. And she brings over the occasional dish, but mostly he lives on TV dinners. Bisa keeps offering to cook for him, but he won't hear it."

That *was* a surprise. From what she'd seen, Bisa only cared about Aaron and her kids. But she'd been Aaron's high school sweetheart, and they'd been married for over thirteen years now, most of which, Shay hadn't been around. She guessed she'd missed plenty while she'd been in the Army. And her efforts to make up for lost time had been more or less useless, except when she was coming to the rescue in one form or another.

She heard the rumble of Eli's bag of bolts truck pull up and let out a deep breath. If she focused on preparing the food, she could stop trying to analyze her daddy's behavior, which everyone else seemed to be trying to find an excuse for. "Light her up. I'll be out with some ribs in ten minutes. And Aaron," she touched his arm lightly, "how about I raid your sauce stash for one bottle...for Momma," she said, her voice cracking.

He frowned. "I don't know..."

"Come on. It's your birthday, and Momma's looking down on us. Let's do ribs in her honor." She took a second and looked up to the sky to stop the tears from escaping. "She'd like that, right?"

Aaron nodded slowly. "One bottle."

She headed to the kitchen and reached the side door just as Cyrus came out of it.

He nodded toward the kitchen. "If Dad's ever gonna be comfortable seeing you with a woman, we figured it'd better be a beautiful Black woman like Nia."

"That's outmoded thinking, brother."

"That's the only mode of thinking he's got."

Cyrus had a point, but she didn't need her relationship with her daddy to get any more complicated, and she didn't need to be responsible for one more person. She moved to go around him, but he sidestepped.

"She's gorgeous, ambitious, intelligent, and single," Cyrus said. "I'd be making a move if I wasn't trying to be faithful to Kali."

"Good to know Kali's still around." Shay hadn't seen her in the melee inside, but she was petite and easily missed. "I'm not looking for serious." She pushed him aside and cracked the door. "I'm not looking for anything." And she already had Rosie for everything she wanted and actually had the time for. "If anything happened with Nia, I'd walk away, but she'd still be Aaron's neighbor. How awkward do you think that gets at every get-together thereafter?"

"That's a poor excuse, sis."

She shrugged. "It's the only one I've got." She went into the kitchen and closed the door behind her.

Nia had already spread out a range of chopping boards on the kitchen island and was creating some kind of a special rub for the meats. She looked up and smiled. "Special recipe for a special occasion."

Before Shay could respond, Eli and Luke hustled in, loaded down with bags of meat and groceries. When they'd put everything on the counter, she held out her hand.

Eli pulled her credit card from the top pocket of his shirt. "You sure I can't keep it to put a down payment on a new truck?"

She snatched it from him and slipped it back in her phone wallet. "You don't need a new truck. You just need to look after the one you've got."

"Aren't you supposed to do that? What's the point of having a magic mechanic in the family if you don't make sure my truck runs like a dream?"

Shay clenched her teeth. "I've told you to bring it to the garage, and I'll check it over."

Eli curled his lip. "I can't come all the way out to Chicago. The truck won't make it."

"Fine." She'd been putting this particular call of duty on the backburner for long enough. "Talk to Anderson and see if it's okay for me to use his garage next weekend, and I'll service your damn truck."

Eli grinned widely. "Thanks, Corporal." He pulled Luke's arm and started out of the kitchen. "Let's go before she goes all Carla Hall on us."

Shay didn't protest. They'd be more hindrance than help anyway.

"So you're good with your hands?" Nia asked, her voice sultry and husky.

Subtle. "So they say." Shay opened the bag with the ribs and pulled them out, then she went to the pantry and had to shift everything on the top shelf to get to Aaron's sauce stash. She should've expected it, but when she saw the label with her momma's handwriting across it, her breath caught, and she nearly dropped the bottle.

She ran her fingers over the delicate cursive with the flourishes on the letters l, s, and t, which Shay had often tried to imitate and always been unsuccessful. Her momma had gorgeous handwriting, reflecting her inner beauty. Shay picked at the edge of the label, but it began to rip so there was no way she could get it off in one piece. She settled for taking a photo of it to print out instead.

She took a long, deep breath and tried to fight the painful burn of her grief, which always simmered closer to the surface whenever she was around the family. She'd run away once, and at times like this, she seriously thought about doing it again.

Chapter Twelve

ROSIE TYPED *TAGLINES* ON the magic keyboard hooked up to her MacBook, then she stood, taking the keyboard with her, and began to pace her living room. She paused at the selection of the special edition tools she'd laid out on her dining room table and ran her fingers over the cool steel. They were so pretty that she actually was tempted to try building something, even if that was just screwing some pieces of wood together. She continued to pace then stopped to look out the window onto the street below and watched for a few minutes as people went about their business, unaware of her scrutiny. She drifted back to the night of Shay's first booty call and the excited anticipation that coursed through her body as she watched Shay get out of her car and wave to her. Like the tools on Rosie's table, she was lithe yet powerful.

She rested her keyboard on the windowsill, thinking about how resilient women and queer folk had to be to survive, and how that was compounded for Shay because of her color. *Tools as Strong as You Are.* She hit return and headed to the kitchen for a drink, grabbing her cup from her cluttered desk on the way. Rosie took her time fixing her coffee while she rolled the remit of Unity Tools around her brain. It would've been easier if they'd chosen to focus on just women *or* the LGBTQ community. She typed *Tools That EmpowHer*, erased it, then hit undo. She'd probably need more than one tagline.

She returned to her desk, freshly caffeinated. *Tools as Diverse as You Are.* The needs, preferences, and experiences across the two groups required a more segmented approach, so this wasn't going to be quite as easy as she'd first imagined. Shay's team ticked the women and L boxes—maybe even the B or T since she didn't know the rest of the group well enough to be sure—but she'd need something different for the guys, trans, and non-binary peeps. These were no homogenous groups: selling something to cishet white men was a piece of cake in comparison. She tapped her nails on the photo that her boss had first tempted her with; the strength and camaraderie of the team shone through even in 2-D. Shay looked delicious in her emerald evening dress, and the memory of it hitting the floor in Rosie's bedroom was still delightfully fresh. *Tools for Every Hand and Every Heart.*

Ugh. Delete. She switched back up to the page entitled *Visual Campaign.* Shay had a visual with wide appeal, but would she be best utilized for the focus on all women or specific sexualities? She scrolled back down to taglines. *Precision, Pride, and Power in Every Tool.* That could work for everyone...maybe. She thought about the photoshoot that she wanted. A mix of candid and professional shots of Shay and the team would work well. Close-ups of their hands working with the tools, emphasizing their competence and enhanced by the amazing tools, *obviously.* She'd need full access to them at work so she could get engaging stories and behind-the-scenes content that showcased the diversity and skill of the whole team. It was a shame they'd contract someone else to do it, because she'd love to be around Shay for that kind of time, watching her work. That fantasy of sex on the hood of Shay's beefy car could become a reality if they worked some overtime after everyone else had gone home. Getting to see the contact sheets and raw video wouldn't be the same, but there'd be something sexy and voyeuristic about pouring over them in the privacy of her office. *Focus.*

She'd need to trawl Insta and TikTok for LGBTQ and women influencers across several generations. God, this was a huge project. Perhaps she should ask Franklin if she could bring another exec in to work with her. She tapped the glass of her mouse, considering her options. She didn't want to seem overwhelmed...

She resolved to wrap her head around the scope of the project and then go to Franklin for someone to work with. She liked Anji; she'd worked with her on the female urinal device trying to compete with the market leader. Rosie laughed out loud, remembering her fascination with being able to pee standing up. Guys didn't realize how good they had it.

Ooh, maybe they could livestream DIY car maintenance workshops at the garage. She could imagine all the *let's ride*, *love*, and *this is fire* gifts raining in for Shay and Gabe. Solo, RB, and Woody were way more average Joe, but that held its own inherent appeal too. She moved down to another page and typed, *Leverage authentic storytelling to build brand loyalty. Focus on women and LGBTQ micro-influencers to create organic buzz. Utilize user-generated content to enhance relatability and trust.*

Rosie took a sip of her rocket fuel and thoughts of Shay pushed for her attention. She'd been trying hard not to think about the intimacy of their conversation at the bar a week ago. Sharing her vulnerabilities and secrets had been terrifying, but they'd also been building blocks which deepened her connection to Shay. That raw honesty had brought them closer together. Shay continued to reiterate her desire to keep things simple, but that night had hinted at the potential to go beyond their physical relationship. But wasn't that what building a stronger friendship entailed? They'd gotten together twice since that night, but Shay hadn't engineered the conversation to her own family and the loss of her mother. If anything, they'd talked even less than before, as if Shay had realized she was overstepping the limits of her own boundaries.

She shook her head and took another gulp of coffee. Right now, she had a marketing plan to create and while Shay was part of that, dwelling on the state of their situationship wasn't helpful. She resolved to keep things simple. That's what Shay wanted, and it had been working well for her too. Rosie would just force herself to ignore the strong pull for something more.

Her fingers flew over the keyboard as ideas poured out of

her, fueled by caffeine and her determination to prove herself not just to Franklin, but also to herself, and to shut Mindy Fletcher up too. If Rosie left this career, it'd be on her own terms, not in one of Franklin's regular house-cleaning furies.

Rosie's phone buzzed and broke her attention. She glanced at the time and then her word count and smiled when she saw she'd managed nearly three thousand words. If it was Shay calling, as she hoped it would be, Rosie would be good to take a break by eight or nine. A bottle of wine and some bedroom time would be the perfect comedown after the exhilaration of creating this strategy.

She found her phone beneath a pile of brochures from other tool manufacturers, all of which unashamedly targeted heterosexual men, with their half-naked photos of long-haired women in plaid shirts tied at the stomach and denim micro-shorts... She was ashamed to admit that she'd stared at some of those photographs for far too long.

Rosie stuck out her bottom lip when she saw there was no caller ID. She briefly considered ignoring it, but curiosity got the better of her, and she hit accept and speaker. "Hello?"

"Is this Rosie?"

The brusque and impatient male voice was unfamiliar. "Yes. Who's this?" she asked.

"My name's Keith. I've been sleeping with your mom."

Rosie's ensuing snort lodged in the back of her throat, and she coughed violently. That was information she didn't need spelled out. Ever. Partner. Friend. So many other options he could have—and should have—chosen.

"She's dead."

Rosie stared at the phone, and the world went soundless and dark like she'd been submerged in tar. She couldn't have heard that correctly.

"You still there?" Keith's abrupt voice pushed through the sticky silence. "She's dead. Your mom. Did you hear me?"

Rosie pulled the phone closer and leaned down to it. "Mom's

dead?"

"What, are you deaf? Yeah, she's dead."

"How?" Autopilot kicked in when she couldn't properly process his words.

"Heart attack, I guess. We were in Tijuana. She's at the Hospital del Carmen. You need to come get her and do whatever it is you're supposed do with dead bodies. I don't do that stuff."

"You can't– Are you serious?" Rosie found her voice in a rush of anger and disbelief.

"Look, I've done my part. You're her daughter. Do yours," he said and hung up.

Her phone beeped three times before returning to a screensaver of her and Lori in front of the Centennial Wheel on Navy Pier.

Dead.

What was she supposed to do now? Would Lori know? She dropped her arms to her side and leaned back in her chair, numb. She knew she was sitting in a chair, but she couldn't *feel* the soft cushion beneath her butt or the firm comfort of the ergonomic support. There was a cold cup of coffee in front of her, but she couldn't smell its tempting, slightly burned aroma. In the breeze created by the A/C unit overhead, a lemongrass candle flickered, but she could take no joy from its scent.

What was it her mom had said she was suffering from? She searched her mind, unable to bring the information to the fore in this dream-like state and wishing she could borrow Lori's hyperthymesia memory thing. Chronic kidney failure. And as it progressed, heart failure followed. That much she remembered from her panicked research. So this meant her mom *hadn't* been lying or scheming; she'd been telling the truth, and Rosie had more or less ignored her. Maybe that wasn't exactly right. She couldn't ignore someone who'd cut off communication from their end.

The world around her seemed to shift back into alignment, and her senses came alive again. She pressed her hand to her chest, and it pulsed beneath her touch, but she didn't feel whole. She didn't feel right, as if her heart was being tugged downward by an anchor and would drop out onto the ground at any moment.

Maybe *this* was another scheme. In all probability, her mom was alive and well, hanging out at a beach bar somewhere sipping margaritas and snorting coke. She just wanted to know that Rosie cared, that she could still pull the mom card, and Rosie would come running. Her mom simply needed some money and, with her twisted logic, figured that Rosie would be so relieved to find her alive in Tijuana that she wouldn't be able to refuse her anything.

But what if Keith is telling the truth?

Rosie couldn't deny that she'd often wondered how her mom would die: a drug overdose; murdered by a jealous lover; shot by a police officer. These weren't the thoughts of a normal kid or even an adult, but they'd plagued Rosie her entire life. Did her eternal question now have an answer? A simple heart attack. If it was true, her mom would be desperately disappointed. She'd always wanted to go out in a blaze of glory and with a story worthy of a Hollywood movie ending.

She pulled a notepad from beneath the folders scattered on her desk and scribbled down the hospital name Keith had given her, then she opened a second tab and typed Hospital del Carmen. She half-hoped not to find anything; if the hospital didn't exist, it was an indication that Keith had lied. When Google did its thing and brought up more information than she could ever want or need, Rosie's heart pounded in her ribs and her breathing labored. The edges of her vision spotted and darkened and began to close in. She pushed her thumbnail hard into the palm of her other hand until the pain was too intense and her eyes cleared. She pushed back in her chair and put her head between her knees, angry at herself for falling into old patterns.

She stayed that way for a few moments then straightened up. *Shay.* Rosie reached for her phone instinctively but stopped herself. What was she thinking? She couldn't burden Shay with her problem. That wasn't just stepping over the boundaries into a serious relationship, that was taking a running jump and diving in headfirst. She could already imagine smashing her head into the brick wall Shay had constructed, and she'd be left laying there, bleeding and unattended because things were no longer "simple." Plus Shay was with her family, which meant she didn't need anything else to deal with.

Rosie called Lori instead, but it went to voicemail. Of course it did. Lori would be doing something wonderful with Gabe, no doubt.

Call me when you can. Need to talk. She hesitated before adding *It's Mom*, hoping that would expedite Lori's response when she saw her text. Rosie entered the number to the hospital on her phone and hovered her thumb over the green icon. But she couldn't do it. Instead, she tabbed to the marketing plan sitting unfinished on her MacBook and closed it, unable to face the project now that everything was overshadowed by more uncertainty. Or was she just praying it was uncertain? She'd come to despise and dread her mom's lying and scheming drama, but right now, she'd prefer that over the very definitive alternative.

Rosie got up and walked over to the bookshelf in the living room. She pulled out the hardbacks on the top shelf and retrieved the small wooden box hidden behind them. She dropped onto her couch and clutched the box to her chest. She couldn't open it. Not yet. She'd promised herself she'd only crack this box when it was over. And she didn't know that yet. Not for sure.

She placed the box on the glass coffee table and dialed the number for the hospital. Time to end the uncertainty.

Chapter Thirteen

"WE MAKE A GREAT team," Nia said as she picked up a tray of meat to take out to the grill.

"Sure." Shay held the door open for her and smiled. They'd worked well together, almost dancing around each other in the relatively small kitchen space, but she wouldn't go as far as saying there'd been anything great about it. Deflecting personal and probing questions wasn't her idea of fun. What was it about civvies that made them so very interested in an ex-vet's service? And why did Nia just assume that she'd be happy to talk about it? Nia hadn't asked once if Shay was okay with the questions she'd bombarded her with. And she'd somehow been oblivious to the many unsubtle clues Shay had given about her reluctance to discuss it.

As soon as she left the kitchen, Cyrus caught her gaze and gave her a questioning look. He was way too invested in her sex life, but maybe that's what happened when someone was curtailing their own adventures to just one person. She could be accused of doing the same thing with Rosie, but that was different. The option to expand her horizons hadn't been taken off the table. Nia had her good points for certain, but her incessant chatter had soon extinguished any interest Shay might have had the moment she emerged from the pantry with her momma's sauce bottle. In the Army, she'd been accomplished at keeping her emotions in check, but the past five years had made her soft, and she was easier to read. Too easy, apparently.

Aaron pulled her closer after Nia walked away, and Shay placed the burgers on the table next to him. "Thanks, Shay. I don't know what we'd do without you."

"You're lucky you don't have to," she said, avoiding the look in his eyes.

He held on when she tried to head back to the kitchen for more of the platters she and Nia had prepared. "I'm serious, Shay. We don't say it enough. The family would've fallen apart if you hadn't come out of the Army to look after us."

Jesus, how was she supposed to keep it together with this kind of gratitude flying around? "It's what Momma would've wanted."

He shook his head and began placing the ribs and burgers on the grill. "I don't think so. She was so proud of you going in the Army."

Shay frowned. "What do you mean?" She'd escaped her family responsibilities once, and she thought her momma had forgiven her but had never been proud of her for running away. "I was supposed to be the good daughter, staying close to home to help Momma with the family, which I would've been able to do if I'd stuck with my original plan."

Aaron scoffed and slapped Shay on the back. "If you'd become a math professor, you would've been miserable. Having a genius IQ doesn't mean that you have to use it the way people expect." He waved the BBQ fork at her. "Look at you! You were blessed with everything: brains, beauty, and physicality. It's kinda unfair, really... Momma loved that you were doing what you wanted to do, and not for one second did she want anything else for you."

Shay sucked in a long, deep breath and released it slowly. If she focused on her breathing, maybe she could make it through the rest of this conversation without breaking down.

Aaron nudged her shoulder. "Don't get all weird on me, Shay Shay. I just wanted to tell you how I feel. Bisa's therapy is rubbing off on me, and she's encouraging me to get 'in touch with my feelings.'"

"Bisa's going to therapy?" she asked, more than a little surprised that something was going on in the family that not only didn't she know about, but also that she hadn't been instrumental in organizing.

"Okay, we're both going." He glanced around then leaned in closer. "She got scared that I was getting too much like Pops, and she wants the kids to have a daddy they can always talk to."

Shay frowned. "What was your reaction to that?" As the first-born son, their father had been the most interested in Aaron, and he'd gotten away with so much more than her or their other brothers. Consequently, Aaron thought their father hung the moon. Maybe he'd started to see the imperfections over the past few years now that Momma wasn't there to soften his edges.

Aaron arched his eyebrows and scowled. "What do you think? It wasn't pretty. But I finally agreed to see someone who helped me view Pops through a different lens. He's not the god I built him up to be."

"Wow." A lengthier response evaded her. "When did you discover that?"

"Last week." Aaron took a long pull on his beer. "So I'm sorry it's taken me so long to appreciate you and everything you do for this family."

Shay smiled and squeezed his forearm. "Thanks, little bro." She gestured back to the kitchen, where she was desperate to go for some emotional respite even though Nia was still hanging around. Aaron had given her too much to think about right now, and she needed to concentrate on his party. She'd consider everything else on the drive back home. "I'll get the rest of the meat."

The guests poured in over the next couple of hours, and the cookout went better than Shay had thought possible under the rushed circumstances. If her momma was looking down on them, she hoped she'd be proud of the party. Shay had thought that her daddy might be tempted to take over grilling duties, but he hovered on the outskirts of it all and busied himself talking to Aaron's in-laws. When he occasionally glanced her way, the distance in his eyes was too much to bear, and she couldn't hold his gaze.

At around seven, she slipped away from the backyard and went around the front to sit on the porch swing. She pulled out her phone and acknowledged the slight disappointment at there being no messages from Rosie. Shay had only been alone a few moments when Nia came out holding two glasses of wine.

"I've been looking for you," she said and offered Shay a glass.

She shook her head and pointed to her car. "I'm driving."

"Nice car." Nia gestured to her house next door with a wine glass. "Or you could not drive until the morning..."

"I'm not really looking—"

"Don't panic," Nia said. "Bisa's told me all about you. I know you're not interested in anything serious." She licked her lips and stepped closer to Shay so that their legs touched. "Neither am I."

Usually, that'd be enough of an invitation, but Nia's connection to the family made a quick hookup too close to home—literally. And that was before Shay considered Nia's need to fill every silence. And why would she think about any of that when she had something sweet and simple with Rosie waiting at the end of a quick text?

Before she could answer, the front door opened again, and her daddy came out onto the deck. From the way Nia reacted—glancing between the two of them as if they might spontaneously combust and then hot-footing it back to the party without another word—it was clear that she had inside information on their relationship. Shay wasn't interested in pursuing anything with Nia, but she disliked the effect her father had on people.

"Where'd you get the sauce for the ribs?"

The accusation in his words was clear, and she inched back into the porch swing. "Aaron had a bottle of Mom's special sauce stashed in his kitchen."

"And you *used* it?"

Shay bit her bottom lip. She wanted to jump up, stand toe-to-toe with him, and not let him stand over her, but her respect for him kept her exactly where she was. "Seemed like a good idea since that's what she made it for." Her respect didn't make it to her vocal cords.

His face reddened and his jaw clenched then twitched wildly. "Who are you talking to with that attitude, Shanae?"

She held up her hands and shook her head. "I'm sorry, Daddy. I'm just tired, and it'd be nice *not* to lock horns with you when I've just busted my ass to save Aaron's party."

"There's no need for that language either."

His expression softened slightly, and she caught a fleeting glimpse of the face she used to love looking up into, the face her momma used to cup in her hands while she kissed his forehead. She drew strength from Aaron's courage in revealing his issues to his therapist. Maybe this would be a good time to finally talk to him and find out what the hell she was supposed to do with the way things had gone between them.

"You've been distant since Mom died. Since I came back."

All essence of softness disappeared, and he turned away. "It's been hard on all of us, Shay. You're not a child anymore. Not everything is about you."

She scoffed quietly and bit back any retort that she'd immediately regret. "I know that. But you're angry and cold, and you've shut me out emotionally. I don't understand why."

"Shut you out? Who do I call when I need help?" He chuffed and slapped his palms on one of the wooden struts. "You shut yourself out when you left... And you came back too late."

"Is that what all this is about? You blame me for leaving, so you punish me every time you see me?"

He turned back toward her, eyes blazing. "See, that's the problem. *You're* the problem. You think it's punishment to come help me out, or fix my car, or spend time with us. I can see you don't want to be here, Shanae. Everyone can see it. But you're too busy blaming everyone else instead of taking a hard look in the mirror."

Shay was glad she'd stayed in her seat. If she'd been standing, the punch of his words would've floored her. She wasn't blaming everyone—just him. But was he right about everything being her fault? Was it obvious she didn't want to be there, to see the family, to act like the matriarch when she wanted none of the responsibility? She *had* run away from the expectations and the pressure, thinking her momma would live forever.

But she hadn't. She'd passed way before her time, and Shay had been drawn back into the trap she thought she'd escaped. *The trap.* So maybe he *was* right. She saw their family unit as a drag, an emotional and financial black hole, a burden.

The slam of the front door jerked Shay from her spiraling thoughts, and she looked up to find she was alone on the porch again. She swiped at her cheek, erasing the evidence of his effect on her, and wished Nia had left one of the glasses of wine. A little alcohol might go a long way to numb the pain or ease the weight of their unresolved issues.

She stood but her legs didn't feel like her own, and she sank back into the cushioned chair. She pulled her phone from her purse. Maybe Rosie would be available later; time with—sex with—her was better than any liquor anyway. She'd be happy to wait for her to come back from a club, or dinner, or whatever else she'd probably be doing on a Saturday night, because it was totally wrong to hope that Rosie would be home alone. And if that didn't pan out, she could always go out with RB and Woody on their weekend prowl. Gabe wouldn't be around though, that much was certain. Shay had gotten used to spending practically every waking hour of every day with Gabe again; living together had been just like old times in the Army, only with comfortable beds and private showers. But with Gabe's focus on Lori, she'd been spending fewer nights at home.

Shay unlocked her phone, deciding not to analyze her order of preference for companionship, and texted Rosie.

I've played the hero, and I'm ready to leave the party. Are you around?

She watched the two checks appear to show her message had been delivered and waited for them to turn blue. When they didn't, she tossed the phone onto the seat beside her. Rosie wasn't waiting around to hear from Shay, and nor should she. She glanced at the time. RB and Woody would be getting ready to go out. She couldn't make it back in time to go with them, but she could drive home, drop the car off, and head into the city to meet them. Sex with Rosie was definitely her preference, but sex with anyone would be better than no sex at all...wouldn't it?

The front door opened again, and Nia emerged, poking her head around the doorframe slowly.

"Do you want some company?" she asked.

Shay looked down at her phone. The checks had turned blue, but there was no response. Any sex was better than no sex, she repeated then sighed, shaking her head as she stood. "I'm heading off. Thanks for the invite though."

Nia tilted her head slightly and shrugged. "You know where I live if you change your mind."

Shay nodded and walked to her car. She wouldn't be changing her mind. She heard the door close but didn't look back. Heavy footsteps thundered up behind her.

"Shay Shay, where're you going? The party's just getting started."

She unlocked the car before facing Aaron. "I've got to work tomorrow." A little white lie would hurt less than the truth, which she was still processing and trying to figure out if her daddy was gaslighting her or if he knew her better than she knew herself. Either way, she still had to get out of there before she did or said something she'd regret.

He didn't look convinced. "On a Sunday. At the business you own?"

"Part own. And yeah, when you're self-employed, you have to work while the jobs are there." She pulled him into a brief hug and opened the car door. "Say goodbye to everyone for me."

"Did Pops say something to you?"

She swallowed. Aaron had always paid enough attention to see through her lies. "He thinks I shouldn't have used Momma's special sauce," she said, hoping that'd be enough to put him off the scent.

He looked back at the house, then gave her a smile that conveyed a hopeful sadness. "Those ribs sure did taste great though. It was like Momma was up there celebrating my birthday with us."

Lord, this therapy stuff had gotten him way too in touch with his softer, emotional side. He was giving her more than one reason to leave without realizing it. "Lucky I didn't use it all then. Maybe you can take on the cookout tradition and organize them even when there's nothing to celebrate."

He nodded. "Maybe."

She clapped him on the shoulder and slid into the driver's seat. "Remind Eli to ask Anderson about me using his garage and get him to call me. I won't be impressed if I come back down here next weekend and don't have a garage to work in."

Aaron shook his head and closed Shay's door gently. She wound down the window, and he leaned in.

"Maybe you should just let him handle it himself," Aaron said.

"Who are you? And what have you done with my little brother?" She laughed, and he shoved her shoulder gently.

"I told you: we haven't been appreciating you enough. We can change even if Pops can't."

Shay's optimism that her family could change left her body like air from a leaking balloon. She was impressed that Aaron was making the effort, though she didn't know if it would last—he'd always been one to be distracted by the next shiny thing—but her younger brothers were a hopeless case. They expected her attention just like they'd expected their momma's, and she couldn't see that evolving. And her daddy's behavior just now indicated he was unlikely to change.

She started the engine and slowly began to reverse, even though Aaron hadn't moved from the window. "Take it easy, little brother."

"I promise you, Shay Shay, we can be better."

She pushed his arms away from the car, wanting to get out of there before the deep rumbling of her engine alerted the rest of her brothers to her departure. "Show me," she said and pulled out into the road.

Shay made it three blocks before she pulled in to check her phone. "Fuck it." She slipped in her earbud and called Rosie.

"Are you really bailing on your brother's party?" Rosie asked.

The humor in her words wasn't backed up by the usual playfulness in her voice, and Shay cursed inwardly. "Hello to you too. Have I...disturbed you?" She didn't want to ask if Rosie was with someone. That'd sound way too weird. But it shouldn't be, should it? Non-exclusive should mean they could talk about other women... Or maybe *that'd* be weird.

"You mean, am I having hot and dirty sex with someone else?"

Shay frowned. The banter was there, but the undertone was harsh. Fuck, she *had* overstepped. "No... Yes? Look, don't worry about it. I'm just driving home." *And I was thinking about you... Fuck. That* was *weird.* "I'll leave you to it."

"Please don't..." Rosie's voice choked.

"Are you okay? Is something wrong?"

Rosie cleared her throat. "Talk to me while you drive. I was... taking a break from the Unity Tools project."

Shay laughed and pulled back into light traffic. "Working on a Saturday night? That's dedication."

"Or stupidity."

"So you were thinking about me too?" *Oh, shit.* She hoped Rosie didn't make anything of that. "Because you're working on our project—your project. The garage stuff." *The Lord save me.*

"I was, actually. Franklin sold me on this project when he showed me a picture of you and the team at the big auction. I had it printed out, and it's on my desk."

"So you can think about me when I'm not there?"

"I have far better photos of you for *that* purpose."

Shay shook her head. Something was definitely wrong. Rosie

was saying all the right things, but there was a missing piece, a distance Shay had never felt before. It looked like she'd be joining RB and Woody tonight, because Rosie didn't sound like she was in the mood for anything other than work. Maybe that was it. Maybe this was Rosie super-focused on a project. Shay joined the highway and opened up the engine. Driving fast would help her ease a little tension if she couldn't work it out with Rosie.

"I was thinking of swinging by, but it sounds like you're swamped with work. Or something." Her attempt at not letting her suspicions creep into her words failed.

"Or something," Rosie said quietly.

The line went quiet, and Shay glanced at her phone screen to make sure she hadn't lost the connection. For a while, the only sound was the deep growl of her engine eating up the road. "We're friends, right?"

"Yeah. We are."

"So even with the obvious benefits of keeping our situation simple, we should still share what's going on in our lives...whether it's related to our work or family, right?"

Rosie huffed loudly in her ear. "Well, I've shared stuff with you, but you got a little squirrelly when you tried it—I'm sorry, that was harsh."

"No, you're right. I know I shut down after talking about my momma the other night. It's just hard for me. It still feels so raw even though it's been...a while." She licked her lips and half-smiled when she could still taste the ribs as if her momma had made them.

"It's hard for me too, Shay," Rosie said. "I'm ashamed of my childhood and my...my mom." Her voice cracked. "And I'm so ashamed of myself for feeling those things."

The line went silent like it'd been muted. "Rosie?" She waited for a few seconds before saying her name again. There was background noise in her ear after another prolonged period of quiet. Then she heard a low sniffling. "Rosie, what's happened? Are you okay?" So many awful scenarios went through Shay's head like a montage of movie clips. Had a hookup gone wrong? Had she been attacked? "Rosie..."

"I..." Rosie's sniffling turned into a full-blown sob. "My... I can't..."

"It's okay, Rosie. I'm on my way. Stay on the line if you want. You don't have to talk." More flashes of what could've happened invaded Shay's mind, and she tried to push the unwanted images out. It wasn't like her to catastrophize, but Rosie wasn't someone to break down lightly either. Rosie's sobbing continued, and she was obviously still unable to talk. The miles ticked by painfully slowly, and Shay prayed that the traffic gods would be kind. She pressed harder on the gas pedal. All thoughts of her own problems receded into the background as she focused on the road; she had to get back to Rosie.

Chapter Fourteen

ROSIE STARED OUT THE window as the last delicate fingers of sunlight were subdued below the horizon. She usually loved this time of day, loved the fragile balance of dark and light, and how they complemented each other, just as they did within a person's soul. But tonight's darkness brought a sense of foreboding with it. As the sun went down on her little part of the world, she had to process the realization that it would never come up anywhere again for her mom.

The silence in the living room contrasted with the chaotic cacophony of screaming thoughts in her mind. Anger, confusion, dread, and grief swirled back and forth, competing to be heard, contradicting each other in their opinions on how she was supposed to feel about the news that had been delivered so callously, and then about the next steps she had to take.

She glanced at her phone. Staying on the line and making Shay listen to her incoherent attempts to voice what had happened while peppering it with her uncontrollable sobbing had been too mortifying to let it continue. She'd allowed herself around fifteen minutes of quiet comfort from Shay's end before she'd forced herself to terminate the call. Lori hadn't responded to her text yet, though Rosie wasn't sure that she'd be able to do anything to help anyway. She'd kept her mom away from every part of her life, so maybe she should continue with that and head out to Tijuana alone.

She got to her feet, her body feeling not quite like her own, and grabbed her MacBook before dropping back onto the couch. She opened Google Flights, entered the details, and hit search. The prices changed depending on what day she chose to return...

How was she supposed to know how long she needed to be down there? And how was she supposed to book space to bring her mom home? Was that even allowed on a commercial flight? She looked at the wooden box she'd pulled down from the bookshelf. Her mom had given her a letter when Rosie turned eighteen and told her it was her last wishes and funeral arrangements. Rosie shook her head. It was quite the unique graduation gift and surprisingly forward thinking. Rosie had long suspected that it was just another desperate bid to be the center of attention, and that she was supposed to be too curious to wait. Then she was supposed to have confronted her mom about the modesty of her requests.

Not opening it had become a matter of stubborn pride, and she'd lost count of the number of times her mom had asked her about it. Rosie was damn sure there wouldn't be a check inside to cover the expenses.

She covered her mouth and choked back another sob at the heartless thought. How could she think something like that when her mom's body was lying frigid in a Mexican morgue? *Experience, that's how*, the angry voice in her head said.

Was Shay still coming? Or had she changed her mind? Rosie wouldn't blame her. It wasn't like she'd signed up for anything like this. Hell, neither had Rosie. She'd pulled the short straw when it came to good moms. The angry voice was far louder and more vocal than the others.

Her front door buzzer sounded, and she headed toward the intercom panel on autopilot. "Hello?" she asked, her throat dry and her voice croaky.

"Hey. I'm here."

Rosie's heart jumped at the sound of Shay's voice before a rush of grief compressed her joy against the wall of her mind like a bully in a school hallway. She hadn't heard the unmistakable roar of Shay's car at all, and she supposed the doorbell had sounded strangely muted.

"Rosie?"

She hit the release button and then pressed her palms to the door, wanting the sensation of something solid to ground her, because it felt like she was becoming distant and disconnected to her senses and surroundings. The knock on the door reverberated through the wood and into her hands. At least she could feel *something*.

Rosie opened the door, and the moment she saw the concern in Shay's expression, she lost all strength in her body and slumped, expecting to hit the floor. But Shay caught her and guided her down gently before closing the door. After a moment, she allowed herself to be lifted to her feet, and Shay supported her unsteady walk back to the couch. Rosie scolded herself. They should be walking the other way to her bedroom. That's what Shay really wanted. That's what they'd agreed on. But friends supported each other too, and that was the other side of this coin. Rosie just hadn't expected to cash it in quite this soon.

"Can I get you something to drink?" Rosie asked, her hostess mode kicking in.

Shay shook her head. "Let me get you something."

She nodded but didn't state a preference. She doubted her mouth would register anything, but the sensible side of her that was hovering stubbornly told her she should drink something. Shay returned from the kitchen with two bottles of water and a glass. Rosie smiled when she heard the fizz of the gas as Shay opened one of the bottles and began to pour it for her. Shay had remembered Rosie's preference for sparkling water. She touched her face and lips. Her heart's response hadn't reached her brain, and she wasn't smiling at all.

Shay offered her the glass, and she took a sip. Maybe the liquid would lubricate her throat and allow her to finally speak. She could see Shay looking around the room, probably trying to find some clue as to what the hell was going on. God, what did she think had happened for her to rush over here like this? Shay surely had so many other things—so many other women—she could be doing instead.

She willed herself to form words, but they evaded her, and her focus fell once again on the small wooden box in the center of her coffee table, taunting her. She was as certain as she could be that her mom was dead. She still had to identify the body, but the doctor's description of her too-numerous-to-count tattoos had done that job really. What did that damn letter say?

"Rosie…"

Shay's gentle voice seeped into her consciousness again, and Rosie lolled her head to the side to look at her. Even through the cloudy grief of her tears, Shay's beauty astounded her. What the hell was she doing here with her?

"Can you tell me what happened?"

Shay looked her up and down but not in the way Rosie had grown both accustomed to and very fond of. No one had ever looked at her with that same primal hunger, like she might starve if she didn't feed on her immediately. She guessed Shay was still searching for visual answers. Physical damage, maybe? Rosie looked back at the screen of her MacBook, and Shay followed her gaze.

"You're going on a trip?" Shay asked gently.

Rosie looked back at her and saw the complete confusion in her expression. Flying to Tijuana clearly had zero to do with the Unity Tools account. Why couldn't she just talk, goddammit? She put her hand on Shay's thigh and looked deep into her beautiful dark eyes. Maybe…maybe she'd feel better if she pushed all of this away for now and lost herself in those eyes, in Shay's embrace. Maybe Shay's touch could make her forget, make her stop overthinking everything. Shay could stop her thinking at all, and she could focus on feeling only good things.

And after, the world would right itself and come back into sharp focus, allowing Rosie to organize everything she needed to. She dropped her gaze to the Cupid's bow curve of Shay's lips, one of the things Rosie had always found so sexy. Her mouth was so kissable, her skin so soft and smooth. If Rosie could just allow Shay to be the center of her Universe right now, she could have one last happy experience before she contemplated her life without...

No, don't think about that right now. Feel. She cupped Shay's cheek in her hand and ran her thumb over her full lips. She dragged her nail along Shay's bottom lip then moved closer to kiss her, desperate to taste her.

But Shay stilled Rosie's hand and pulled away slightly. "Rosie, talk to me."

Rosie shook her head. "Please, no talking. Not yet." She saw the hesitancy mixed with confusion in Shay's expression, like she was trying hard to read her and failing. Rosie didn't need Shay to understand; she just wanted her fingers on her skin, reminding her she was alive, reminding her that she could still experience joy. And what greater joy was there than a few of the earth-shattering orgasms Shay could give her?

"I don't get what's happening," Shay whispered, still gently holding Rosie's hand.

"Please. I want this." She got up, her legs feeling steady once more, and pulled Shay to her feet. "No words." She tugged Shay down the hallway to her bedroom and was grateful when she resisted no further.

"What do you want?" Shay asked as she stood at the foot of Rosie's bed, her eyes searching for more information than Rosie was currently able to give.

"I want you to fuck me. Hard." She pulled off her linen pants and T-shirt and dropped back onto her bed, completely naked. "Fuck me harder than you've ever fucked anyone before."

Shay's uncertainty was clear, but the biggest part of Rosie didn't care right now. She didn't need Shay's hesitation or moral conscience. She wanted to be fucked senseless and delivered onto the shores of oblivion on a wave of pleasure. "Simple, remember?"

Shay's expression flickered, but she began to open the buttons at the front of her dress. She untied the fabric belt around her waist, and Rosie exhaled as Shay let her dress drop to the floor, revealing a matching burgundy lace bra and panties set. Shay's gaze never left Rosie as she knelt on the bed between her legs, and finally, there was a hint of the hunger Rosie was used to seeing in her eyes.

"You're sure you want this?"

"Yes," Rosie said, already breathless with the tension of her need pressing on her chest and humming between her legs. "Please. No more words."

Shay spread Rosie's lips with her left hand and pressed two fingers against her. She slid in easily, and Rosie saw the flicker of satisfaction dance across Shay's face.

And then Rosie closed her eyes. As stunning and beautiful as Shay was, Rosie was done with interpreting her visual cues and body language, something that, after years of being a therapist, she couldn't flick a switch to turn off. The ink-black darkness of her eyelids was the perfect non-stimulus to focus on the sensations between her legs and all over her body as she felt Shay's lips and teeth drag over her stomach, her breasts, and her collarbone. Shay sucked hard on Rosie's neck, her teeth scratching her jugular, while her fingers pumped rigid and strong.

Rosie opened up wider, demanding more, and Shay gave her more fingers until she paused just long enough to fold her thumb into her palm. Rosie screamed as Shay slowly curled her fingers inside her and completely filled her. Shay picked up her pace, steady at first, while Rosie exhaled and relaxed around Shay's fist.

She searched blindly for Shay's body, refusing to open her eyes, and her hand finally made contact with Shay's back. She dragged her nails hard across Shay's skin, hoping that it would encourage her to drive deeper.

It did exactly that, and just as Rosie had wanted, everything but the feeling in the hidden depths of her core, a depth that could only be reached this way, fell away. Intense, unforgiving, and unyielding. This was where the fundamental essence of herself resided, patient yet desperate for someone to have the strength to reach out for her this way.

Rosie rode Shay that way, losing time and thought, for as long as her body would take it. She didn't count the number of times her body clenched and crushed Shay's hand inside her as Shay took her over and over the highest crests of desire. It wasn't until she was fully exhausted and Shay was breathless above her that Rosie said, "I'm spent."

Shay removed herself slowly and carefully, and Rosie kept her eyes closed as she breathed around the discomfort. When Shay had withdrawn, Rosie felt her weight settle beside her on the bed, but she still remained locked inside her black cocoon of blissful ignorance, the hot pulsing between her legs the only thing she was truly cognizant of. She couldn't—wouldn't—acknowledge the deep trust it took to let someone in that way, nor the feeling of being so perfectly taken.

She placed her hand flat on the space between them and tentatively inched across the mattress in search of Shay's skin. Not just her skin; Rosie wanted her hand. Her fingers touched a smooth, long nail, and she followed it until her hand completely covered Shay's. When Shay didn't pull away, Rosie intertwined their fingers and went still.

They lay like that for a while until Shay moved beneath her touch, and Rosie found herself being gently maneuvered onto her side. The heat of Shay's skin warmed her cooling body, and the soft material of her underwear felt comforting against her back. Shay's slow, hot breaths caressed Rosie's neck, and as she listened to Shay's steady breathing, it lulled her into an easy semi-consciousness.

Every muscle in Rosie's body relaxed, and all her tension ebbed away. Shay was staying for a while then. That was new. And so very welcome.

Chapter Fifteen

Shay stayed awake in a semi-guard role as Rosie fell into a deep sleep following their intense sex. She'd fucked women that way before, though not as hard or for as long, but it had never felt that *important*. It seemed like it hadn't just been sex for Rosie, that she'd needed it as much as she needed air. And Shay had a sense they were communicating on the deepest level possible without words.

That complicated things, didn't it? Or maybe these were just special circumstances, and Shay didn't have to *let* it complicate things between them. But she'd been the one to wrap her arms around Rosie and pull her close, like she knew that was exactly what Rosie needed. And what the hell did that mean? She and Gabe had never comforted each other that way, but they were both Army, and they'd had to keep their feelings and vulnerabilities pretty much hidden. They weren't ever having sex either. Maybe now that they were civilians and living together, it might be different. If Lori dumped Gabe, and she came home one evening, devastated and messy, would Shay lay with her, hold her as she cried—if Gabe was actually capable of shedding tears? She'd come close when Lori had walked out on her before they were even together, but full-blown sobbing... She didn't think so.

Shay had no idea what it was that had brought Rosie to this place but guessed that she would tell her when she was ready, just like Shay would tell Rosie about her complicated family eventually. There'd been no signs of the worst-case scenarios that had haunted Shay's mind all the way from Aaron's house to Rosie's apartment, but that didn't necessarily mean anything. Something could've happened elsewhere, and Rosie could have come home and cleaned herself up.

She edged even closer to Rosie and breathed in the tangy scent of sex that hung in the air. Even that smelled different. Did emotions have a scent? Rosie pushed her butt back into Shay's crotch, but her deep breathing indicated she was still sleeping, something Shay should try to do too. She had a sleep cap in her purse, but there was no way she could shift Rosie to get to it. She'd just have to hope none of her hair broke and deal with the dry hair situation in the morning. She closed her eyes, but her pupils bounced behind her eyelids, and her mind smirked at her attempt to rest. She concentrated on her breathing and repeated the nonsensical mantra that always helped clear her thoughts: *Black is black. White is white. You don't get gray without a fight.*

When Rosie shifted in her arms, Shay woke with a start. The daylight streaming in through the half-closed blinds meant they must've slept as least six hours, and her numb arm under Rosie's body tingled, underlining her guess. Rosie wriggled out of her rubbery grasp, and the feeling rushed back into Shay's left arm, making it buzz and ache.

Rosie sat up and pulled the sheet over her breasts. "You're still here?"

"No. You're hallucinating, and I'm a figment of your imagination," Shay said and winked. "Though it's tough to tell from your face whether it's a good or bad illusion." And the way Rosie had covered herself with the sheet indicated it was the latter.

As if aware of her reaction, Rosie dropped the sheet. "It's a good one."

She smiled, but it didn't last long, and the unspoken sadness in her eyes invaded her whole expression, just as it had last night. She sighed deeply and looked away, but not before Shay had caught the tears edging Rosie's eyes.

Shay ran her tongue over her teeth and shuddered. She had an overnight kit in the car but didn't want to go out just yet. "Do you have a spare toothbrush?" She got up and headed toward the bathroom after grabbing moisture spray from her purse, more concerned with how unruly her hair was going to be than how bad her breath stank.

"Middle drawer on the left."

When Shay returned, Rosie was no longer in bed. She looked around for a T-shirt or hoody but couldn't find anything. She didn't want to hunt through Rosie's space, so she walked to the kitchen in her underwear, not quite ready to pull on her dress again. She found Rosie eating cake straight from the fridge, and she turned around with an adorable look of guilt before that too dissolved into grief.

Rosie slammed the fridge door and tossed the fork into the sink. "My mom's dead."

Shay wished she'd gotten dressed. That was a hell of a bombshell to drop before she'd even had coffee. How could Rosie have pulled Shay to the bedroom with that news fresh in her mind? "Rosie...I'm so sorry." Jesus, those words were too rote, too shallow and lacking. And they couldn't provide comfort, but neither could Shay. Her own unresolved grief spewed to the surface like lava to the top of a volcano, and she leaned against the countertop for support, assuming Rosie wouldn't notice given that she had her own shit to deal with. "How?" From what Rosie had already told her about her mom, Shay figured it wouldn't be a simple story.

"Keith said it was a heart attack. She was admitted to the hospital with cardiac arrest, but she died of a pulmonary edema brought on by an opioid overdose."

The words came out in rapid fire, as if Rosie had to eject them before her emotions closed her throat and made it impossible to speak. Shay stepped forward awkwardly and held out her arms, still painfully aware of her inappropriate half-naked state. Images of her momma's grave assailed her mind, and she blinked them away, trying desperately to focus on Rosie's pain and this moment.

Rosie held up her hand. "I can't... If I let you hug me, I'm afraid I'll lose it." She closed her eyes and took a couple of deep breaths.

"I'm barely hanging on, and there's...so much to do."

Shay nodded and motioned back down the hallway. "I'm going to get dressed, and then we can talk more." She thought about how disinclined she'd been to talk to anyone, even Gabe, when she'd gotten the news that her momma had died. "If you want to."

"I'll make coffee."

Shay rushed back to the bedroom, grabbed her dress, and locked herself in the bathroom. She flipped the toilet seat up and dropped to her knees. She held her braids back and retched into the bowl, but only bile came up. When the nausea receded slightly, Shay rocked back on her ass and held her head in her hands. "Momma, I miss you so much." She would've known what to say in this situation; she always had the words.

And she wouldn't have run off to the bathroom to vomit. Shay recomposed herself, cleaned up, and got dressed then headed back to the open plan living space. A steaming mug of coffee sat on a coaster, while Rosie sat with her feet tucked beneath her ass in the furthest corner of the couch. She seemed to be gripping her own mug so tightly that it was in danger of imploding in her hands.

Shay positioned herself sideways on the opposite end of the couch and faced Rosie. "I'm here for you." She wanted to mean the words so much but wasn't sure she was capable of seeing them through.

Rosie lifted her phone from its place on the sofa beside her. "I've missed fifteen calls and messages from Lori. She came over last night, but I guess I silenced the intercom after I let you up." Her lips twitched in an apparent attempt to smile. "She wants to be here for me too, but I think I'd be better off facing this alone."

"Have you called her?" Shay already knew the answer. Sound carried easily in Rosie's apartment, and she'd heard nothing but the bubbling of the coffee pot. "She'll be worried sick."

Rosie tapped her phone and shook her head. "You're MIA too. She and Gabe will probably just think we're together somewhere."

Shay sucked her teeth and arched her eyebrow.

Rosie sighed deeply. "I'll do that now, I guess."

Her flat, almost emotionless tone rang alarm bells, signaling that Rosie was keeping her grief at bay. But who was Shay to dictate how anyone dealt with death when she was still struggling to process it herself?

Rosie put the phone on speaker in her lap and went to sip her coffee, but Lori answered before the first ring was complete.

"Rosie? What's happening? Where are you? Are you with your mom?"

"Mom's dead." Rosie took a drink in the moments of silence that followed.

"Oh, Rosie, I'm so sorry."

Shay glanced away at the repetition of her exact words. Even coming from Rosie's best friend, they sounded just as hollow and useless. Death had a nasty habit of stealing people's ability to comfort their loved ones, rendering them mute but for the one pedestrian phrase.

Rosie retold the story from Keith and the doctor almost verbatim, and she stared beyond Shay, her eyes distant and empty.

"Keith's disappeared. I have to go to the hospital to identify the body."

"You're going to Mexico?" Lori asked.

Rosie nodded. "I'll get a flight today." She shrugged. "I don't know how long I'll be gone. The hospital said they'd email details of a local funeral home they use. There are permits I need to bring her remains home."

Shay frowned. She had no idea how it worked when a US civilian died in another country, but she'd expected Rosie to want to bring her mom's body home, not just her ashes. She checked herself. Rosie had a different history with her mom than Shay and her momma had, and different cultural traditions too. From the little Rosie had told Shay about their relationship, she could see why Rosie wouldn't want to celebrate that life. Her own momma's funeral had been attended by almost the whole town, though Shay had been unable to sing or dance. She'd spent the entire time numb and cold despite the near-hundred-degree heat. "When You Hear of My Homegoing" hadn't lifted Shay's spirits or allowed her to be okay with the Lord calling her momma *home*. Her momma wasn't just another soldier going home to be with the Lord; she was Shay's momma, being dragged away before her time. She couldn't have *wanted* to go. Heaven *wasn't* home.

She drew in a long, deep breath through her mouth until she could pull in no more air, then she exhaled slowly and quietly. If she was doing that, maybe she could stave away the rising tide of her own grief that lurked, ready to wash her away. Six years and she was no closer to healing than she had been when she saw her momma in the open casket and finally accepted she was really dead. None of this was about her. She had to concentrate on being Rosie's friend, on being there for her when she needed her the most, and she had to park her own painful past.

She tuned back into the conversation to hear Lori saying something about wearing a gas mask, but Shay had totally missed the rest.

"It's okay, Lori," Rosie said. "I'm not asking you to go, and you can't risk spreading COVID or making yourself sicker."

"What if you waited a couple of days?" Lori asked. "I'm sure I wouldn't test positive by then."

"No. I can't. I have to get there as soon as possible. I need it done."

"Is Shay with you?"

Rosie flicked her gaze up as if to ask for permission, and Shay nodded. "Yeah. She got here last night."

"Oh... That's good. I'm glad you're not alone. Could Shay fly with you?" Lori asked. "Gabe's here. They could chat now about her not being at the garage for a few days."

Shay's phone vibrated quietly in the pocket of her dress, and she knew instinctively it would be Gabe asking her if she was supposed to agree to that proposal or not. She finished her coffee and got up, pointing down the hallway. Rosie nodded, and Shay headed to the bathroom.

Do u want 2 go 2 Mexico?

Of course she didn't. She didn't want to be mistaken for a Haitian migrant and not live to tell the story. But despite her own trauma, a big part of her felt an increasing urge to support Rosie, especially now that Lori was unable to step in.

Tough call. Leave it with me.

Shay flushed the toilet and ran the faucet for a few seconds to really sell the subterfuge. She turned her cell to flight mode and slipped it back into her pocket before walking back to the sofa. Rosie's phone was face down on the coffee table.

"Talking to Gabe?" Rosie gave her a half smile. "You don't have to make excuses, Shay. I didn't ask Lori to go with me, and I won't ask you. This is my family drama, and I don't want to drag anyone else into it." She looked into Shay's eyes. "Especially not you, because this is far from simple."

Rosie was handing her a pass. She'd refused her best friend's help, and she was telling Shay the same thing. But Shay couldn't get beyond the overwhelming sense of isolation Rosie must be feeling, and she wasn't saying outright that she didn't *need* Shay's support. Her distress was blatantly obvious, and what kind of friend ignored that? One who only took the benefits and ignored the other expectations of friendship. "Let me go with you."

Rosie looked as surprised as Shay felt when the words emerged from her mouth. But the offer had been made now, and she'd work it out. This was the kind of thing her momma would do without hesitation, and Shay could almost sense her presence and guidance.

"I couldn't ask—"

"You're not asking; I'm offering." Shay sat beside Rosie, much closer this time, and took her hand. "And I won't take no for an answer." Of course, she *would* if Rosie was insistent that she didn't want Shay's help, but the relief that seemed to wash over Rosie's expression indicated that wasn't the case.

Rosie hung her head, but she didn't pull away from Shay's embrace. Her chest began to rise and fall more rapidly, and tears fell onto her sweatpants, creating dark spots on the soft, gray material. Her shoulders began to shake, and then she fell forward onto Shay's chest. She wrapped her arms around Rosie and held her close. She eased back into the sofa, and Rosie huddled down onto her lap, sobbing softly. Shay stroked Rosie's hair slowly and gently while Rosie death-gripped her other hand.

Rosie tried to choke something out, but it was incomprehensible, so she simply continued to comfort her as she cried herself out. Shay swallowed back the memory of herself in a similar fetal position on her old bed when she'd gone home for her momma's funeral. No one had held her like this, and maybe if they had, she might not have felt so abandoned. Gabe had wanted to go home with her but hadn't been given permission. She'd said she'd go AWOL, but Shay refused the offer and went home alone. Her brothers had been too wrapped up in their own loss and expected her to comfort them and to take her place as the new matriarch instead of recognizing her grief.

But that didn't have to be the same for Rosie. There was no reason for Shay not to provide the same support she'd needed.

Rosie's sobbing subsided, and she turned in Shay's lap to look up at her. "Why would you waste your time coming with me?"

Shay smiled lightly. "Being there when a friend needs you isn't a waste of time."

The look of absolute and unguarded vulnerability in Rosie's eyes reached out and squeezed Shay's heart so tight, she had to catch her breath. There was no way she could or would leave Rosie alone. Not now, when she was most in need of...solace, a friend, someone to care. Rosie's expression and words made it clear she didn't take any of those things for granted, even from Lori. And now, not from Shay either.

Rosie's brow knitted tightly. "Are you *sure*? I don't think I could bear to drive you away with this. I'd rather not impose on you at all. Keep things simple."

"Simple can be supportive too." Shay cupped Rosie's cheek and smiled. "And you're not imposing, I promise. I want to do this for you, and you really shouldn't be doing it alone. Okay?"

Rosie gave a small smile. "Thank you." She glanced away. "And thank you for last night. I needed to be claimed that way. I needed to be taken that absolutely."

Shay nodded, not knowing quite how to respond to that. *Claimed?* She held no *claim* on Rosie. She pushed away the urge to analyze Rosie's words more deeply—Rosie was the ex-therapist, not her. Shay was just a well-educated mechanic, trying to keep things from getting complicated and working hard to stay afloat in a sea of her own grief.

Being by Rosie's side as she faced this wasn't going to make either of those things easy, but Shay had never been capable of taking the easy route to anything. Why change that now?

Chapter Sixteen

Rosie stayed silent and still on the sofa for a good while after Shay left to pack a bag and grab her passport. She drifted to sleep and dreamed that her mom had jumped up from the slab in the morgue and cackled like a maniac.

"Got you, Rosarita!" she'd screamed and then jumped into the arms of the hospital's mortician and proceeded to make out. He turned out to be Keith. His stubby, broken, and blackened teeth had been a clue she'd ignored.

Rosie woke up screaming too, but that was as much from the desire to get away from seeing her mom starting to have sex than it was from the shock of her being alive. She tugged her sweaty T-shirt from her chest and took deep breaths to steady her racing heart. She picked up her phone to check the time and jumped up from the couch when she saw it was nearly noon, and Shay would be returning soon.

She hustled into the bedroom, opened all her closets and drawers, and stood in the middle of her room, staring at all her clothing options. The weather in Tijuana was only a few degrees higher than Chicago right now, so her choices should be simple. But what was she supposed to wear to identify her mom's body? Something formal? She tugged a few sweaters, blouses, skirts, and dresses from their hangers, half-heartedly folded them, and stuffed them in her small suitcase. They were joined by three pairs of pumps and sandals, a selection of underwear, and her ever-ready travel toiletries and cosmetics bag.

Rosie still couldn't quite believe Shay had offered to go with her. She'd never envisaged going away with Shay for a couple of days at all, but for this? Rosie couldn't imagine a less desirable reason to travel. She zipped her case and put it by the door along with her purse before heading into the living room to write to Franklin, explaining what she had to do and why. She intended to continue working on the proposal on the plane and during any other time she could squeeze it in so that she'd still meet the deadline. He didn't need to panic, and he definitely didn't need to reassign the account to someone else.

After sending that email, she closed her MacBook and put it in her purse, along with her passport. She stared back down the hallway at the letter from her mom. It *had* contained her mom's last wishes, and they *were* as outrageous as Rosie had thought they might be. She shook her head and grabbed the piece of paper from the coffee table. She wouldn't need it in Tijuana, but she had a strange desire to show it to Shay so they could share a laugh over on the plane.

She probably shouldn't even be thinking of laughing right now, but she'd been preparing herself for this moment for most of her life and now that it was finally here, she had to admit to a deep sense of relief. She couldn't share that with anyone else, or they'd think she was a cold-hearted, poor excuse for a daughter, but she'd been a therapist too long to ignore her own emotions, as ugly as they were.

Rosie heard the distinctive sound of Shay's car engine roaring up the street. Funny, she'd never taken any notice of how a car sounded before, nor had she reacted to one quite like this either. Her Pavlovian response wasn't quite dog drool, but even today, when the engine cutting out wouldn't signal the start of another marathon sex session, she couldn't ignore the buzz of anticipation and excitement in the usual places. The other things she was beginning to feel... Well, she didn't need to acknowledge them right now, and she reminded herself that she was an *ex*-therapist, so repression was a normal human response.

She headed back down the corridor to put the letter in her

purse, gathered her things, and went downstairs to greet Shay. Rosie put her case in the trunk and got in the car. "Thanks again for doing this."

"You don't have to keep saying that."

"I know, but I probably will." Rosie clicked her belt into place as Shay pulled into traffic. "I'm pretty much used to being self-sufficient and having to fend for myself. I'm definitely not used to someone being willing to inconvenience themselves to help me."

Shay glanced at her briefly and frowned. "Lori's always there for you, isn't she?"

"Yeah, she is," Rosie said, "but we've only known each other for just over six years. I've been like this for over three decades, and it takes a lot longer to unlearn responses than it does to learn them." She stared at Shay's profile, thinking that this would probably change everything. After Shay had seen Rosie ugly cry, and after all that was to come in the next however many hours, she probably wouldn't want to touch Rosie again. The veil had officially been dropped, and there was nothing sexy about watching someone dissolve into their grief.

"Do you think those responses are reversible?" Shay asked.

"I used to think so." Rosie shifted in the bucket seat so she could stare at Shay without getting a cricked neck. "That's mostly why I followed the career path I did; I wanted to know that people could change, that *I* could change...and that my mom could too."

Shay wrinkled her nose. "But now you're in marketing..."

Rosie laughed. "Now I'm in marketing."

"Because leopards don't change their spots, or whatever cliché you want to go with?"

"I honestly don't know anymore." Rosie sighed deeply. She hadn't had this conversation with anyone, including herself. "I had clients coming to me every two weeks for years, and it just got to the stage where I didn't think we were making progress. They just didn't want to put the work in, or they felt like they *couldn't* put the work in. Whatever it was, there was no real change, and I started to feel jaded, like I was wasting my time and their money."

"Come on," Shay said. "You've got to have had clients who got better, or improved, or something."

"I guess so, but sometimes, people just stop coming, and you don't ever get to know what their outcome was." Rosie shrugged. "I needed a change of scenery, so now I—"

"Use psychology to manipulate people into buying expensive shit they don't need?"

"Wow, that's harsh." Rosie gently shoved Shay's shoulder. "You really know how to beat a girl when she's down, huh?"

Shay turned quickly, her eyes wide and her expression concerned. "I'm sorry, I didn't mean to upset you. I was trying to lighten the mood and keep your mind off...y'know, things."

Rosie smiled. "And it's working. I'm teasing you. And honestly, it's hard to grieve someone who was never really fully there." She bit her lip, a little unsure how comfortable Shay would be talking about the loss of her own mom. "I'm sure it's different for people who had good relationships with their parents. But I feel like I might've grieved for her the most when I was a kid, when I really needed her, and she never came through." She took a moment to dig deeper and think about her initial reaction. "I've got a whole mixed bag of emotions running roughshod through my mind right now, including guilt."

"Why guilt?"

"I told you that Mom said she had to go to Mexico for medication for kidney disease, but I didn't really believe her." Rosie wiped her nails as if they were covered in a fine sprinkling of dust. "I called Aunt Sheila, but then I ignored the situation, thinking Mom'd just come back like she always does—did. I left a message asking her to call me back, but I didn't keep calling. I didn't find out what medication she needed to see if I could get it for her without her going to Mexico."

Shay slowed the car to join the end of the traffic line on Airport Road then half-turned toward Rosie. "She died of an overdose, so none of that mattered."

"She took the drugs without the hospital staff knowing, yes," Rosie pressed her lips together tightly and shook her head, "but the doctor I talked to said that Mom had been admitted with complications arising from her kidney disease. That's why she was there. And if I'd done more, maybe she wouldn't have been there at all." She wanted to continue but had to stop as the guilt seemed to wrap around her lungs, making it difficult to breathe, let alone speak. Of course guilt would be her overriding emotion, even stronger than her grief. It was her overdeveloped sense of guilt that her mom had played on all her life.

Shay pulled into the airport parking lot and switched off the engine. "You haven't told me everything about your mom, but it sounds like she always did what she wanted to do whether you tried to help her or not. You shouldn't carry that kind of guilt around with you. It only gets heavier as the years pass."

Shay sounded like she was speaking from experience, but Rosie didn't press. She was conscious of the time, and their last-minute flight was due to depart shortly. They got their luggage and headed into the terminal enveloped by a weighty silence. Rosie was too preoccupied to make small talk, and Shay seemed lost in her own thoughts. Only then did it occur to Rosie that Shay might be dealing with unresolved feelings around the death of her own mom—did she say it had been six years? Shay had choked up and been unable to talk about it, other than to say that she thought her father blamed her in some way. Her offer to come with Rosie now seemed like even more of an imposition. Supporting her when she was still clearly grieving the death of her own mom was like exposure therapy. Rosie began to worry that it might all be too much.

She caught Shay's wrist just as they were about to go through security. "I really appreciate you coming this far, but I think it might be best if you let me go alone."

"What? Why?" Shay asked, not pulling away.

"You've got your own grief over your mom's death to deal with, and I think traveling with me as I face mine probably isn't the wisest move." She released Shay's arm reluctantly and hoped she'd infused her words with a genuine encouragement she didn't feel. Having Shay by her side for this already felt natural and comforting, and she really didn't want to do this alone. But the hesitancy in Shay's response and the multitude of emotions that flashed across her eyes told Rosie that she'd said the right thing...for Shay. "I'll text you when I land and let you know when I'm coming home."

"Uh, but I've got a ticket, and I'm here now." Shay held out her phone and pointed to the boarding pass on the screen.

Rosie smiled and touched Shay's arm. She wanted to caress her cheek, but that seemed too intimate and not friend-like at all. "But you're not really here, are you? You're in your head about losing your own mom—" she held up her hand when Shay opened her mouth to protest, "and that's okay. Honestly." She tapped her purse. "Lori's sent me a whole raft of information about the American Citizens' Service and how they can help me get my mom home and sort her estate, what there is of it. I'll be fine."

Shay continued to look torn between the sense Rosie was making and her sense of duty, which solidified Rosie's resolve not to let Shay come with her. She took a few steps back, and Shay followed.

"Shay, please. I'll be okay. Go home." Rosie turned and walked away, rolling her small suitcase behind her. She didn't look over her shoulder as she showed her ticket and passport to security, or when she rounded the corner to join the line of people taking off their belts and sorting their electronics and liquids from the rest of their luggage. She sucked in a deep breath. She'd always been alone, whether she was barricading herself in her bedroom to keep her mom's boyfriends from coming in or graduating from college with honors. Bad or good, Rosie had learned to rely only on herself, just as she had to now. So what was that gnawing disappointment doing lurking in her gut? And why did this time feel that little bit different?

An announcement for a delayed flight came over the speaker, and everyone in the airport paused to listen in case they were affected. Shay watched Rosie disappear around the corner to security and frowned when the back of her eyes began to burn. She couldn't just let Rosie face one of the worst moments in her life alone.

Could she?

A slew of passengers parted around her like the Red Sea. She stepped to the side and pulled out her cell.

Gabe answered on the first ring. "Aren't you supposed to be on a plane?"

"I'm at the airport, and Rosie's already through security. I'm still in departures," she said as if that explained everything.

"You're not going," Gabe said. "It's too hard, right?"

Shay's lips quirked. After twenty-plus years of friendship, they were practically in each other's heads, pulling out thoughts without the need for explanation. "I'm being a coward."

"Hey, no. No, you're not. You've never been a coward, and you never will be. Pretty sure cowards don't pull their unconscious buddies out of the line of fire."

Shay laughed lightly. "That was a long time ago. It's about time you forgot that."

"I'm *never* going to forget that you saved my life." Gabe cleared her throat. "Anyway, Lori's isolating because of her COVID, so I'll be home from the garage in a half hour if you want to get dinner. Though I'd drop everything even if Lori wasn't sick, *obviously*. We can shoot some pool and *not* talk about everything you need to talk about."

Not talking sounded tempting. She looked up at the line of airport staff checking tickets and passports, half-expecting Rosie to be behind them trying to get her attention, but she was nowhere to be seen. "I need your advice, Gabe."

"You do?" Gabe chuckled. "You never need my advice when it

comes to women. And you won't *take* my advice when it comes to your family."

"I want to support her through this, but it's bringing all my own stuff a little closer to the surface than usual. Things got strained at Aaron's birthday, and Momma was already on my mind, then Rosie told me what had happened to her mom and–"

"You got pulled in. Your overwhelming desire to do the right thing took over, and you offered to get on a plane and go with Rosie to Mexico. I get it. But I'm going to ask you a question, and don't jump down my throat. Just sit with it for a minute before you answer, okay?"

Shay groaned. "Okay. Do it," she said, not quite sure what the hell Gabe was about to say.

"When I was getting my boxers in a bunch over Lori, you asked me how she'd become so special to me so quic–"

"This isn't the same–"

"I said not to jump down my throat. I hadn't finished."

Shay huffed. "Fine. But it's not the same."

"Shut up and listen. You asked me how Lori had become so special to me so quickly when I didn't let many people in. You and me get along so well because we're the same in a lot of ways, so I can ask: is Rosie special to you?"

Shay resisted the urge to answer immediately and allowed herself some time to really think about her answer. "Yeah, she's special to me but *not* in the same way as Lori is to you, or even was at the time I asked you that question."

"Okay. And you're always there for the people who pierce that strong outer membrane of yours, aren't you?"

"Of course I am. My momma taught me how to treat people." Beyond the immediate stab of loss that her momma was no longer around to keep teaching her lessons, Shay could see what Gabe was trying to say.

"The problem with that–"

"Whoa, what? How can there be a problem with being someone

people can rely on?" Shay had lost the point she'd thought Gabe was making.

Gabe sighed heavily. "The problem is that you don't leave room for people to look after you. Lori's told me that Rosie is pretty self-sufficient and doesn't like inconveniencing people. So I'm guessing that she's said she doesn't need you to go with her because you've got your own stuff going on. Is that about right?"

"That's exactly right." Shay glanced at the departures screen. The flight to San Diego was already boarding, and she was still no closer to deciding what to do. "I get what you're saying, but you know why there's no room for people to look after me. There are only two people in the world who've ever really done that: one's dead, and I'm on the phone to the other one."

Gabe grumbled. "What was it you recently told me about opening up and letting new people into my life? Was that a 'do as I say, not as I do' piece of advice?"

"That's the only way I know how to give advice." Shay laughed, despite the situation.

"Look, buddy, all I'm saying is Rosie is obviously special to you, and she's trying to look after you. Maybe you should let her. It sounds like she's a tough cookie, and she'll be fine. But—"

"Did there have to be a but? That was beginning to sound like a direction I could follow."

Gabe laughed so loudly that Shay had to pull the phone away from her ear.

"We're not in the army anymore, Shay. I don't give you orders or directions," Gabe said. "*But* maybe going with her would be good for both of you if you go because you want to and not because you think you have to."

Shay ran her hand over her braids and blew out an exasperated breath. "How am I supposed to know the difference?"

"I don't know the answer to that question, and maybe you don't either. You're usually pretty tuned in though, so maybe you should be asking yourself and not me."

"That's great, Gabe. Really helpful. I'm so glad I called you."

Gabe chuckled. "You didn't call me so I could tell you what to do, buddy. You called me so you could hear yourself saying it all out loud and figure it out for yourself."

"A little push in the right direction would be well-received this time." Shay looked toward the security gate, having gotten closer to her decision.

"Okay. Then I'll ask you this: when Rosie told you to stay, why did you?"

Shay bit her bottom lip as she contemplated Gabe's question. "Confusion, I guess. I'm not sure what I'm feeling or where it's coming from."

"Mm. Then I'd push you to follow her and see what happens. I think you'll soon find out if you're by her side because you want to be or because you feel obligated. What's the worst that could happen?"

"My grief for my momma could become the focus of the whole trip."

"So what if it does?" Gabe asked. "Rosie isn't close to her mom, so maybe the distraction would be good for her. There's only one way to find out. You staying here means you'll only have questions that you can never get the answers to. And if I know anything about you, it's that you like answers and solutions. Not knowing would drive you nuts."

"You're right. Okay, I'm going." Shay grasped the handle of her cabin bag. "You're sure everything's going to be good at the garage? It's been crazy busy since the auction."

"We'll cope, and you won't be gone that long. You're doing this?"

"I'm doing this... Thanks, Gabe."

"Anytime, Shay. Let me know when you've landed."

Shay smiled at the slight hint of concern in Gabe's voice. "This civilian life is making you soft," she said and laughed.

"Nah, it's loving Lori that's doing that," Gabe said and hung up.

Shay bypassed the growing line and went to the express security lane, which she navigated in less than two minutes, and hurried to her gate. Final boarding had been called and as she approached, she saw the gate staff were about to retreat onto the plane. "Hey, wait!"

The two stewards turned to look at her and waved her forward. "Cutting it fine, ma'am," one of them said as he inspected her phone and passport.

"Sorry. My friend's mom just died, and this was a last-minute thing to go get the body."

"Oh, I'm so sorry." He snapped her passport closed and handed it back before stepping aside.

There were those words to taunt her again. But now she was doing something that felt more useful than the empty sentiment. Shay rushed down the tunnel and onto the plane. She paused when she saw Rosie seated by the window, staring out and looking so incredibly alone. Even when Shay slipped in beside her, it didn't pull Rosie's attention.

Shay snapped her seatbelt into place and cleared her throat. "I'm not letting you face this alone," she said quietly.

Rosie's head snapped in Shay's direction and for a moment, she seemed confused before she sighed deeply. Tears edged her eyes, and her bottom lip quivered slightly.

"Why?" Rosie asked.

"Because I'm your friend, and friends support each other, especially at times like this."

Rosie gave her a half-smile and shook her head slowly. "I'm used to supporting myself. You really don't have to be here."

"I don't have to, no. But I want to."

"Thank you." Rosie looked like she might dissolve into a sob, then she threw her arms around Shay's neck. She pulled back and looked into Shay's eyes as if she were searching for something. "I know how hard it is for you to be here."

Shay nodded. She wasn't about to deny that. Even though Rosie wasn't a shrink anymore, it was clear her skills were still sharp, and she'd probably see through the untruth before Shay had even finished verbalizing it. "Did you get the car rental worked out for San Diego? It's too bad there were no direct flights straight into TJ."

Rosie rolled her eyes. "I did, but I had to take out special Mexican liability insurance. They were eager to stress that I couldn't have a one-way rental. The coroner's office has picked up Mom's body, so that's our first stop. And I had a little time to skim the details Lori sent me; I need a death report from the Justice Center before I can get a funeral home to pick her up." She patted the purse on her lap. "Mom wanted to be cremated, and that makes it easier to get her back—"

The air stewardess came over the speaker system and loudly announced details of their departure, silencing Rosie for a moment. Shay took Rosie's hand and held it tight.

The announcement finished, and Rosie smiled. "Let's just get this part of the journey out of the way." She nodded to the screen set in the headrest. "We've got time to watch a couple of movies or binge-watch a show."

"Sure." Shay hadn't been as calm as Rosie when she was traveling home for the funeral, but she reminded herself that their situations were poles apart, and she had no idea what Rosie was hiding inside, if anything. "What kind of movies do you like?" she asked then frowned. "How do I not know that?"

Rosie arched her eyebrow. "My viewing habits don't really come up when we meet. We're usually a little preoccupied with ripping each other's clothes off," she whispered.

Shay hadn't felt guilty about that until now. "I guess we've been focusing on the benefits and neglecting the friendship." She tapped her watch as the airline staff began their safety presentation. "We've got four hours to rectify that. Do you want to start with movies and TV?"

Rosie's answering smile calmed Shay's racing heart, something she hadn't been aware of until just then. The confusion she had about whether or not she should be here fell away, and she could almost hear her momma's voice telling her this was the right thing to do, not just for Rosie but also for herself. And Gabe had been right too. Shay would get her answers in the next few days, and her life could go back to normal. She and Rosie could go back to normal.

The niggling doubt that was calling their situationship into question at the back of her mind? For now, she'd park that and deal with it when she got home.

Chapter Seventeen

ROSIE COLLAPSED ONTO THE hotel bed face down, groaning. "I think that might have been the most exhausting eighteen hours of my life." Between the flight, the drive across the border, and then heading straight to the coroner's office, it was like someone had pulled the plug out of her, leaving her drained in every way possible.

"That could be partly due to a lack of fuel. You haven't eaten anything since that granola bar you found at the bottom of your purse," Shay said. "Do you want to get room service?"

Rosie rolled over and dragged herself higher up the bed. She pressed her hands over her stomach, trying to decide if she *was* hungry, or if she was over it and just needed to sleep.

Shay waved the menu in her hand. "They've got a tasty-looking grilled club sandwich with fries."

Rosie smiled. They'd talked about so many things on the flight to San Diego and in the car to Tijuana, from food and movies, to pets and travel. She was impressed Shay had remembered such a tiny detail. "Someone was paying attention on the journey here."

Shay shrugged and sat on the edge of the bed beside her. "What kind of friend would I be if I asked the questions and didn't pay attention to the answers?"

She laughed. "You'd be like every other friend I've ever had since childhood—apart from Lori. Though I guess with all the moving around I did, the other kids didn't really have much of a chance to get to know me."

Shay handed Rosie the menu. "You know, with all you've been through, it's a wonder you're quite so well put together."

Rosie chuckled. "You think I'm 'well put together?'" She bit her bottom lip and shook her head. She was pretty certain that there was no way back to their friends with benefits situation after all of this, so there really was zero point in keeping her mess in a box. "It's a lot of work. I told you why I became a therapist, but part of the qualification involves a lot of your own therapy. Even though I don't have to do that anymore, I still see someone. Three and a half decades of being Brenda Morgan's daughter is a lot to unravel." She glanced away from Shay's intense gaze. "Maybe it'll get easier now that she's...now that she's gone." She took in a stuttering breath and clasped her hand to her chest, as if that might help. It didn't, and her breathing became more erratic.

Shay took her hand. "Rosie. Relax. Take some deep breaths," she said gently.

"I'm sorry," Rosie said between mini gasps. She pulled in some oxygen and tried to calm herself. Slowly, her breathing returned to normal, and the rhino sitting on her chest faded away. "I probably shouldn't say things like that."

"You should be able to say anything to a friend, shouldn't you?"

And there it was again. It was as if Shay was subtly pulling back from their situationship and confirming Rosie's belief that, after this, they could only be friends. No more spectacular sex or late-night booty calls because how could Shay still find her attractive after she'd seen behind the veil? Maybe another friend wouldn't be so bad. "Because of your mom. I sound like I'm relieved it's over, which I probably shouldn't say out loud, when you'd probably give anything to have your mom back."

Sadness flickered across Shay's expression, and Rosie wished she hadn't drawn attention to her highly inappropriate emotion, even though it was competing with a kind of grief too. Though if she said that now, it'd just seem like she was trying to dial back her original feelings. And she knew better than that.

Shay folded her leg beneath her to sit sideways on the bed, facing Rosie. "I'm not a therapist, but even I know that people should be allowed to feel what they feel." She looked away briefly.

"Our experiences with our moms were so very different, and it's not a comparison or a competition when you tell me how you're feeling. I'm glad that you're comfortable enough to share with me."

"How did you get to be so good with emotions when you seem to keep them at bay most of the time?"

Shay frowned. "What do you mean?"

"Like how you are with intimate relationships. You keep people at a distance and don't get involved. You like everything simple."

"Oh, I get it. If we're going to get heavy, we should both get some brain food." Shay tapped the menu on Rosie's lap.

Rosie didn't look at it and opted for her favorite comfort food. "Will you order? I'm going to shower before the food arrives." She dragged herself off the bed and closed the bathroom door behind her. She'd been tempted to ask Shay to join her, but she felt a little too grubby to get sexy, *and* she was exhausted. The judgmental part of her brain raised its eyebrow at the fact that she could even *think* about having sex when the ink was barely dry on her mom's death certificate. She silently countered that argument with the logic that being around death made her realize just how precious and fleeting life was, so every last drop of existence should be squeezed out of each moment.

Her skin tingled when the hot water hit her body, immediately invigorating her. Rosie pumped the shower gel into her palm and inhaled the refreshing lemongrass and bergamot scent before soaping up. She ran her hands all over her body, washing away the grimy feeling of the travel day and the gritty sensation she'd had since going to the coroner's office to see her mom and to collect the medical examiner's report. She shuddered despite the warmth of the water and blinked away the image of her mom's lifeless body on the metal table they'd pulled out of a cabinet door on the wall, like she was in an oversized safety deposit box. Her mom definitely hadn't looked like she could've gotten up and cackled, "Rosarita!" like in Rosie's weird dream. That total lifelessness had been so misplaced; while she'd often thought her mom would end up like that, she'd never stopped to *imagine* it. Death was certainly an equalizer and had dragged away all sense of the power her mom held over her. At least it had in *that* moment.

Tomorrow, they had to go to the Justice Center to file the death report, which she'd been advised would take a couple of hours, but for now, she wanted to focus on getting clean and continuing to process the gamut of emotions assailing her as she faced the reality that her mom was actually gone.

Rosie washed the suds from her body, wishing that it could be as easy to do the same with her parental baggage. Logically, she knew she didn't owe her mom anything other than to follow the last wishes she'd detailed in her decades-old letter, and maybe not even that. But she didn't want to miss the opportunity for personal growth. She patted her skin dry with a fluffy towel and decided she'd just let the situation be what it was going to be. No amount of second-guessing or trying to see into her subconscious would expedite the process. There were stages, and she'd work her way through them.

She pulled on a light cotton robe and tied it at the waist before going back out into the bedroom to see Shay lying on the other queen bed by the window. Rosie wrinkled her nose. "Do you think they assumed we were just friends when they allocated this room?"

Shay's lips quirked before she seemed to school her expression. "They were probably just playing it safe. Does it bother you?"

Rosie sat on the edge of Shay's bed. "Kind of. I don't like when people assume two trad feminine women can't possibly be lovers— or friends with benefits," she added quickly, hoping there might be one last connection possible. *To hell with it*. If this was going to be the last time she was this close to Shay, especially in a nice hotel room, she'd damn well make the most of it. Most people didn't know when their last time for anything would be, so they didn't get the chance to treasure it properly. She wasn't going to let their last time be on the same day she'd learned her mom had died.

But now wasn't right. Her growling stomach let her know she

wanted food more than she'd realized.

"But you didn't correct them."

Rosie frowned. "What?"

"You're not happy that the guy on reception assumed we'd need two beds, but you didn't correct him or ask for a room with just one bed."

"I don't think I was paying enough attention," she said. "*But* if I hadn't been emotionally and physically exhausted, I definitely would've called him on it."

Shay grinned. "I'm just messing with you. I've always thought you were feisty."

"Really?" She liked the idea of Shay thinking of her before they'd gotten together, as much as they *were* together. "Tell me more."

Shay shook her head. "You don't need to fish for compliments, do you?" She laughed when Rosie nodded enthusiastically. "Okay, okay. Gabe told me how you warned her not to hurt Lori, and when I saw you the first time at the garage, I could see you weren't someone to play with."

Rosie arched her eyebrow and caught hold of Shay's bare foot. "But you have played with me," she said hoarsely.

The knock at the door came before Shay responded, and Rosie reluctantly got up to answer it. She tipped the server after they'd brought everything in and laid it on the small table by the window. When they server left, she turned back to the table and moaned. "*That* looks amazing." She gestured to Shay's plate of quesadillas. "Are you eating in bed?" Rosie giggled at Shay's mortified expression as she practically jumped off the bed.

"No way. You should know I hate crumbs in the bed."

Rosie pulled out a chair and sat down, not sure what to make of that statement. On the one hand, it implied they might share a bed again, but on the other, it implied Shay had chosen to sleep in the second bed and not join Rosie in the one she'd flopped onto earlier.

They ate in relative silence. Shay was clearly as hungry as Rosie was, but when Rosie finished her entrée first and uncovered the third plate, she moaned in appreciation again. "Brownies!" They were her favorite dessert, which had been another thing they'd discussed on the journey here. Shay really had been paying attention.

Shay laughed. "It's like you enjoy food as much as sex. I don't think I've ever heard anyone moan like that over a grilled sandwich and cake."

Rosie clasped her hand over her mouth. "Oh my God, do I make the same noises when I'm having sex?"

Shay tilted her head one way then the other as if she had to seriously contemplate the question.

"Shay..." Rosie said when she still hadn't answered.

"You're more...enthusiastic when it comes to sex," she said and bit into the last quarter of her quesadilla.

"God, I wish I hadn't asked at all, because now I want to know if I'm too loud."

Shay chewed and swallowed then took a too-long pull on her beer, knowing damn well what she was doing.

Rosie shoved Shay's shoulder. "Well?"

Shay shook her head and smiled. "You could never be too loud for me. I'm not a fan of quiet sex. It's like people are ashamed they're having such a good time."

"Mm, that's not exactly fair," she said, though relief washed through her, knowing that Shay wasn't turned off by the noises she made.

"What do you mean?" Shay dipped the final piece of her food into a cup of sour cream and popped it into her mouth.

"Lots of people like to be quiet so they can appreciate the sound of their lover's breath," Rosie said. "Some people are in their heads with a fantasy, and making noise is a distraction from the movie playing in their mind. And plenty of people enjoy the intimacy of silence as a direct juxtaposition to the noise of everyday life."

Shay grinned. "They all sound like case studies from your time as a therapist. Did you do a lot of couples' counseling?"

"Sorry." Rosie made what she hoped was an apologetic expression. "It's hard to forget over a decade of your working life."

Shay frowned. "Why would you want to? And there's definitely no need to apologize."

Rosie didn't answer for a moment while she considered the implication of her reaction. "That's a good question that I don't instantly know the answer to. I'll have to ponder it and get back to you."

"It seems like you still like therapizing people," Shay said.

"I'm sorry." Rosie recalled their pre-room service conversation. "Your behavior and feelings around intimate relationships are none of my business. Forget I said anything." She pulled the plate of brownies toward her; if she couldn't have Shay as her dessert, these would have to suffice. She took a bite and made a conscious effort not to moan out loud.

"I don't get involved because I don't have time for more complications," Shay said after the silence had stretched on. "My family takes up all of my emotional bandwidth, and intimate relationships are exhausting."

Rosie laughed. "You understand that being with someone in an intimate relationship could be extremely supportive and help you with your family stuff, don't you? They're two-way streets, or at least, the good ones are. I've seen them in action, even if I haven't had one myself. You don't have to look far to see that Lori and Gabe fit perfectly into that category."

"But you're a shrink, and you still haven't managed to have a successful relationship."

"Ouch." Rosie smiled, but that one stung a lot more than she would've liked. "I just haven't met someone who fits me yet, that's all."

"And you said that you'd stopped searching."

"I have." Rosie sighed and looked at Shay, trying to stop herself from following a train of thought that would only derail the moment she vocalized it. A change of subject was required before one of them said something they couldn't take back. "And that led me into our simple situationship, which I'm thoroughly enjoying." She ran her fingers along Shay's forearm and tilted her head toward the bed. "And which I'd like to enjoy tonight, if you're willing." She stared into Shay's eyes, checking for clues as to where her head was at right now.

"I'm always willing," Shay got up and held out her hand, "if you're sure that's what you want."

Rosie took it and allowed herself to be pulled to her feet. "I'm sure." She'd seen no sign of hesitation or disinterest in Shay's expression, only concern and perhaps a little relief at the end to a tricky conversation. Maybe she'd gotten it wrong, and they would be able to continue this when they got back to Chicago. *Stop.* She should quit overthinking everything and go with the flow. The shower and the food had combined to combat her fatigue and honestly, being in such close proximity with someone as sexy as Shay made sleep far less appealing than it should be right now.

Shay guided her to the closest bed and gently pushed her down, falling to the mattress with her. Rosie inched up higher until her head was on a pillow, and then she relaxed, content to let Shay take the lead. Shay seemed to understand that's what she wanted, and she slowly untied the robe and pushed it away from Rosie's body. Her unhurried touch somehow transmitted a soft vibe to Rosie's brain, and she sank deeper into the comforter, her body taking on a weightless sensation that was a little surreal.

Rosie stretched out as Shay kissed her neck softly before working her way along Rosie's collarbone, down between her breasts, and then to her stomach. Her strong hands cupped Rosie's breasts and squeezed gently, making her gasp. Shay's lips were fire on her skin, everywhere all at once as everything else on Rosie's mind dropped away like heavy raindrops from a fragile leaf, leaving her light and empty in only good ways.

Shay pressed her body to Rosie's, and her slight weight

grounded her even more deeply in the moment, and then Shay kissed her with such intensity that it carried Rosie away on a wave of emotion so powerful, she almost lost herself in it. They'd kissed before, that wasn't new, but this was—*No*. She pulled back on the intrusive and destructive notion. This could still be the last time, and that's what she needed to feel and think about. She needed to memorize the way Shay traced her tongue along Rosie's skin in circles, the way Shay's lips felt pressed against hers, the way Shay used her fingers to bring her to orgasm. *Those* orgasms. Powerful and life-affirming like nothing she'd ever felt before. Shay knew how to play Rosie's body to hit the high notes of pleasure.

Rosie opened her eyes, and Shay met her gaze. The connection electrified the room, and every sensory cell in her body rose up and cried out for more. More of this. More of Shay. Shay's dark eyes held such untapped depths, like she was both desperate for and terrified of someone truly seeing her. Rosie moaned and lifted her hips to grind herself into Shay's body, counting on that to break Shay's concentration and take her back to the sex, to the sounds she'd said she liked Rosie to make. The sounds she liked *any* woman to make, not just her. Rosie had to stop herself from getting carried away by something that wasn't there, by a connection that was purely physical and nothing more.

Shay's eyes remained intently on Rosie as she trailed her fingers slowly along Rosie's body and to her core. Rosie opened her legs wider, already wet and ready for Shay to take her, already hungry for the inevitable release but simultaneously dreading the shattering of her defenses. She could feel it rise inexorably to the surface, no longer willing to remain unacknowledged and silent. Simple. Friends with benefits. No strings sex. *Fuck all that.* This thing inside her wanted so much more. This need inside her wanted Shay, *all* of Shay. Everything Shay allowed people to see and everything she never gave voice or freedom to. Everything that Shay was and would ever be.

Fuck it. I've fallen in love.

Chapter Eighteen

She flashed the keycard, and Rosie followed her in. Shay had never been so happy to see the inside of a hotel room. Their time at the Justice Center had reminded her how much she *didn't* miss government institutions, with all their red tape and bureaucracy. And even though she'd never been to Tijuana before and the hotel concierge continued to urge them to visit Zona Rio and the Plaza Fiesta, she had no desire to explore any of it.

Her lack of interest was unusual, but she figured it was probably just the situation. Being here to do all things death-related for Rosie's mom wasn't conducive to tripping down La Revolución and sampling all this vibrant city had to offer. Then last night had happened, and she realized there were other things at play directing her not to indulge in vacation-type activities. Confusing things. Emotional things that had no right to be lurking in her brain.

Shay placed the full ice bucket on the side table and scanned her mind for something safe to talk about. "When the justice guy commented on your name, you said you had a good story to tell me about it..."

Rosie kicked off her Converse and dropped onto the nearest bed. "Did I say it was a good story?" She shook her head. "Turning trauma into humorous anecdotes is a bad habit of mine. I think someone said that everything becomes funny eventually, but I'm not so sure."

"Laughter is better than tears, isn't it?" Shay dropped some ice cubes into two glasses and took a Coke from the fridge.

Rosie smiled. "Not always. Emotional tears can detox the body." She locked eyes with Shay. "And there are other benefits I won't bore you with."

"It's not boring." Shay poured a double measure of Abasolo whisky over the ice in her glass, and the cubes crackled. "I like the residual knowledge you've got from your therapy days; it's educational."

Rosie chuckled. "Because that's what you want from your friend with benefits: educational tidbits."

"Knowledge is power, right?" Shay looked away from Rosie's intense gaze and added Coke to their glasses. She didn't know what she wanted right now. Part of her wanted more time like this, and another part of her wanted to run to the nearest club to bed another woman. "So, your story," Shay said, ignoring her clashing contemplations.

"It's nothing, really. And it's kind of a downer. Are you sure you want to hear it?"

"I do." Shay handed one glass to Rosie before sitting sideways in the giant armchair between the two beds and draping her legs over the edge. Rosie tugged off Shay's pumps and began to rub her feet. Shay's instinct was to pull away, but she distracted herself from the intimate gesture with a long drink.

"I'll start with a question, if you don't mind. Who named you?"

"My momma." Shay's resulting smile surprised her as the memory of her own story rushed into her mind, ready and willing to be told. "She said that it means the Lord is gracious, but that's not what I like about it. I like it because my daddy wanted to call me something else, and she wouldn't let him. I don't even remember what that was, or whether I would've liked it more. I just remember the look on my momma's face every time she told that story. She was a strong, proud Black woman who fought for what she wanted, even when it was for something as simple as her child's name."

Rosie squeezed Shay's foot and smiled, but there was a sadness in her eyes that made Shay want to wrap her arms around Rosie and hold her until it went away.

"That's beautiful. I was named by a nurse," Rosie said, shaking her head as she looked up at the ceiling. "When my mom told this story, she was strangely proud of it."

Shay took another drink, partially hiding her face to conceal her reaction to the beginning of yet another devastatingly heartbreaking story about Rosie's mom. She'd learned a lot more than she needed to in order to conclude that Rosie's mom was a piece of work who had no business becoming a mother. But every story that Rosie told also encouraged a beautiful memory from Shay's childhood, and she'd been wrapped up in a protective bubble of love and kindness that shielded her from the acidity of Rosie's mom. The worry she'd had about stirring up her own unresolved grief by coming with Rosie had been unfounded. And more than that, it had been helpful in transforming her grieving thoughts into ones of celebration and happiness at the love she'd shared with her momma. "Your mom let a nurse name you?" she asked, unable to hold back her judgment.

"Yep. The nurse said that Mom should call me Rosie on account of how rosy my cheeks were when I was born. Mom was still vaguely high on cocaine, so she went along with it." Rosie shrugged. "I always thought I'd gotten away lightly. In my mom's heightened state, God knows I could've ended up being called Mary Jane or Molly."

Shay flexed her feet under Rosie's grip, which she'd tightened considerably since starting the story.

"Oh, sorry." Rosie lifted one of Shay's feet and kissed her toes.

She laughed. "Did you really just kiss my feet?"

Rosie shrugged. "Well, you are kind of a goddess, and they get their feet kissed *all* the time."

"They do?" Shay wrinkled her nose, though she liked that Rosie thought of her that way. "Exactly how many goddesses do you know?"

"Just you," Rosie said and glanced away as her cheeks pinked slightly.

Lord, she was adorable when she got all shy. *Adorable?* Since when did Shay think *anything* was adorable? "Have you ever thought about changing your name to change your story?"

Rosie looked up at the ceiling, as though the question had taken her deep into unpleasant memories. "Only every time Mom told that tale."

"Is there a reason you never have?" If she'd experienced half of the things Rosie had gone through, Shay would've used any means necessary to distance herself from her mom, and a name change seemed a relatively simple and easy action. She reprimanded herself almost before she'd completed the thought. "Ignore that question," she said. "I wouldn't have done that or anything else to get away from my family. They're my blood, and I can't turn my back on them even though they're far from perfect." She shook her head and sighed. "I only have to think of all the times I've bailed my brothers out of bad situations, or the times I've done things that were detrimental to me just to help them, and all the crap I've put up with over the years. I really can't begin to wonder why you didn't change your name or do anything else, especially with the state of my relationship with my daddy."

Rosie frowned. "But you joined the Army, so you did get away from your family."

Shay pulled on one of her box braids and inspected it like it was the most interesting thing she'd seen in a long time. They were looking dry; she'd probably have to bite the bullet and spend eight hours with her hairdresser getting an inch off and having them redone.

Rosie tugged on her foot. "Shay?"

She dropped her braid and looked back at Rosie. What was it about this hotel room that was encouraging all these deeply intense conversations? "I was a stupid kid when I made that decision, but you're right. I'd convinced myself there was too much expectation on me to be some kind of light-bringer for the whole family. I couldn't handle it, and I didn't want it. I graduated from Yale and joined the Army the following week. I met Gabe and found the friend I'd been looking for my whole life. After that, leaving didn't occur to me at all. But I didn't turn my back on my family, and I still can't do that to my daddy even though it feels like he's turned away from me."

"Maybe you need to talk to him about that."

"Ha. Like hell I do," Shay said. "Can we change the subject?"

"Do you think it's weird that I'm having Mom cremated instead of organizing a proper funeral when I get home?" Rosie asked without missing a beat.

Shay shook her head, glad to be talking about anything other than the crazy thoughts running around her head. "Everybody has different ideas about that final send off, don't they? And you said that's what your mom wanted, so none of this has really been your choice."

"My mom wanted some strange stuff though, right?" Rosie pulled out the paper list from her purse.

"One person's weird is another person's normal. It can't be the first time someone's had hard rock playing at their funeral." Shay had seen it yesterday when they were at the coroners' office and had tried hard not to react.

Rosie arched her eyebrow. "You don't have to be diplomatic. You were desperate to laugh when I showed you this yesterday."

"Hey, you wanted to laugh too. Your eyes went all crinkly." Which had been something else that Shay found adorable at the time.

"Maybe. But it definitely wouldn't have been appropriate to burst into laughter since we were surrounded by a hundred mini metal doors, each of them with a dead body hiding behind it."

"No." Shay shook her head rapidly. "Definitely not. Do you think you could get kicked out of a morgue for inappropriate behavior?"

Rosie winked. "Do you want to go back and find out?"

Shay blew out a long breath. "With your mom behind one of those doors?" She tilted her head slightly. "Hard pass." She gestured to the list in Rosie's hand. "I guess some of the requests are unusual. But it's been a while since she wrote it. Maybe she had an updated version you haven't seen."

Rosie shook her head. "Every time one of her old friends or someone she knew from way back died, she'd bring it up and ask if I'd read it yet. She hated getting old... I think in a lot of ways, she was stuck in that same time when she wrote these instructions, so she wouldn't have wanted to change them."

"Does anyone *like* getting old?" Shay looked at Rosie's soft, unlined hands and imagined the dark age spots that would inevitably mar her pale skin. "Although I don't have to worry much. Everyone in my family looks about fifteen years younger than their actual age."

"You can be okay with getting older. I think that's different from getting old." Rosie shrugged. "But over the last ten years or so, my mom always said that she didn't recognize the woman looking back at her in the mirror. And she was angry about it, about losing that past version of herself, the one she loved the best."

"What about you?" Shay asked, eager to divert the conversation away from Rosie's mom. The day had been all about her, which was fair given why they were there, but every moment of that seemed to weigh heavy on Rosie. Her color had faded slowly throughout the day, as if her mom was still there, washing her brightness away. "Which version of yourself do you love the best?"

Rosie laughed. "Who said I loved *any* version of myself?"

Beyond the humor of Rosie's words, Shay detected a truthfulness to her flippancy. "Don't you have to love yourself before you can expect anyone else to love you? Isn't that therapy 101?"

"Maybe that's where I'm going wrong," Rosie said quietly then stopped stroking Shay's feet and tucked her knees up to her chest. "Although, Lori loves me, and Aunt Sheila is convinced she does too, even though she only says it after a half bottle of whiskey." She waved as if the words she'd just said out loud were hanging in the air, and she needed to shove them away. "Anyway, can I ask about your mom's funeral?"

Shay hesitated before answering, not only because that topic was too painful to talk about, but also to keep herself from pursuing Rosie's dropped conversation. The room was already supercharged with emotions, and Shay was having difficulty parsing out what was real and would stick around, and what was only the result of the situation and would fall away once they went back to Chicago.

"I'm sorry," Rosie said, "I shouldn't have asked."

"It's okay." Shay stretched to tap her foot Rosie's. "You can ask me anything," she said, though she really hoped Rosie wouldn't take her word for that. She might have answers, but they might not be answers Rosie would want to hear. "There was a lot of music. And singing and dancing. That's the way it's been at all of my family's funerals. The energy is supposed to be healing, so we express our emotions any way that works... People read out poetry, sang psalms and her favorite songs." Shay thought about the funeral program she'd tucked in the back of a photo frame of her and her momma at Shay's Yale graduation. She'd played no part in the preparations because it had taken her so long to get home; her CO at the time had been one of Major Nelson's old cronies, and he'd pulled every string he could and put every delay possible in her path just to fuck with her. She sometimes thought that might be one of the reasons her daddy had pulled away from her, but she couldn't be sure because he simply wouldn't talk to her about it. But Rosie was dealing with her past and moving forward. Maybe Shay could too. She resolved to visit him when they got back, just like Rosie had suggested; it was beyond time to sit with him and have an uncomfortable conversation.

"Shay?"

She became aware of Rosie's hand on her arm, and she looked up to see Rosie had come to the edge of the bed. Concern etched lines across Rosie's face, and Shay ached to trace her finger across those contours. *Damn it.* Last night's sex had affected her more than she'd wanted it to, more than she wanted to acknowledge.

Without asking, she pressed her lips over Rosie's, seeking to deal with her tension the only way she knew how. If they could just have sex again, the fun, unemotional, and purely physical kind they'd been having in Chicago, then the confusion would melt away, and she could get back on track.

But even the kiss was different now. Soft, tender, full of intimate promise, and beyond simple sexual satisfaction. She opened her eyes to see those same emotions reflected in Rosie's gaze. Shay shifted to sit properly in the armchair, and Rosie slipped smoothly off the bed and straddled her. Shay placed her hands on Rosie's hips and leaned back, but Rosie followed her, her mouth seeking hers, giving her the green light. Shay really couldn't say what she was asking for, so how could Rosie know what she was consenting to?

Rosie cupped Shay's face and kissed her hard, and Shay grasped at the tiny sliver of simplicity, responding with a similar pressure, as if she could kiss away a slowly dawning reality. Damn, why did Rosie have to be so beautiful inside and out? Wouldn't it be easier to stick to her rules if Shay could find one thing that she didn't like? One thing that irritated her was all she needed to hold onto.

But as their kiss deepened, and the heat of Rosie's body filtered through Shay's thin cotton tank top, she stopped thinking and let go. She rose slowly from the chair, and Rosie wrapped her legs around Shay's waist. She guided Rosie onto the bed and pressed her body against her, not wanting even a millimeter of air between them as she continued to devour her as if she might never taste her again.

Rosie thrust herself against Shay's core and squeezed her legs so tightly around Shay that it made it difficult to breathe. But the strength of her embrace served only to stoke Shay's fire for her all the more. When she rolled onto her back, Rosie came with her then sat up briefly to tear off her own shirt before tugging at Shay's.

"Oops," Rosie said as Shay's tank top strained and tore.

Shay didn't care. She could buy more clothes, but moments like this weren't anywhere near as easy to come by. Rosie tore it off and discarded it before falling back onto Shay's body, pressing her lips to Shay's with a passion that could've set the room on fire. Shay absorbed Rosie's energy and returned it two-fold, desperate to take everything and anything Rosie had to offer.

Rosie's hair fell over her shoulders and fanned around Shay's face, the errant strands tickling her nose. She reached up and brushed them over Rosie's ear while her body begged for more. She stroked her other hand along the length of Rosie's side until she got to the edge of her short skirt. Shay raked her nails up along Rosie's thigh, bringing the soft material of Rosie's skirt up higher until she felt the intricate lace of Rosie's panties. Shay had admired the matching set when she'd watched Rosie get dressed in the bathroom earlier that day, but she'd kept her desire to rip the bra and panties off to herself.

She hooked her fingers in the band of the panties and pulled them down just enough to give her access. Rosie lifted herself slightly higher to give Shay the space to move inside her, and she moaned loudly when Shay slipped two fingers into her wet pussy.

"You were ready for me," Shay whispered, her arousal ramping up even higher at Rosie's vocal appreciation.

Rosie ran her tongue along Shay's bottom lip before sucking it into her mouth. "I'll always be ready for you."

Always. Permanently. Forever. Things no one had any business promising anyone else. And yet, Shay wanted to believe her, wanted to believe that Rosie's desire for her could be everlasting...

She'd looked into Rosie's eyes last night and seen something she hadn't thought possible: a future happiness, a connection beyond their shared sexual appetite. How the hell had that happened? "Always?" Shay was unable to stop herself from asking as she thrust harder inside Rosie, who moaned loud enough to make their neighbor bang on the wall.

Rosie raked her nails over Shay's chest, and she hissed in

response, pushing in even deeper.

"Always," Rosie whispered, breathless, and she rode Shay's hand hard until she cried out her release and collapsed onto Shay.

Shay stroked slow circles on Rosie's back while she panted into Shay's neck until her breathing steadily evened out. Rosie lifted her head and smiled. And while there was a definite post-orgasmic Zen quality to her expression, Shay saw something more, saw Rosie in a way she hadn't registered before now. It was as though she was completely relaxed and one hundred percent her authentic self. No masks, no filters. Just pure Rosie. Although maybe they were just the things Shay was feeling. Somehow, through all their intensely pleasurable sex and deep conversations, and despite Shay's determination not to let things get complicated, Rosie had stripped away her defenses and left her with an unguarded heart.

But it didn't matter what her heart was feeling, or what nonsense it was trying to fill her head with. She'd made up her rules two decades ago, and they'd been working great, keeping her personal life simple and giving her the outlet she needed when she needed it. She had Gabe, RB, and Woody for everything else. Hell, she could even rely on Solo if she was desperate, though she was chest-deep in her own problems right now. Shay didn't need, and didn't have time for, a time-sucking, emotion-filled, complicated relationship. Rosie was just a friend with *extremely fantastic* benefits.

So why did thinking of Rosie as just a friend leave her feeling so hollow?

Chapter Nineteen

ROSIE SET THE URN in the footwell and clamped her feet around it. Nope, that wasn't going to work for the next hour. She could already imagine Shay braking sharply for some haphazard driver, and her mom's ashes exploding all over her feet before they were even out of the city. She could feel Shay staring at her from the driver's seat, and Rosie glanced over. "What?"

Shay grinned. "There's a Home Depot nearby; we could stop and get some duct tape."

She raised her eyebrow and gave Shay her best wicked little smile. "Do we have time to roleplay? Our flight is in four hours."

"That's not where my mind was at," Shay said, her grin growing wider, "but it is now."

Rosie rolled her eyes and got out of the car. She popped the trunk and wedged the urn into a neat side pocket, then she shoved their cases and purses around it. She looked through the back windshield at Shay's silhouette and couldn't stifle a guilty giggle at the thought of being "kidnapped" by her. Rosie hadn't expected the somber trip to Mexico to pick up her mom's remains to turn into the sex-fest that it had, but she was far from sorry. It had made the whole thing bearable, and it hadn't been the death knell on their situationship like she'd thought it was going to be either. As for that pesky love thing, she'd harbor that quietly and talk to Lori when they got back.

"All good?" Shay asked.

She slid back into the passenger seat. "It'll be fine as long as you don't drive like you're in a *Fast and Furious* movie."

Shay looked incredulous and started the engine. "In this

piece of modern junk? It's so slow, it's got a calendar instead of a speedometer."

Rosie shook her head and laughed. "Missing your car much?"

"More than I should."

She had no response for that. Rosie liked her new Mercedes 400E, and she enjoyed driving it, but she couldn't imagine *missing* a pile of metal.

Shay pulled out of the hotel parking lot and into traffic on the Avenida de los Insurgentes, and they fell back into easy conversation by the time they were driving past Parque Morelos. The journey to the San Ysidro border crossing was stupidly busy, and Rosie began to wonder if she should've booked a later flight. "Do you think they'll check the urn for drugs? We don't need any more delays," she said when they got to the checkpoint and, unlike on the way in when the light remained green and they drove straight into Mexico, it turned red for them to stop. Shay glanced her way, and Rosie couldn't interpret her expression.

"You're white, and you look like a nice, respectable woman. You don't need to worry."

"Does that mean that you do?"

Shay nodded. "Relax. I know how to handle myself around cops."

Rosie bit the inside of her lip. "I'll kick their ass if they mess with you," she said with a brave edge that she didn't particularly feel. But she'd find it if Shay was threatened.

Shay turned in her seat and looked at Rosie seriously. "You do nothing, Rosie. This isn't a game. Keep your hands visible, and don't give them any sass, you understand me?"

"I understand," she said quietly and placed her hands on her thighs. An icy chill ran up her spine even though the wind blew the eighty-degree heat in through her open window. She'd always felt safe when the police were nearby, but Shay's unease evaporated that security like water in the Mojave Basin.

The American border patrol officer seemed nice enough.

He inspected the car thoroughly, but Rosie expected that in the current climate of post-Trump America and the ongoing struggle with immigrants. She explained the nature of their trip, and he asked her to pop the trunk but to stay in the vehicle.

"It's going to be okay," she said to herself as much as to Shay, who was gripping the steering wheel so hard, Rosie thought she might tear it off the dash.

Shay huffed. "You don't know that," she said quietly.

When the officer appeared beside her window like he'd materialized from thin air, Rosie jumped. He held her mom's urn in his hands at such an angle that she was worried the top might fall off, and her mom's final resting place would be all over the ground in... Were they technically still in Mexico? Or were they on American soil? She imagined her mom might be inclined to haunt her if the officer didn't have steady hands.

"Are these your mother's remains?" he asked.

Rosie felt the white heat of Shay's glare without needing look at her. *No sass.* If she'd been in the car with Lori, she wouldn't have been able to hold back a smart-ass comment. But the tension radiating off Shay quashed that desire. "Yes."

He thrust the urn through the window. "Open it, please."

Rosie wrinkled her nose and bit her top lip. What if she fumbled and ended up dropping it all over herself? She took the container and secured it between her legs to remove the lid, then she tilted it toward him slightly so he could inspect the contents. She didn't look inside. She'd seen the ashes of her friend's dog when she was fifteen and had been shocked at the amount of bone fragments. Whenever they threw ashes in the movies, it was like a fine powder, and she had no idea whether the process was different for humans or not. Whatever it was, she didn't want to investigate.

He shifted his head from side to side and even shone a Maglite into the urn. Did he think it had magical properties and was some sort of bottomless genie urn with a million-dollar stash of drugs held within?

Stop it. She bit her lip harder.

"I need to see the paperwork," he said and put away his flashlight.

"Can I close this and put it back in the trunk?"

He shook his head. "Close it but leave it there for now. Paperwork." He held out his hand.

Rosie replaced the lid on the urn, wondering what her mom would've thought of being pulled over by cops even in death. No doubt she'd make some sort of joke about it. And Rosie would've done the same if it wasn't for the tangible terror filling the inside of the car. Maybe terror was an exaggeration. Shay seemed calm enough, just extremely tense and on high alert.

"The papers are in the pale blue leather tote bag in the trunk," she said. "Would you like me to get them for you?"

"No," he said and headed back to the rear of their car.

Rosie pulled down her visor and watched him rifling through what she assumed was her purse through the vanity mirror. He stayed there for a damn sight longer than she thought he needed to be, but when she shifted to call out to him, Shay shook her head, so she froze in place like a statue.

He slammed the trunk closed and came back around to her side of the car. "Everything appears to be in order." He shifted slightly to peer back into the car and stare beyond Rosie at Shay, then he turned his attention back to her. "Sorry for your loss," he said and waved them onward.

He didn't seem like the kind of man who was ever sorry for anything, and his words were as hollow as his cold eyes. But she didn't retort. She simply looked straight ahead.

"Is it okay to ask if you get pulled over a lot?" Rosie had waited until Shay had driven away before breaking the silence.

"More than you, for sure."

"Good thing we didn't get that duct tape, and you didn't stuff me in the trunk," Rosie said and nudged Shay's shoulder lightly. Shay rewarded her with the smile she'd been hoping for, and she relaxed her own shoulders a little.

"Don't think that means we won't try it in a safer environment," Shay said and winked.

"Is that what it's like for you every time?"

When Shay nodded, Rosie wanted to convey how awful that must be, but everything she thought of sounded trite and patronizing. "It was scary," she said, though that word didn't quite encapsulate her emotions. She couldn't even begin to imagine what it must've been like for Shay.

"I try to think that they're just as scared," Shay said. "They don't know who's in the car, or how someone might react if they're doing something illegal. The window could roll down, and they could be facing the business end of an AK-47."

Rosie sighed and shook out her arms, trying to lose the steel wire that had wrapped around her entire torso during the encounter. "That's very philosophical of you."

"That's the only thing I can be in those situations. Philosophical and docile as a drugged cow."

Rosie looked down at the urn in her lap. "Would you mind pulling over so I can put this in the back again?"

Shay flicked a glance in the rearview mirror. "Sure, but let's put some distance between us and the border."

She stopped the car after a mile, and Rosie opened the trunk to discover all of their bags had been opened, and the contents were strewn everywhere. "Motherfucker," she hissed.

Shay got out and shook her head when she joined Rosie at the back of the car. "Good job you didn't *pack* pack."

Rosie giggled. "Now I know exactly what I want to do with you when we get home." *Shit.* "I mean, when you drop me at my place. You can come in. If you want. But you'll probably be tired and just want to go home. To your home." *Stop rambling.* She began to stuff all of her things back into her bags, and Shay did the same without responding, thankfully.

She'd need to play this way cooler to have any chance of

keeping her love for Shay under wraps.

***

"You're in love, aren't you?" Lori shook her head, but her smile was gentle.

Rosie gave an exaggerated shrug to make sure Lori saw it on the screen. "It was inevitable, wasn't it? You knew it, and I knew it. Shay's a goddess. My heart would have to be made of stone *not* to have fallen for her."

"Does she know?"

Rosie chuckled and wafted her hand at the screen. "I haven't told her, if that's what you're asking. She probably knows in the sense that she knows all women who spend any time around her fall in love with her." She pointed at Lori. "And you can't tell Gabe. Promise me you won't spill your guts to your new best friend."

Lori started coughing hard. "Damn COVID," she said when she'd finally stopped.

"Promise me."

Lori sipped a glass of water. "I promise you Gabe isn't my new best friend," she said and winked. "I could never replace you. Gabe hates shopping, for starters, and I need your impeccable fashion sense in my life, always."

Rosie arched her eyebrow and leaned in toward the screen until her nose touched it. "*Promise* me you won't tell Gabe I'm in love with her best friend."

"I promise." Lori rolled her eyes. "But why aren't you telling her?"

"Duh." Rosie lightly tapped her forehead with her knuckles. "Our situationship is supposed to be super simple. There's certainly no room for complications like lovey-dovey feelings. Shay has a very specific view of how intimate relationships work, and she's convinced herself that they're more trouble than they're worth. She's got a lot of family stuff going on, and maybe, if she ever sorts through all that and its inherent baggage, she'll come to realize that having a partner is more balanced than she thinks it is. Right now, she just sees them as a black hole for her time and emotions, and she's got enough of that with her family."

"Goodness." Lori made a funny face. "Sounds like she needs you to be her therapist, not her bed buddy."

"She could probably use some therapy, but couldn't we all?" Rosie rolled her neck and sighed. "And I like being her bed buddy best, so I'm just going to ride the train until it crashes. I don't want to miss a single moment of being with her. My heart is going to break anyway; what's the point in rushing that along?"

"If that's what you want, I'll support you." Lori held up her wine glass, and it went fuzzy as she tapped it close to the screen. "And when your heart's breaking, I'll be ready with a few bottles of this to drown the pain, just like you were when Katherine broke mine."

Rosie almost choked on her drink. When she'd stopped spluttering, she widened her eyes and looked at Lori with her best serious face. "You just said her name."

Lori laughed. "Katherine."

"Oh my God, don't say it again, or she'll materialize right behind you. Since when did she stop being *the lawyer*?"

"Since we sold the Brewster. I closed the chapter and let it all go." Lori bounced in her chair a little. "It feels good. She doesn't hold any power over me anymore, so it doesn't matter if I use her name or her job title. It means nothing."

Rosie smiled and sighed deeply. "It's so good to see you happy again. I thought that woman might've broken you for good."

"No way." Lori's expression went all dreamy. "I had to heal so I could be with Gabe."

Rosie pretended to gag. "Where's the real Lori? This one's way too soppy to be my best friend. You'll be talking about fate and destiny next."

Lori stuck out her tongue. "No, I won't. But I do believe the right people come onto your path at the right time. And I was ready to move on when Gabe came into my life."

"But why did she have to put Shay on my path when I'd just given up trying to find Princess Charming? Or is she just here to tease me?"

Lori pressed her lips together and wrinkled her nose. "I don't have the answer to that. But it could be that you're on *her* path to help her figure out her family stuff. And when all that is done, maybe she'll be ready to be your Princess Charming."

"That's some romantic bull crap." Rosie snorted. "The only way I can get a girlfriend is by being their therapist first to help them pick through and process their baggage. Great."

Lori shrugged. "Maybe the reason you became a therapist was to find yourself a woman," she said and laughed.

Rosie swatted at the screen, but Lori's words brought her thoughts back to her mom, and her smile dropped. "You know why I got into therapy. Then I got disillusioned with it and left it behind. But while I was in Tijuana with Shay, we did a lot of talking—"

"*That's* why you've fallen in love," Lori said. "All the talking. You were fine when you were just having oodles of hot sex."

Rosie wouldn't deny it. "Of course it's all the talking. The amazing sex has just compounded my feelings." She grinned. "Shay is *fantastic* in bed. And on desks. And in showers. And—"

"If we'd been having this conversation three months ago, I might've been jealous, but I've got my own sex machine now, so I'm not... Although, I probably wouldn't have been jealous, because I didn't know what I was missing until Gabe." Lori motioned with her finger. "Carry on."

"I was saying that all the talking made me remember how much I loved being a therapist. Now that Mom's gone, I feel like..." Rosie leaned back in the chair, grabbed her wine glass, and took a long drink. She couldn't finish that sentence, couldn't be that selfish.

"Hey, please don't do that," Lori said when Rosie didn't continue. "You don't ever need to censor yourself with me."

Rosie bit her bottom lip, unsure if she could say the words out loud for the first time. Doing that would make them all the more real. "I feel like I've got a clean slate, and everything I do can be for me. It can be because I want to do it, not because I feel like I have to do it, or because Mom needs me to do it. Does that make sense?"

Lori gave her a small smile. "All of it makes sense. I've always thought you were a great therapist, Rosie. I mean, I'm sure you're great at being a marketeer too—you've certainly got Gabe and the gang excited about those tools—but I feel like therapy's a calling more than a career, you know? So are you saying that you want to go back to being a therapist again?"

"I'm not sure. I haven't had time to think about it properly, since I've only just become aware of it." Rosie glanced at the urn on the bookshelf. She'd put it in five different places before settling on that position, as temporary as it might be. Everywhere else had creeped her out. "I've had other things on my mind."

"Is she there?" Lori shuddered visibly when Rosie nodded and jutted her chin toward it. "How are you feeling about everything? About your mom?"

Rosie topped up her wine glass before answering. "I'm grieving in a way, but I think I've been grieving all my life for the mom I never had. It could be that I'm all cried out."

"Have you cried?"

She nodded. "But I find myself wondering what I'm crying for. It can't be for all the good times we had—"

"God knows, the only good thing your mom ever did was give birth to you."

Rosie couldn't argue with that. And she appreciated that Lori always had her back. "Do you think your parents will adopt me now that I'm an orphan?"

"I don't see why not. I've always wanted a sister." Lori chuckled. "It figures that you've processed quickly. Your relationship had been bare minimum for a while now."

"Yeah, I guess it has. I've been pulling away since college, but I've never been quite able to make that final separation." She shrugged. "Now I don't have to because Mom's done it for me."

"Did you get the full story of how she died?"

Rosie recounted the details of her mom's demise. When she finished, she waved the piece of paper with her mom's last wishes on it. "Now I've got the memorial to organize, which includes some weird-ass requests, including black roses, which I don't think even exist. And her estate to finalize, though that shouldn't take long since she didn't own anything, and I'll bet that if she had anything of value at her house, Keith will already have taken it. Not that I have that address anyway."

"So you never met this guy?" Lori asked.

"Nope. I suppose I should be grateful that he even called me. He could've just left her there in Mexico, and I would never have known what happened."

"Small mercies.. How did Aunt Sheila react?"

"She didn't. Not really. It was like I'd told her I painted my nails a different color." Rosie shrugged. "She just wasn't interested."

"Is she coming to the memorial?"

"She said she would, yes."

Lori took another sip of her wine, and Rosie took the opportunity to drink away some of the bile that had risen when she thought of Keith. She hadn't spoken to him for long, but he'd managed to leave quite the impression.

"So what do you need me to do?" Lori pulled a notepad into focus and held a pen in the air. "I'm poised and ready to scribble."

Rosie waved the offer away. "That's okay. You're sick. I can handle it on my own."

Lori shook her head and wagged her finger. "I tested negative today. I've just got this nasty cough and some residual symptoms, but I'll be fine. I'm really sorry that I couldn't go with you to Tijuana, but nothing's stopping me from helping you any way you need."

"You not coming turned out just fine." Images of Shay, mostly naked, and all the positions they'd taken each other in, covering almost the entire hotel room flicked through her mind, and she grinned. "Is it bad that I had such a good time with Shay when I was handling my mom's death?"

"No. I think celebrating you're alive is the best thing to do when you're dealing with someone else's death."

Rosie liked the instant nature of Lori's response. "That sounds like a bumper sticker."

Lori laughed. "It'd have to be a pretty big sticker."

"Anyway, enough about me." Rosie shifted to lay on the couch to get more comfortable. "Tell me what's been going on with you and Gabe."

Lori groaned and harrumphed. "I haven't been able to see her, except on screen and through the window when she brought Max back from Ellery's."

"Wait—what? Is Max okay? Did something happen while I was away?"

"Yeah," Lori said. "Gabe was exercising Max off the lead, and he jumped over one of the fences. But he landed funny and went lame, and Gabe had to carry him back." She clearly tried to suppress a grin.

"And that makes you smile because?"

"Because Max weighs seventy-five pounds, and Gabe carried him for over a mile." Lori flexed her arm and sighed deeply. "I do love her muscles..."

Rosie rolled her eyes. Gabe's arms were almost bigger than her thighs. That kind of physique had never done anything for Rosie, but Shay's lithe, yoga body was another matter entirely. She snapped herself out of her little fantasy and refocused. "And Max?"

"Gabe took him to Ellery for an X-ray, but it was just a bad sprain, so she bandaged him up and sent him home. Now he has the cone of shame on his neck and is staying with Beth for a few days. She says he's feeling very sorry for himself and keeps trying to bite it off."

Rosie chuckled at the image. "Even a gorgeous dog like Max can't make one of those look good," she said. "How did Gabe react?"

"She acted like she was okay, but I think she was disintegrating inside. After everything that they've already been through together, they didn't need a broken leg or a torn CCL. She wanted to take care of Max herself, but the garage was too busy."

Rosie dipped her chin and fought to relax the tightening vice around her chest. "Because Shay was with me."

"Stop that." Lori wafted at the screen again. "We had plenty of people here to care for Max. Shay was the only one able to care for you."

Rosie sucked in a breath and nodded, recognizing the reaction borne from years of not being important enough to her mom to care for her. Maybe now that her mom was gone, she might be able to finally rid herself of that stubborn behavior pattern. "So how long before Max is fully recovered?"

"About a month, to be safe."

"That's good," Rosie said. "And Gabe? How long before she's safe to see you in the flesh again?"

"She's coming over tonight." Lori wiggled her eyebrows. "I can't wait."

"Given the size of her truck, I suppose Gabe doesn't need a U-Haul, but when is she moving in?"

Lori shook her head. "That won't be happening for a while. It's going great, and neither of us want to rush anything."

"Isn't she already staying at your place most nights?"

"You're getting insider information." Lori grumbled. "But it's wrong. She's not here *every* night."

Rosie narrowed her eyes and pointed at the screen. "But your little pouty face tells me you want her to be, even though you don't want to rush things."

"Yes," Lori said. "I know, they're polar opposites. But this is Gabe's first serious relationship, and I'm trying to stay a little cautious after the divorce. Of course I want to dive headfirst into a new life, but taking things slow isn't so bad. I look forward to the time we spend together even more."

Rosie could relate wholeheartedly to that last part, though she didn't want to say that and bring the conversation back to her again. When Shay had dropped Rosie off at home, she'd declined the offer to come in. Even though Rosie had expected that response, it still stung. She wanted as much time with Shay as possible because it was only a matter of time before she realized their situationship had been complicated by Rosie inconveniently falling in love.

Once she figured that out, Shay would bolt faster than her muscle car could do zero to sixty, leaving Rosie to pick up the pieces of her broken heart again. Except this time, Rosie had a feeling it would hurt a whole lot more than it ever had before.

Chapter Twenty

SOLO DROPPED TWO GIANT bags of food onto the engine block table and placed a tray of coffee beside it. "Bonnie's set a tab up for us to pay monthly. Is that okay?"

Shay looked up when Gabe didn't answer, and she realized Solo's question was directed at her.

Gabe laughed and shoved her shoulder lightly. "You're our math whizz. We've entrusted all the financials to your capable super-brain; you know that."

"I guess I haven't quite gotten used to you not giving all the orders and being our go-to yet."

Gabe grinned and winked. "I'll always be your go-to."

"So is it okay or not?"

Shay looked back at Solo and arched her eyebrow. "Someone get out of the wrong side of bed this morning?"

Solo dropped heavily onto a couch. "I didn't get out of bed; I rolled off the sofa."

Shay glanced at Gabe, who frowned. So she was genuinely worried this was more than a little hiccup. "Didn't you have therapy last night?"

Solo nodded. "It was our second session, and Rae gave us homework like we're college kids. *Active listening.*" She opened one of the bags and tore open the first wrapped package. "What the fuck does that even mean? Either you're listening or you're not. Putting another word in front of it doesn't change anything, does it?" She took a huge bite of the bagel, and cream cheese oozed out of the back to drop all over the front of her shirt. "Fuck and damn it. Now I need a new shirt for the photo shoot."

Under normal circumstances, one of them—usually RB—would've snatched Solo's bagel from her hand, flipped it open, and smushed it in Solo's face. But even RB wasn't that insensitive, so they all took their own lunch packets from the bags quietly and waited for one of them to spread wisdom on the situation.

"Isn't it about focusing just on the person who's talking and not having other distractions around?" Shay asked when no one else ventured an opinion. "Like your phone, or the TV, or in your case, your kids?"

Solo glared at her. "I can't just ignore my babies to make Janie feel like I'm listening to her."

"But isn't Janie's main problem that you're giving all your attention to the triplets and none to her?" Gabe asked.

"That's bullshit," Solo said around a messy mouthful of food. She wiped her mouth with the heel of her hand, and then wiped it on her cargo pants. "If you and Lori ever have kids, you'll understand that. You can't take your eyes off them for a *second*. A second. That's all it takes for them to run out in front of a bus and get squished like a pancake." She dropped the rest of her bagel back into the bag as if she'd just lost her appetite.

Shay looked at Gabe and raised her eyebrow. They'd talked last night about how she and Lori were taking it slow. But talk like this would likely wipe the thought of starting a family off the table totally. It was certainly reinforcing Shay's rules about keeping it simple, despite her long-buried soppy side trying to convince her otherwise.

"I felt like a fucking parrot, repeating everything Janie said as if I didn't understand it when she said it the first time or like she didn't remember what she'd just said. Bullshit. And I'm supposed to acknowledge her feelings even if I don't agree with her. Isn't that just lying?"

Shay shook her head. "No, it isn't. That's just about seeing her point of view and recognizing what she's feeling. Everyone reacts to situations differently, and that comes from who we are as people.

If you acknowledge her point of view, you're trying to understand her better."

Solo wrinkled her nose like she'd just sniffed gasoline. "Can't tell you're fucking a therapist, can you?"

Shay clenched her jaw, and Gabe touched her forearm lightly. Solo had always been their problem child and dealing with something this volcanic would only exacerbate that. She reminded herself that it'd only been a few weeks ago that she'd had to stop Gabe from going for Solo after she'd opened her mouth at Lori's birthday dinner.

Gabe leaned forward and fixed her gaze on Solo. "Wanna rephrase that?"

Solo banged her head against the back of the couch and closed her eyes briefly. "I'm sorry, Shay. I'm all fucked up. I *want* to understand her better, I do. But she needs to understand what it is to be a mom too, doesn't she? It can't be all about us anymore, not when we've got three little humans to raise."

That was a point Shay wouldn't argue with, though she also understood Janie's fear of losing her sense of self within the family dynamic. That had been Shay's main driver when she'd joined the Army. But this was a time for solidarity, not a "side with the enemy" moment, because Solo didn't seem to be in a space where she might be able to grasp the flip side of the argument.

"That sounds like a good enough reason to stick with the therapy," Woody said.

Solo bent over and put her head in her hands. "I've got a hundred and one reasons to stick with therapy, but my three main ones are my girls." She swallowed hard, looking like she was on the edge of breaking down. "They need their mom."

And there was something else Shay couldn't disagree with, at least from her experience anyway. If Rosie was sitting here with them, she'd have a different perspective. Kids needed a parent, sure, but that person wasn't necessarily the one who'd brought them into the world. And if Janie was more concerned with herself than her kids, maybe she wasn't cut out to be their mom.

"So how'd you end up on the sofa?" Woody asked.

Solo leaned back and dropped her hands into her lap. "I couldn't face sleeping alone in our bed."

Shay frowned, preparing for a response to the inevitable question that no one really wanted to ask. "Where was Janie sleeping?"

"In the guest room," Solo said and grabbed her cup to take a big slurp. "Shit!" She jerked away as she crushed the cup in her grasp, and the coffee spilled all over her already-ruined shirt. She tugged it away from her skin and muttered more expletives.

RB handed her a bunch of napkins from one of the food bags, and Solo pressed them against her tee.

"She moved into the guest room the day after Lori's dinner party." Solo shook her head and sat back on the couch. "I haven't slept next to my wife for nearly two weeks."

The giant bell sounded, saving all of them from trying to find something comforting to say in response. The last time Shay had gone without sex for more than a week was during the Iraq War. But she recognized that, in a more permanent relationship, it was the intimacy of sharing a bed that was perhaps more important than actually having sex. If she was ever going to have a real relationship, she'd want both, and she'd want them to have similarly equal importance. She blinked, the weird thought surprising her. She'd never considered entertaining anything permanent before; why would she now? She admonished herself for even attempting to delude her own mind. The reason was damn obvious, and she'd just arrived downstairs in killer heels and a pencil skirt.

Gabe clapped Shay on the shoulder and stood. "That'll be your girl."

"She's not my girl." Shay shoved her away. "We're just casual."

"Keep telling yourself that," Gabe said and walked away. "Solo, don't forget to change your shirt," she called after her.

Shay's phone pinged as she and the rest of the gang made their way downstairs to let Rosie and her crew into the building.

I haven't seen you at your brother's house since the big party. When do we get to play in the kitchen together again? xx

Nia. She'd be an easy way to prove to Gabe that she didn't think of Rosie as "her girl," but she wasn't going there, and why did she think she needed to prove anything to Gabe? Maybe it was more about proving something to herself.

She pocketed her phone and headed to the stairs at the sound of Rosie's voice. They hadn't seen each other since they'd gotten back from Tijuana, both of them saying they were swamped with work. In her case, it had been true, but she wondered if Rosie's distance was genuine, or if she'd needed to take a breather from the intensity of their situation. Their emotions had reached boiling point in the cauldron of grief they'd swum in together, and maybe now that they'd had some time apart, things could go back to a steady, simmering heat.

And that's what they both wanted, right?

***

"I'm sorry the stylist tried to touch your hair. The director told me she's new—not that that's an excuse or makes it okay," Rosie said. "He's happy to fire her—"

"What? No, I don't want that," Shay said. It might've been different if the stylist hadn't been ultra-apologetic, but she had. "Your director's at fault too. He should make sure his staff are properly trained."

Rosie nodded, looking as guilty as if she'd been the one to cross the line. "I'll speak to Franklin on Monday, and I'll get him to authorize a sensitivity trainer right away. I'm really sorry; I didn't realize that wasn't a standard element of their induction."

"I appreciate that."

"Your finger coils look amazing, by the way."

"Thanks." Shay smiled and instinctively touched her curls. "I had them done yesterday 'specially for the shoot."

'Well, they're gorgeous and looked amazing on film. I was watching the monitor while they were shooting you." Rosie bit her bottom lip and sighed. "You could definitely have been a model. Blake said they're a little bit in love with you."

Shay glanced at Blake, the photographer. They had their long hair pulled into a ponytail and bunched under a ballcap, revealing a high undercut and a head tattoo Shay hadn't been able to quite make out but didn't want to stare at. She shook her head. "They're not my type."

"Phew." Rosie held the back of her hand to her forehead in an exaggerated motion. "I kind of like them, so I didn't want to have to kill them."

"Possessive much?"

Rosie raised her eyebrow. "I can't be possessive over someone I don't have."

Shay wrapped her arms around Rosie's waist and pulled her closer. "You've had me plenty."

Rosie's eyes half-lidded, and Shay grinned at how easy it was to turn her on.

"You're laughing at me, aren't you?" Rosie wriggled from her grasp. "It's not my fault you're so damn sexy. You should have a warning sign."

"Should I?" Shay put her hand on Rosie's hip. "What would it say?"

Rosie swatted her away. "Danger. One hundred percent flammable."

Shay smiled widely. "I like that." And she also liked the way they seemed to have slipped back into the easy nature of their situationship. The fervor of their Mexican mini vacation had clearly receded, leaving much-needed oxygen for their friends with benefits fire to burn again. Her concerns had clearly been unfounded, and normal service had resumed.

In some form, anyway. The connection they'd forged in those

short days had drawn them closer together with an invisible linkage, one that Shay couldn't seem to break, even if she wanted to. Which she didn't. Their friendship had become stronger, and they knew so much more about each other. Just as Solo's therapist was encouraging her to understand Janie more, Shay felt like she understood Rosie more. And that understanding made Shay *want* to be a good friend. That she was able to have that *and* a blazing-hot sexual bond was almost too good to be true.

Rosie waved her hand in front of Shay's face. "Are you in there? I was trying to say thank you for doing this on a Sunday."

"Sorry." Shay winked. "You made me think dirty thoughts."

"Make sure you share them with me later," Rosie said. "Bonus points if it's something we haven't done already." She gestured back to the shooting area. "You're up again for some group shots. Go glitter and sparkle."

Shay joined her friends on the makeshift stage, and Blake issued directions, getting them all to move this way and that in a vertical version of Twister with tools.

"Solo," Blake said. "Could you maybe smile and *not* look like you're going to commit murder with that wrench?"

Solo took a half-step forward, and Shay and Gabe caught hold of her arms before she advanced farther.

"Don't do that," Shay said. "You just said the triplets need their mom."

Gabe wrapped her arm around Solo's shoulders. "Come on, buddy. Let's just get this done with and sell the shit out of these tools. Think of all the building blocks and teddy bears you can buy the girls with the money we're making from this."

Solo held up her hands and nodded. "Okay, okay. I'm all good."

Shay gave a thumbs-up to Blake, who look dumbfounded by Solo's reaction. "Keep talking. What do you want us to do?" She glanced across at Rosie, who pressed her palms together and mouthed *thank you*.

Blake continued to give directions, although they were a little more cautious with their delivery and word choice: a good move on their part. When Rosie moved behind Blake and their camera, Shay concentrated on just her, knowing she'd be giving her most genuine smile.

After another hour, Blake called for a break and headed for something Rosie had called craft services. Shay had seen something similar on movies, but she hadn't expected it for this. The spread of food and all the dietary options were pretty incredible, and her stomach rumbled in response. She checked her watch and was surprised to see it was already nearly one p.m.

"Are we nearly done?" she asked Rosie when she came up beside her.

Rosie smiled. "Do you want to be done? I haven't even had you on the hood of a car yet."

Shay tilted her head and grinned. "That might have to be something we do without an audience."

Rosie gave her a playful shove. "I didn't mean that, but it's good to know that's where your head's at for a change." She gestured back to the set. "I booked you until six because I thought it would take all day, and it might even be that Blake still won't get all the shots they want. They might want to come back for another full day."

Shay rolled her eyes and blew out a long breath. "Please don't let that happen. Solo is struggling to slap a smile on her face already."

Rosie looked over at Solo piling a plate high with sliders and fries. "Things are still rough at home?"

Shay nodded. "We're all worried she might start to spiral. She's never been that hot at handling stressful situations—"

Rosie frowned. "And she was in the Army for how long?"

"Thirteen years. I know what you're saying, but she didn't see much action." She glanced over at Solo and thought about all the conversations she and Gabe had over the years, trying to figure out if Solo was fit for duty and protecting her from as much of the horrors as they could. But Solo was determined to stick it out, and she was still there when Shay left. "And her go-to numbing agent has always been alcohol."

Rosie snapped her head back to Shay, her eyes wide. "You're concerned that she'll go there even though she's got the girls now?"

"I hope not. They're going to the therapist you recommended, but Solo seems to be having trouble getting on board with what she's being asked to do."

Rosie didn't look surprised. "It's early days. And you have to be open to it. If she really wants to fix her marriage, Rae will be able to help her." She wrinkled her nose and tipped her head to the side. "But if she's not prepared to put the work in, with all the will in the world, Rae won't be able to do a damn thing." Her gaze shifted to the floor, and she went silent for a moment. "I had my share of clients like that, and it was so frustrating."

Shay rubbed Rosie's arm. "And now you've got a whole different set of problems with your marketing clients. Like models who won't smile," she said and winked.

Rosie smiled, and her expression brightened. "And models who can't wait for the end of the shoot."

Shay's phone vibrated in her pocket, and she looked away from Rosie, a weird blanket of guilt falling over her like a shroud.

Rosie's brow furrowed. "What's up?"

Nia, probably. "Nothing. Why?"

"You look like you've just stolen some little kid's lunch money." Rosie tapped the phone in Shay's pants. "Got a hot date and don't want to shove it in my face?" She smiled widely. "I'm still good with our arrangement, Shay. You don't need to hide anything from me."

Shay thought she saw the slightest flicker of something across Rosie's eyes that belied her sentiment, but then she dismissed it. More likely it was her own discomfort with the situation reflecting back at her. She had the urge to tell Rosie about Nia, and why not, since she had no intention of doing anything about the one-way attraction? "My brother's given his neighbor my cell. He's trying to do some unwanted matchmaking."

Rosie's eyes lit up mischievously. "Why unwanted? Is the woman in question all butchy butch?"

Shay scoffed. "He knows my type; he wouldn't do that. She's nice enough, but it's too close to home."

"In case you break her heart?" Rosie clamped her lips together like she was trying to keep from bursting into laughter.

"I'm so glad I'm a source of amusement for you. And actually, no. She said casual was her thing too." *Just like it's supposed to be my thing...which it is.* She pulled her phone from her pocket, almost tempted to agree to see Nia out of... Out of what? Spite? That was stupid and unnecessary. If Shay was getting everything she needed from Rosie, and vice versa, maybe they should just be exclusive friends with benefits. That would fix everything, wouldn't it?

But it wasn't Nia contacting her, it was Aaron. Her stomach dropped when she read the text, and a chill ran over her skin.

Dad's had a fall in the yard and banged his head. We're at Saint Mary's General Hospital. Come when you can.

She conveyed the text to Rosie and leaned against one of the food tables for support. "I have to go."

Gabe rushed over and grasped Shay's shoulder. "What's going on? You look sick."

Shay held up her phone for Gabe to read the text.

"Do you want me to come with you?" Rosie asked.

Her instinct was to say no. She always handled her family problems alone. But another part of her wanted Rosie by her side.

"You should let her," Gabe said. "Your pops will think she's just a friend."

There was no reason to change the way she'd been doing things for six years. It'd been working up to now, and it'd continue to work. And if her daddy did realize what Rosie was to her, she wouldn't hear the end of it. *Why aren't you seeing a pretty Black woman? Your momma wouldn't be happy.* Shay shook her head, her mind made up. "No, I'll go alone. You should stay here and make sure Blake gets all the shots they need. I don't think anyone except RB's enjoyed this, so we shouldn't elongate the process."

Gabe huffed. "Speak for yourself. Blake says I'm a natural." She flicked imaginary long hair over her shoulder. "Seriously though, don't worry about this. Just get going."

She nodded and looked at them both. "I'll let you know what's happening." Shay quashed the desire to lean into Rosie and kiss her goodbye. Instead, she pulled Gabe and Rosie into an awkward three-way hug before jogging away to grab her keys from upstairs. Her heart pounded against her ribs like it was trying to escape, and she tried to quell the worst-case scenarios battling for her attention. Broken hip. Coma. Brain damage. All the things left unsaid between them. All the misunderstanding and unresolved issues. Rosie seemed almost relieved that her mom had died, and Shay couldn't blame her for that, but she was nowhere near that state of mind. Maybe this could be the wake-up call they both needed, and they'd be able to fix whatever had broken between them...if it wasn't already too late.

Chapter Twenty-One

"ARE YOU SURE THIS is the place?" Lori asked as Rosie parked outside The Flower Loft. "It looks kind of small."

"I'm sure. Franklin gave me the details, and he wouldn't use anywhere half-assed. Maybe it goes way back." Rosie got out of the car and looked up at the façade of the three-story building. "Or maybe it uses all these floors."

"I guess it doesn't have to be big as long as they can do what you need."

"Exactly." Rosie stooped to smell the snow-white gardenias at the front of the store. "Though I'm not sure anyone will be able to do what Mom wanted." She pushed open the door, and a quaint little bell tinkled above her head.

A bundle of vibrant red soft-looking curls was the first thing Rosie saw as she ventured farther into the store. The woman to whom they belonged was hunched over the desk carefully writing a notecard Rosie presumed would accompany the stunning bouquet also on the desk. She waited until the woman had finished a sentence before she said hi.

The florist peered at her then clamped her hand over her mouth. "Rosie Morgan!" she said at the same time as Rosie said "Alyssa Wilson?"

"Oh my, what a treat." Alyssa hurried around the counter and threw her arms around Rosie. "It's been too long. What are you doing here? I didn't know you lived in Chicago."

"I don't. I'm in Burnham." Rosie eased out of the unexpectedly buoyant embrace. "This is my friend Lori," she said, strangely and ridiculously ultra-conscious of her history with Alyssa. She should know better than to fall into old patterns so easily.

Lori gave her an awkward wave and hung back, clearly trying to avoid the same effusive greeting.

Alyssa's eyes sparkled. "Hi, Lori," she said and then focused back on Rosie. "So what have you been up to? I bet you've got your own therapy practice, haven't you? You were always so single-minded and driven."

Heat swept over Rosie's face, and she took a breath to control the youthful stutter that hovered in the background. Christ, she hadn't had speech issues for over a decade. "Actually, I work in marketing now. I gave up my private practice a little while ago."

Alyssa frowned. "Really? That's quite a shift in careers."

There was no edge or judgment to Alyssa's words, but Rosie couldn't help but feel that she'd let Alyssa down, like she had high expectations of Rosie that she no longer met. All of it was her own baggage and nothing to do with sweet, cute Alyssa Wilson. Her curious reaction gave Rosie more to consider as she continued to process her current career path and yet another possible change. "I don't know that it's working out," she said by way of compensation.

"Oh, I don't believe that. You can do anything you put your mind to, Rosie."

Rosie gestured at the shop to shift Alyssa's focus. "I think you're describing yourself. You always said owning a flower shop was your dream. This place is amazing."

Alyssa smiled widely. "Thank you. It's taken a while to get here, but I'm really happy with it. I love what I do."

She motioned to the notecard she'd just written, and Rosie recognized the beautiful handwriting that she used to admire in college. "I see you're still using fountain pens. Do you remember the mess you made of our dorm carpet?"

Alyssa held up her hands, both of which were stained with oxblood red ink. "You caught me on refill day."

Her unrestrained laughter transported Rosie back to that dorm and the wonderful times they'd shared, and she smiled. Beyond the vague awkwardness that had crept up on her, it was genuinely nice to see Alyssa and better still, it appeared she hadn't changed. Her free spirit and refusal to be bound by societal norms had been the main things which had attracted Rosie to her...way back.

And now there was Shay, another woman who refused to be traditionally coupled or tied down in a monogamous relationship. Rosie was in love with someone who wouldn't love her back. Was she destined to keep repeating that pattern?

"So I'm taking from your surprise that you're not here just to see me," Alyssa said. "What do you need?"

"Memorial arrangements." The ease with which that tripped off her tongue would probably sound callous to most people, but Alyssa was one of the few people in the world Rosie had confided in about her fucked-up family.

"Your mom?" Alyssa seemed to struggle with a half-grimace, half-smile as if she wasn't sure which would be most appropriate.

Rosie nodded. "She died in Mexico, and I've just gotten back with her ashes." She swallowed, and her pulse thudded against her temples. She hadn't been in the room to see the cremation, but right now, it felt like the heat of that furnace was licking at her spine... And the darkness invaded the edges of her vision.

"Rosie? Rosie, are you okay?"

Lori's voice grounded her, and she came back into the room, unsettled and uneasy.

"I'm sorry. I don't know what happened." She shifted and realized she was sitting on a couch, then she peered around Lori's shoulders to see the front door of a store forty or so feet away.

"You're in the back of the Flower Loft," Lori said. "You fainted, and we caught you before you hit the ground."

"We?" Rosie switched her gaze to the other shape in front of her, and Alyssa came back into focus along with the past twenty minutes. *Great. My college crush saved me from a concussion.*

"Has this happened before?" Lori sat beside her and brushed Rosie's hair over her ear.

She shook her head. "No. I'm confused."

"It's okay. Let's just sit for a while."

"No." Rosie stood. "I mean, I'm confused as to what just happened and why. What you're describing is like a dissociative incident." She raised her eyebrows and shrugged. "I'll talk to my therapist about it. I'm sure it's nothing." She hadn't drunk much water or eaten anything since Shay had left the photoshoot abruptly yesterday afternoon. "It's probably low blood sugar. We should get lunch after this."

Alyssa put her hand on Rosie's shoulder. "Wait right there. I've got a blueberry cheesecake donut with your name on it."

After Alyssa had left, Lori got up and took Rosie's hands in hers. "Are you sure that's what it is?"

"I am. I haven't eaten anything since I had a Cubano at the shoot yesterday. I've been too worried about Shay and her father."

"You haven't heard anything?" Lori's eyes widened, and she nibbled her top lip.

"But you *have*?" Rosie threw her hands up. "Of course you have. Because if Shay was going to call anyone, it'd be her best friend, not me." The stab of jealousy went deeper than it should have, and she tried to rein in her irrational emotion.

"I'm sorry. I thought she'd called you. I was so focused on this stuff with your mom that Shay and her dad didn't figure into my thought process. He's still unconscious, and Shay stayed overnight by his bedside. Have you called her?"

Rosie shook her head. "I texted last night and this morning, but I don't want to crowd her. She knows where I am if she needs me." She shrugged. "She's so used to handling her family stuff alone, it probably hasn't occurred to her to call anyone but her friend of twenty years. I'm being silly."

Alyssa returned with a plate laden with the biggest donut Rosie had ever seen.

"I've cut it into smaller pieces." Alyssa handed her the carb-killer and a wet wipe. "And this is because you don't like getting sticky fingers."

In her peripheral vision, she saw Lori's eyebrows raise almost high enough to touch her hairline. Lori would have a hundred and one questions about their time in college when they left. "You remembered?"

"Of course." She touched Rosie's hand gently. "What kind of an old best friend would I be if I forgot something like that?" Alyssa laughed and winked at Lori. "Not to step on your toes, obviously."

Rosie smiled, touched by the gesture and the sentiment behind it. She'd been so focused on Alyssa not being her girlfriend in college that she'd missed out on the possibility of a best friend. After she'd managed a quarter of the donut, she nodded back toward the shop. "I'm refueled, thank you." She hooked her hand through Lori's arm and went back to the front counter.

"I'm sorry about your mom," Alyssa said when she took her spot on the other side of the desk. "I know your relationship was difficult, but that doesn't necessarily make all of this any easier."

Rosie waved off Alyssa's concerns. "I'm doing okay, actually. All the stunts she pulled about her health were good practice for when the day finally arrived, I guess." She'd had small pockets of tear-filled episodes, but they passed relatively quickly. Her overriding emotion was still a strange kind of relief coupled with a soft sadness at not having the loss of a positive relationship to grieve. "Anyway, Mom wanted black roses at her funeral. That ship's sailed, but we're having a memorial instead. Are black roses a real thing?"

"They are, in a way," Alyssa said. "They don't occur naturally, but people do create them in a variety of ways." She pulled out a large folder from under the counter and opened it for Rosie to see. "These are black baccara, and they can grow to nearly three feet. They're not a true black though. If that's what you want, we can dye them with a special pigment."

"We?" Rosie asked. Could it be that someone had finally snagged Alyssa?

She looked up from the folder and arched her eyebrow as if she knew exactly why Rosie was asking. "Harry and me."

That was inconclusive, but it served her right for snooping.

"Do you think your mom wanted roses because of your name?"

Rosie snorted. "I wouldn't put it past her. That's probably why she went with black and not those lovely rainbow roses you can get, or something at least a little bit colorful."

"There's a beautiful song called 'Black Roses' about a mother and daughter relationship... I mean, it's beautiful, but it's haunting too. Maybe your mom was trying to tell you something?"

"Do you know when it was released?"

"Ten years or so, I guess. It was on a TV show about country music."

Rosie shook her head and tapped her purse, which still contained her mom's wishes. She'd taken to carrying them around with her and hadn't processed what that meant yet. "She gave me the orders when I was eighteen. The only thing my mom told me was that I was never good enough." *Too much.* "Sorry. Ignore that. Seems like I might be passing through the anger stage of grief," she said and smiled. Seeing someone from a past when her mom still very much had her claws in Rosie was triggering, apparently.

Alyssa's jaw twitched. She reached over the counter and rubbed Rosie's upper arm gently. "Your mom never realized that she created someone as special as you." She shrugged. "Or maybe she did, and her jealousy made her such a bitch."

Rosie placed her hand over Alyssa's and gave a tight-lipped smile. "I really appreciate you saying that." She didn't believe it, of course. Deconstructing the framework of negativity her mom had built around Rosie continued to be a work in progress.

"How many would you like? They're fifteen dollars each."

Rosie gulped when she did the math. Seemed like a lot of money to spend on something only about ten people were going to see. And she couldn't imagine anyone wanting to take them home. "Fifty-one. Mom wanted one for every year of her life."

"It could be worse. At least she didn't want roses dipped in twenty-four karat gold." Alyssa made a note with an elegant flourish of her pen.

"Well, she did want gold foliage."

"No problem. We can use regular gold spray paint for that," Alyssa said and winked. "When is the memorial? It takes a few days to get these in stock, and we're quite busy getting our Halloween orders prepared."

"Saturday."

"Oh." Alyssa laid her pen down and looked serious. "*This* Saturday?"

Rosie dropped her shoulders. "Is that not going to be possible?"

Alyssa pulled a giant, overstuffed diary from under the counter and dropped it with a thud. "Let's see."

As she flipped through the diary, Rosie could see how incredibly busy Alyssa was from the ink-filled pages. "Wow, you're very popular."

Alyssa looked up and grinned. "Isn't it great? Speaking of which, how did you find out about us?"

"My boss recommended you." Rosie stopped herself from saying any more. She knew from Mindy Fletcher that Franklin sent a lot of business Alyssa's way, but she didn't want to be an unprofessional gossip like her. "I don't really have occasion to send flowers much. I'd rather receive them," she said and smiled.

"Noted," Alyssa said and winked. "Who's your boss?"

It took Rosie a second to regain her composure. Why had she said anything about receiving flowers? And why did Alyssa note it? "Billy Franklin of Mandele."

"Ah, Billy Franklin." Alyssa tapped her diary repeatedly with her pen, and ink dripped onto the pages. She dabbed it away with some leftover tissue paper from the bouquet on the desk. "He's probably my best private customer. Spends more than most companies, but I bet you know that already."

Heat prickled up her spine. She was embarrassed for him.

Someone had to be, because he had no shame about the number of people he "liaised with," as he called it. Rosie didn't indulge the office gossip, but she had to admit to being intrigued as to whether it was just the women he sent flowers to, or if he was equal opportunities in his brush-offs with the men and the enbies who passed through his doors. She liked to think he wasn't sexist, since he was all about equal opportunities for everyone in his sex life. Not that she wanted to think about his sex life. She shook off the thoughts. *This* was why she didn't like gossip. There were some mental images she just couldn't shake.

Alyssa sucked in her breath sharply, recapturing Rosie's attention.

She flipped back and forth between two pages. "Okay, I'm going to squeeze you in and work late on Wednesday. It means that your flowers will be ready Thursday, which isn't ideal." She rolled her fountain pen under her palm on the counter and shook her head. "Ideally, I'd do them first thing on the morning of the memorial. They don't last as long as regular roses because of the dye, so they'll start to droop on Monday. But they'll still look nice on Saturday."

"Are you sure?"

Alyssa frowned. "Am I sure they'll still look nice? Of course I am. I wouldn't deliver bad flowers to anyone, let alone my favorite best friend." She glanced at Lori and smiled. "Again, no offense. You're clearly an upgrade."

Lori chuckled. "Thank you."

"No, I meant, are you sure you're able to fit me in?" Rosie asked.

"Absolutely. But you owe me a coffee so I don't fall asleep dipping your roses."

Fire whipped across Rosie's face when Alyssa winked again. Was she flirting? That would be too weird, after all this time, but Rosie did want the opportunity to catch up. "I'd like that. I'm slammed this week—"

"Could I crash the memorial?" Alyssa managed to look hopeful and a tiny bit mischievous at the same time. "I'd like to be there for you, if that's okay?"

"Uh, yeah. Sure. We're having a wake of sorts at Bonnie's Brew on West Chicago Avenue. I could buy you a vodka Red Bull…if that's what you still like?"

Alyssa grinned. "You remembered?"

"What kind of an old best friend would I be if I didn't remember your poison?"

Alyssa laughed. "I see what you did there. Clever. Are you sure you don't mind?"

"I don't mind at all," Rosie said. "I'd love for you to come. It'll give us the chance to talk properly."

She gave Alyssa her cell number and the details of the record store where they were holding the memorial, and when Alyssa began to flip through the possible bouquet combinations for the black roses, Rosie stopped her. "I trust you to create something perfect." And besides that, she had no idea what memorial flowers were supposed to look like. The only thing she knew she didn't want was MOM spelled out in roses.

Rosie pulled her wallet from her purse, but Alyssa waved her away.

"We'll sort all that out after the memorial."

"Okay. Thank you. I'll see you on Saturday."

Alyssa nodded. "You certainly will."

She and Lori left the store and got back in Rosie's car.

"You gave me crap about Gabe being my new best friend when you've been unfaithful to me all this time?" Lori asked with mock incredulity. "I can't believe she even remembered your obsession with not having sticky fingers. And what were you up to, remembering her favorite drink? Did you two sleep together?"

"Stop." Rosie started the engine and pulled out into traffic. "Let's get lunch, and I'll tell you all about it." As she drove away, she thought about Shay, who said she'd be at the memorial too. What would she think of Alyssa? But with her dad being in the hospital,

Shay might not make it. Not that it mattered. Rosie wasn't looking to rekindle her unrequited college crush flame, and the pesky little thing called love wouldn't hear of it anyway.

Chapter Twenty-Two

"Do you think there's a special place where all the rejected coffee beans go?"

Shay looked up from the fascinating patch of worn carpet on the hospital waiting room floor and glared at Cyrus. "What?"

"The foul-tasting, rejected coffee beans, y'know. Like the ones that don't make it to Dunkin' or Starbucks." Cyrus held his Styrofoam cup aloft. "I think there is. And that's where all the hospitals get their machine coffee from. All the crappiest beans in the world."

Shay squeezed the arm of her chair hard. Their daddy was lying unconscious in a hospital bed, and her brother was more concerned with the quality of his java. "Don't drink it. They have soda too."

Cyrus laughed. "They should have beer."

"You should shut up," Aaron said. He stood beside Shay and put his hand on her shoulder. Cyrus kissed his teeth but didn't say anything else. "Any news?"

Shay shook her head and sighed. "Still waiting. Bisa and the kids okay?"

"They're not too bad considering they saw it all happen." Aaron dropped into the chair beside her. "Bisa's keeping them home from school."

She lightly punched Aaron's thigh. "They're bomb-proof. They'll be okay."

He tilted his head slightly. "That might depend on..."

Aaron gestured to the double doors they were all focused on, desperate for more information about their father. Shay knew what he couldn't give voice to: his kids would be traumatized if their gramps died and the last time they'd seen him was in the yard laying in a pool of blood with EMTs surrounding him. "Daddy's not going anywhere, little brother."

"I hope you're right."

So did she. Shay's prediction was nothing but wishful thinking. She glanced around the room at the rest of her brothers. Matthew hadn't raised his head from his phone since he'd arrived after his night shift, Luke and Eli were deep in conversation about cars, and Cyrus still seemed fascinated with the contents of his coffee cup. It'd be just like a normal family gathering at Aaron's place if it weren't for the fact that their father's life hung in the balance in a sterile room down the hallway.

"Do you want to go to my place and freshen up?" Aaron asked. "I'm assuming you still have a permanent overnight bag in your car."

She did, though she hadn't used it for a while now. She now had a toothbrush in Rosie's bathroom, a sleep cap in one of the bedside drawers, and if she needed fresh clothes, she borrowed Rosie's sweats and returned them the next time she stayed over. She shucked off the lurking knowledge of what that might mean. "Are you trying to say something?"

"Nah. If you were rank, I'd tell you. You know that." Aaron gave a weak laugh then looked at her, his expression serious. "Have you called anyone?"

Shay frowned. "Like who?"

He shook his head. "Like someone you care about. Someone who can support you. A friend? Someone you spend a lot of time with?"

She eyeballed him. "You're being serious right now?"

"Yeah, I am." He shifted sideways in his chair to face her fully. "My therapist says that even the strong one in the family needs someone to have their back... Who's got yours?"

"Gabe," she said. "Gabe's had my back metaphorically and literally for the past twenty years. And the rest of my team are always there for me." And then there was Rosie. She hadn't been in Shay's life for long, but she'd already become an integral part of it, and they'd been spending the most time together. Shay had barely seen Gabe outside work since she and Lori had gotten together.

"Okay, so have you called her?"

Shay pushed herself further back in the chair. "I texted to let her know what was happening and that I wouldn't be at work."

"What are you, a millennial? Go call her."

"Oh my Lord, fine." Shay jumped up and pulled her cell from her purse. "I'll call if it'll shut you up."

Aaron grinned. "It will."

"I liked you better when you were self-centered." She walked out and headed to the front of the building, needing some fresh air to cleanse her nose of the nauseating antiseptic and sickness scent unique to hospitals. She squinted when she emerged into the midday sun, but the heat felt good after the chilly a/c in the waiting room. She shivered, not realizing she'd gotten cold to the bone, and closed her eyes, soaking up the sun's rays like she was a walking solar panel.

After a few revitalizing minutes, she became aware of the weight in her hand again and the reason she'd come out there. She unlocked the phone and opened her contacts' favorites. Rosie would probably be having lunch with Lori if the visit to her boss's florist had worked out. Gabe would be working.

"Hey, I'm so glad you called. How are you? How's your dad?"

Just the sound of Rosie's voice relaxed all the muscle tension making Shay's body ache. "I'm fine."

Rosie scoffed. "No, Shay. How *are* you?"

"One second." Shay looked around and found an unoccupied bench close by. She sat in the center of it, hoping that would discourage anyone looking for miserable company. "I'm holding it together." She stopped short of saying that she wished Rosie was there with her. She'd slowly concluded that she missed the way Rosie held her tight on the nights they'd actually slept in Mexico, and just the thought of her embrace right now was weirdly comforting. "My brothers are here, so I'm not alone."

"Are you sure about that?"

Shay laughed, but there was no humor in the sound. She'd shared more of her family background with Rosie than anyone, other than Gabe. "I suppose I was alone when Aaron went to see his family. The rest of them are too self-absorbed to consider I need support too." She played with a finger curl and smiled a little when she recalled how good Rosie had said her hair looked. "But Aaron's back now. He even suggested that I call..." *someone who can support me.* When had that person become Rosie? With only brief consideration, Shay knew it wasn't just because she'd done the same for Rosie. It was more than that, *way* more than that.

"Good. I know you won't feel like it, but have you eaten anything? You need to keep your body fueled."

Shay touched her stomach reflexively, and it grumbled beneath her fingers. She smiled a little more at Rosie's attempt to take care of her. "I haven't had anything since yesterday, but I'll grab something from the hospital cafeteria when we're done talking."

"Can you talk about what's happening with your dad?"

There was the therapist in Rosie's gentle voice, the compassionate seeking of consent to talk about something that might be difficult. Shay should've texted her yesterday to tell her how things were at the hospital, but a stubborn part of her just wanted to stick with her form: text Gabe and handle it alone. "Sure. He was confused when I got here, and he didn't seem to know any of us except Aaron. They were waiting on results from a CT scan. That didn't show anything, but the doctor wanted to keep him under observation for twenty-four hours. That's normal, right?"

"It is, yes," Rosie said, "and they should've woken him up every few hours to make sure his symptoms hadn't gotten worse. Is that what happened?"

"Yeah, yeah. That's exactly what they did. The nurses put a sleeper chair in his room, and they went into the waiting room a couple of times to let my brothers know how things were going. Me and Aaron took shifts through the night." She paused for a second to steady her breath when she realized she was racing through her explanation, and all the dark thoughts that had zipped through her mind while she'd been in her daddy's room watching his too-still body came rushing back.

"Are you still there?"

"Yeah, sorry. I was just taking a beat." *Hell, no.* She glared at a young man approaching her bench with a purposeful swagger and a broad grin, but he U-turned before she was forced to say anything. She'd expected sad relatives of other patients wanting to sit with her and share their stories, but she hadn't expected assholes thinking they could hit on her because she was emotionally vulnerable. "It seemed to get harder for them to wake him up every time, and when they came in at seven thirty, it took them forever. He vomited immediately, and he wasn't able to answer any of the questions. The next thing we knew, they rushed him out of the room for another CT scan."

"Oh, God, I'm sorry, Shay. That must've been terrifying."

"Scarier than facing enemy fire." She blew out a long breath. "I bet that sounds stupid."

"No, it doesn't at all," Rosie said. "We're talking about your dad, probably the strongest man you've ever known. It's difficult to see him in a position that compromised."

Shay leaned forward and put her elbows on her knees. "The second CT scan took longer than the first one, and we were going crazy in the waiting room. The doctor came in about an hour later to say Daddy had developed acute hydrocephalus and that they were prepping him for emergency surgery to relieve the pressure and..." She swallowed against her dry throat, wishing she'd stopped to grab a cup of coffee, regardless of how terrible it was.

"They're worried about brain damage?" Rosie asked gently.

"*Further* brain damage." Shay squeezed her tired eyes closed then rubbed at them with her fingers. "What if—"

"Don't," Rosie said. "You shouldn't get into that mindset. Don't give anything to or take anything away from your father before the doctors have spoken to you."

"Okay." She nodded, watching her shadow agree. "That's good advice. Anyway, they took him to the operating room just over an hour ago, so we're just waiting and hoping."

"Well, just know that I'm thinking about you, and everyone's praying and sending good wishes into the Universe."

"Thanks. Did the rest of the shoot go well?"

"We got everything we needed for this campaign. But forget about that; it's not important right now."

Shay leaned back on the bench and tilted her face to the sun. "It's important to you."

"Mm."

"What does that mean?" Shay asked. "I thought you were really excited about it."

"Forget I said anything. You don't want to be talking about this with everything you've got going on."

Shay opened her eyes and stretched out her legs, feeling warmer and a little more energized. "Actually, I'd like to talk about anything other than what's going on in the faceless, concrete building behind me. It'd give me something different to focus on... unless you have to go. Are you with Lori? Did you get the flowers handled?"

"No, I'm not with Lori; yep, we got the flowers organized; and no, I don't have to be anywhere. I'm here for you."

Here for you. Rosie's words echoed in her mind and found a place to hook on to her memory, to make it real and true. To make Rosie more, so much more, than a friend with benefits. She cleared her throat and blinked to refocus on the conversation. "So why the ennui about the tools?"

"It's not this account, per se. I think I'm just having a mini career crisis. Again."

Shay got up from the bench and headed in the direction of

a signposted peace garden. She'd been sitting for the best part of twenty-four hours, and she needed to take this opportunity to move. "Tell me more."

"Do you want me to tell you that it's your fault?"

"How's that? Because you didn't get the shot of me naked on the hood of my car?" Shay surprised herself with the question. It didn't seem right that she should still be able to have fun with Rosie when her daddy was under the surgeon's knife with his head cracked open. Still, Rosie's laugh made Shay smile as she took a right.

"Well, that *was* disappointing," Rosie said huskily. "But no, that's not the reason. It's all the talking you made me do on the Mexico trip. I mean, it wasn't a trip, but you know what I'm saying."

Shay reached the end of the alley, and it opened up into a huge square exploding with color. "Wow." She took a deep breath, like the oxygen was pure and clean. "And also, wow. You're blaming me for talking to you?"

"Why were there two wows?"

"Oh, just a second." Shay switched to video call and gave Rosie a panoramic view of the peace garden as she began to walk the circular route. "I don't know what all these flowers are, but they're beautiful."

"Wow, indeed. Glad to see there aren't any black roses."

Shay pressed the front camera icon, and her breath caught when she saw Rosie's smiling face. "So they do exist?" she asked, ignoring the ridiculous flutter in her stomach.

"Yes and no. A story for later, maybe, along with a blast from my past." Rosie rolled her eyes. "Anyway, yes, I am absolutely blaming you for talking to me. It made me remember how much I loved being a therapist. Also, you almost look tired, which means you're probably exhausted. Is it okay that I'm a tiny bit relieved that you can occasionally look less than perfect?"

"If you're good with what that says about you as a person, then sure, that's totally okay." Her heart lifted with every smile Rosie caused. "But I'm happy to shoulder that blame if it made you realize the huge mistake you've made closing your practice and selling out to corporate America."

Rosie clasped her hand over her mouth. "Oh my God, that's harsh. Couldn't you sugarcoat it just a little?"

Shay shook her head. "You like me being direct. It's one of the great things about our relationsh—friendship."

Rosie raised her eyebrow. "Relax. A friendship is a relationship. It just means we're connected, that's all. It's if you start calling me your girlfriend that we're going to have to have a serious talk." She grinned widely. "But you think I made a huge mistake?"

It took everything Shay had to not react to the girlfriend comment, and she wiggled her eyebrows mischievously. "Do you?"

Rosie pointed at the screen. "Hey, no turning the therapist tables on me. Is that your honest opinion? Or are you just messing with me?"

Shay shrugged. "It's not for me to tell you that. Any decision is a judgment call, and if you're lucky, you learn from it. If you're unlucky, you regret it. But those decisions take you down different paths and mold you as a person, and I think it's important not to dwell on whether you were right or wrong. Otherwise, you can spend your whole life drowning in a sea of regrets."

"That's a good way of looking at it, but it sounds like you're talking from experience too."

"Maybe."

"Do you regret going in the Army?" Rosie asked.

Shay shook her head. "Most of the time, no. But sometimes I wonder if things might've been different if I'd followed the path from degree to PhD and become a math professor. Would I have spent more time with Momma before she died? Would Daddy still be mad at me?"

"But then you'd be drowning."

"Exactly." Shay stopped to look more closely at a vibrant tulip, one of the few flowers she did know, and switched to the rear camera again. "Orange was my momma's favorite color, and these were her favorite flowers." She smiled, then realized the words had come out so easily. They hadn't been choked by the grip of grief before being allowed to escape her mouth. She looked up toward the heavens. *I love you, Momma.*

"Would it creep you out if I told you they were my favorites too?"

Shay laughed. "Yes, it would."

"Then I won't tell you." Rosie gave her crazy eyes and stuck out her tongue.

"So what are you going to do about your mid-life crisis?"

"Hey, I'm only thirty-two! It's a career crisis, not a life crisis. I'm very happy with the rest of my life, thank you very much."

Shay smiled, taking that description to include her. "Happy to be of service. So what are you going to do about your *career* crisis?"

"I don't know yet, but I won't rush into another decision, and I'm definitely not doing anything until the rollout of this campaign is over. That gives me a few months to figure out what I want to do."

"Sounds like a good plan." Shay had finished the circuit and was back at the entrance. As much as she wanted to keep walking and talking to Rosie, she had to face what was happening with her daddy. "Thanks for this. You took my mind off things for a while. I better get back inside."

"No problem. Can I call you later? Or would you prefer to call me when you can? Because I'm assuming you'll want to call me since I'm so good at this talking thing," Rosie said and winked.

"I'll call you, I promise." Shay hung up, briefly wondering why she was making promises. *Because that's what you do with people you care about.*

Chapter Twenty-Three

"I'M SORRY, TOOTS," AUNT Sheila said. "I'm just not going to be able to make it."

Rosie lowered her cell and looked at the screen as if she couldn't quite believe what her aunt was saying, which was stupid, because she should've anticipated something like this. Aunt Sheila was her mom's sister in more than just blood. "Is it money?" she asked, even though the direct roundtrip would cost less than Aunt Sheila spent on whiskey in a week.

"Of course it isn't."

"Is it Uncle Roger? Doesn't he want you to come? I know he never liked Mom, but she was your sister, Aunt Sheila. Surely he understands you need to say goodbye?"

"It isn't Roger, toots. He wouldn't stop me from doing anything; he never has, and he never will. I'm my own woman, you know that."

No. No, Rosie didn't know that. She knew very little about her aunt other than she was an alcoholic narcissist, much like her mom. "So what is it?" She hated guessing games and just wanted a straight answer.

"It's just that... Well, it turns out that I'm banned from flying for life."

Rosie rubbed her eyes and took a deep breath. "You're telling me you're not allowed to fly on *any* airline at any time?" She put her cell in the crook of her neck and googled *can you be banned for life from flying?* The search engine promptly confirmed that yes, a person could be barred on one airline, and they'd share the details with other airlines.

"Yep. They kept threatening me with it, but now they've dropped the hammer, I guess."

"You guess? You don't know for sure?"

"No, I know for sure."

God, this was like having a conversation with a vocally challenged teenager. Why couldn't Aunt Sheila just provide all the information without constant prompting? "And you only just found out today?"

"No. They told me a couple of months ago when I tried to fly to New York." Her aunt groaned loudly. "Ended up missing a Bon Jovi gig."

Rosie googled again to discover Bon Jovi hadn't toured since 2022. She could spend more time pressing Aunt Sheila into increasingly outrageous lies, but her aunt clearly didn't want to make the trip, and in reality, there was very little Rosie could do to change that. It wasn't like she hadn't briefly entertained the thought of missing the memorial too, but she needed the closure more than she needed to avoid dealing with her errant emotions. "Is there anyone else Mom knew who might want to come?"

"We haven't been close for decades, toots. I don't know who she's been running with."

She'd been "running with" Keith, but Rosie had no way of contacting him. So apart from Rosie, no one her mom knew or had spent any part of her life with would be there. The friends Rosie had called were dead, in rehab, or had flat out refused to come. Some kind of memorial this was going to be. "Okay. Well, thanks for the help."

"Before you go, toots, what music are you playing?"

That was a random thing to be interested in, and Rosie was tempted to tell her aunt to come if her curiosity was that strong. But what would be the point, other than proving nurture was a very powerful factor in deciding how a person acts? And more than anything, she didn't want *any* of her mom's personality traits or behaviors. "She wanted 'Welcome to the Jungle' by Guns 'n

Roses as people come into the memorial and 'Highway to Hell' by AC/DC as people leave. She loved her eighties rock like you do."

Aunt Sheila chuckled. "I bet you're tempted to have 'Ding Dong, the Witch is Dead,' am I right?"

Nope, not right at all. The only temptation had been not to have a memorial and then there would've been no music at all. But that temptation was brief and petulant and quickly overcome by a sense of duty. "Okay, Aunt Sheila, I have to go."

"You know, toots, I tried to protect you from your mom. I tried to take you away with me, but she wouldn't let you go."

"Yeah, I know, Aunt Sheila." She heard the same story every time they talked. Frying pan and fire. Devil and the deep blue sea. Rock and a hard place. Clichés abounded for how Rosie felt about that option. The only discernible difference between the two had been Aunt Sheila's capacity to stay in a relationship with a man for longer than a month. Roger might well have been preferable to the parade of would-be papas her mom brought home. And if she'd had a model of what a long-term intimate relationship actually looked like, maybe Rosie wouldn't have such a hard time staying in one either. *Hypocrite.* At some point in adulthood, you have to decide not to let your past negatively influence your future anymore. She'd lost count of the number of times she'd parroted that to clients. And aside from the lack of monogamous commitment, Shay was turning out to be the healthiest relationship she'd ever had, so maybe she'd already turned that corner.

She tuned back in to hear Aunt Sheila still rattling on about her regret at not being able to tear Rosie away from her mom and not having kids of her own. Some people just weren't meant for parenthood, and Rosie gave silent thanks to whoever or whatever was responsible for not allowing her aunt and Roger to procreate. "I'm sorry, Aunt Sheila. I've got a lot to figure out for the memorial and not a lot of time to do it. Talk soon." She hung up without waiting for a response, which was usually a lie about keeping in touch and talking more often anyway. With her mom gone, there was even less reason for Rosie to reach out at all, and since communication never came from the other direction, she anticipated that could have been the last conversation they ever had. Strangely, that possibility didn't bother her.

Rosie pulled the legal pad to the front of her desk and looked at the catering arrangements again. She'd given Bonnie her estimated guest numbers and didn't want to mess her around on such short notice. *Guests.* Was that what people were at a memorial? The people that'd be there were Rosie's *guests.* Apart from the last-minute addition of Alyssa, no one coming had met her mom once, let alone established any kind of relationship or connection with her. But they'd be there for Rosie, and that would have to be good enough. She googled homeless shelters in the surrounding area and figured they'd pick up any leftover food, or Lori could get Gabe to drop it off in her truck.

When her phone rang and Rosie looked at the time, she realized she'd gone down a rabbit hole with homeless charities after rediscovering the one for LGBTQ kids which Unity Tools was going to donate some of their profits to.

"Am I speaking to a Ms. Rosie Morgan?"

Rosie glanced at the screen to see it was a California area code. "You are. To whom am I speaking?" she asked, matching their formal tone with wry amusement.

"I'm Gary Brown from the Lancaster Bank of America branch. I'm calling about the missed payment on your home improvement loan. Do you have a moment to chat?"

Like she had time to entertain a scam call. "Give me one second, please." Rosie scribbled the guy's name and number on a blank sheet of the pad then googled the number to find it was legit. "I'm sorry, Gary. I don't hold a loan with the Bank of America right now. Are you sure you've got the right Rosie Morgan?" She googled *Rosie Morgan America*, and there were more than sixty just on LinkedIn.

"Is your mother Brenda Morgan of 51638 West Truro Drive?"

Rosie swallowed, and a ball of dread sank heavy in her gut. "Yes, that's my mom. I don't know if that was her last address. She died nearly two weeks ago."

"Ah, I see," he said. "I'm so sorry for your loss. Under the circumstances, we can forego the late penalty charge for a missed payment, and we can offer you a three-month payment break. Does that sound like something you'd be interested in taking advantage of?"

"That's a very nice offer, Gary, but I don't need it because I don't have a loan with you."

"Erm, I'm a little confused, Ms. Morgan. I've got the details right here. You co-signed a loan for $30,000 with Brenda Morgan right here in this branch three months ago."

She wrote *Thirty thousand!!!!* on the pad and underscored it four times. "And I'm more than a little confused, because I wasn't in Lancaster three months ago. I haven't been anywhere near California since Christmas last year, so there's no way I signed off on any loan at your, or any other, branch."

"But I have everything right in front—"

"I'm sorry, Gary, but I think my mom's somehow managed to convince you to give her money without my help."

"We don't just give that kind of money away without extensive checks, Ms. Morgan," he said, sounding a little less friendly. "I'm afraid if you insist on denying responsibility for this loan, I'm going to have to pass this onto our legal team."

"Gary, I have to insist because I'm not responsible for the loan at all and not because I'm trying to duck out of something I've committed to. Can you please send the details you have to my email so I can get my lawyer to look at them?"

"The email we have on file is rosie dot morgan one nine nine two at hotmail dot com; is that still correct?"

She couldn't stop a scoff from escaping. At least her mom had remembered her birth year when she was committing fraud in Rosie's name. "That's not my email, and it never has been my email."

"Oh. Well, that's the email that was given at the time of the loan and where all the electronic paperwork was sent for signatures. And it's the email associated with your checking account."

Rosie shook her head. "And how long has that checking account been open?"

Gary's key tapping sounded harsh and slow. "Six months."

"So she set up a checking account in my name three months in advance of taking out the loan," she said more to herself than Gary, who was just following protocol and probably couldn't help her at all. "How did you get this number?"

"From Sheila Morgan, the emergency contact on your mother's account."

"Because you tried the number that was supposed to be mine, and it was dead, right?"

"Right," he said after a slight pause. "So should I send copies of the paperwork to that email address?"

Rosie sighed. Gary obviously wasn't quite as intelligent as he sounded. "No, Gary. Because I don't have access to that email. It's not mine." She gave him her real address, and seconds later, a message from Gary Brown and the Bank of America popped into her inbox. "Can you give me a moment while I check the paperwork, please?"

"Of course," he said and popped her on hold.

Sure enough, her name and details were listed as the co-signee on a loan for $30,000. "Jesus Christ, Mom." It wasn't like Rosie didn't already have enough debt with student loans. She had a feeling her mom hadn't used it for home renovations since she wouldn't have had any intention of staying in the new place longer than twelve months. But was there anything left of it? If her mom hadn't spent it before she'd died, Keith would sure as shit have gotten his hands on it. She scrolled down to the fees. *Fuck.* The sixteen percent interest of nearly twenty thousand took the total to just under $50,000, and then there was the fifteen-dollar monthly loan service fee. Nausea roiled in her stomach, and she took a long, deep breath. Her mom was gone. How was she still inciting such visceral reactions to her behavior?

She refocused and got to the signature part. That was her mom's scribble, but whoever had attempted to forge Rosie's had failed quite miserably, which was a relief though she wasn't sure whether that alone would be enough to prove she'd had nothing to do with this damn loan. She blew out a long breath and waited for Gary to take her off hold. She knew two lawyers: Lori's piece-of-work ex-wife and Solo's wife, though she didn't have a number for Janie and would have to call Lori.

"Are you still there, Ms. Morgan?" Gary asked when he finally came back on the line.

"Yeah, I'm here."

"And now that you've seen the paperwork..."

She waited for the end of the sentence—the accusation—but it didn't come. "That's not my signature on the paperwork. It looks more like a drunk spider dropped into an ink pot and then crawled all over the page."

There was a long pause from Gary's end. "It looks like we have a little problem, Ms. Morgan."

"Little? I don't think you can call $50,000 worth of debt little." She took a breath, trying to keep her voice even against the volcano erupting inside. "Look, Gary, obviously this isn't your fault, but also, this isn't my loan or my financial responsibility."

"But your name is on—"

"Yes, Gary. I know my name is on the paperwork, but this is clearly fraud by my mom."

"Your mom?"

His incredulous tone would've made her laugh. Of course the average person would find such a notion ridiculous, but then the average person wasn't unlucky enough to have had a mom like hers. "Yes, Gary. My mom."

"I'm afraid that isn't my department. I'm going to pass the case onto our legal team, and they'll be in touch."

"Great. Thanks, Gary." She hung up. "And thanks, Mom." She flipped to her favorite contacts and was about to call Lori when her cell vibrated in her hand. *Shay*. Rosie had replaced a semi-naked picture of Shay with one of them together in Tijuana, and the new photograph made her smile despite the serious conversation she'd just had. She answered the video call and waved. "Hey, you. How're you doing?"

"Hey, yourself."

Shay's bright smile pushed away the last thoughts of her potential new debt so she could fully concentrate on being in the moment, and she hoped Shay's apparent happiness meant her father's surgery had gone well. "Any news on your dad?"

"Great news, actually. He came out of surgery just after I spoke to you earlier, and he's been conscious and lucid for the past few hours." Shay switched the camera around to show she was in the peace garden again. "I'm back in my new happy place."

Rosie could see the orange tulips in the foreground and wondered if there was any significance to Shay choosing that spot to call her again, or if Shay had attributed some importance to seeing her mom's favorite flowers just before she'd received good news about her father. "That's wonderful, Shay," she said, putting aside her therapy hat. "Does he seem like his usual self?" The question was a bit of a double-edged sword.

"Yes and no. He isn't showing any signs of confusion, and he knows all the family. But he seems to be keeping his usual crankiness dialed down." Shay shrugged. "Could be he just needs to get his strength up before he clicks back to normal."

Rosie nibbled on her lip, switching between choosing to say nothing and interfering. Was their friendship strong enough that she could offer her thoughts and gently push Shay toward reconciliation with her father? "I know you weren't interested last time I brought this up, but do you think you might take this as an opportunity to mend fences?" A wave of relief washed over her when Shay grinned.

"Get out of my head."

Rosie smiled and winked. "That's a yes. Five psychic points for me."

"Only five?" Shay jutted her chin at the screen. "I think you might deserve ten."

"Ooh, you're so generous. Thank you."

Shay shook her head. "Seriously though, yes, I'm going to talk to him when we've finished chatting. Everyone but Aaron has gone home, and he's in with Daddy now."

Rosie clenched her toes and held onto her judgment that most of Shay's brothers were leaving everything to her again.

"It doesn't matter, Rosie."

She frowned. "What doesn't matter?"

"It's okay that they've gone home," Shay said. "You'd make a terrible poker player. The condemnation was all over your face."

"It was not." Rosie blinked and placed her palm over the screen briefly. She liked that she was paying attention and didn't stop the slight smile at Shay's reading of her.

"It really was. But it's good. This way, I get to talk to Daddy alone, and no one's going to interrupt us. And," Shay put her finger up, "progress with Aaron continues. He made a genuine offer to stay, but I told him to go home to his family. See what therapy can do? That's the kind of difference you used to make."

"But now I just manipulate people to spend money they don't have on things they don't want." Rosie made a face and clutched her hand to her chest. "Ouch."

Shay cocked her head. "Your words, not mine. This time."

Rosie stuck out her tongue but didn't argue. Words were powerful indicators of emotional state, and her own choice of them was telling.

"What's been happening in your world? Do you miss me?"

More than you'll ever know. "So much stuff. And no, not at all."

Shay gave her cockiest grin. "Liar. You're just saying that to hurt me."

Rosie arched her eyebrow. "You want me to miss you?" The question was out of her mouth before she could marshal her thoughts.

Shay glanced away and shrugged. "Maybe."

The idea of that was enough, and Rosie didn't press for more. It was a good sign their situationship was still solid and that Shay had no idea Rosie was head over heels in love. "No one's coming to the memorial, including Aunt Sheila, and my mom forged my signature on a loan, so I have a new $50,000 debt."

Shay's eyes widened. "What? You're kidding?"

Rosie shook her head. "I wish I was. I need a lawyer."

"I'll text you Janie's number," Shay said. "I don't know what kind of lawyer she is, but she should probably be able to help."

"Are you sure that's okay, given how things are with her and Solo?"

"I'm positive. And if she can't help, I'll bet she can give you the details of someone who can."

Rosie smiled tightly as the gravity of the situation dawned on her a little more. Her mom really never thought of anyone but herself. "Thank you." She didn't want to drone on about her problems, so she thought about what it meant that Shay was calling her again, and she tried for a more genuine smile. This one came far easier. "Have the doctors told you when your dad will be allowed to go home?"

"He's got to stay in the ICU for another forty-eight hours for round the clock observation, then they'll move him to a ward, where he has to stay for a week minimum." Shay shook her head and laughed. "You'll guess he's not happy about that."

"What about you? How do you feel about it?"

Shay rolled her eyes. "Getting back into practice, counselor?"

Rosie opened her mouth to protest, but Shay waved at the screen.

"I'm kidding. I'm okay with it. Me and Aaron will figure out a schedule and corral the others into it, so there'll always be someone here for visiting hours. I'll probably take most of the weekend."

"Oh." She quelled her selfish disappointment down and hoped Shay hadn't heard it in her voice.

"Don't worry. I'll still be there for your mom's memorial on Saturday."

"You will? It's fine if you can't make it. You've got your own family stuff to manage. You don't need mine too." Rosie didn't want to prove Shay right and be just another emotional time suck she didn't have the capacity for.

"I'll be there." Shay's teasing disappeared, and her expression was serious. "I promise."

A kaleidoscope of colorful butterflies fluttered in Rosie's stomach. That made two promises in one day, and Shay had kept the first one, which was one more than any of her previous partners had. She caught herself. Shay wasn't her partner; she was her friend with benefits.

Words were powerful and reflected emotional states, she reminded herself again. Love. That was *her* overarching emotion right now, and keeping a lid on it was proving more difficult than she thought it would be.

Chapter Twenty-Four

Buzzing with the energy from her conversation with Rosie, Shay took the stairs back to the ICU unit on the third floor. Rosie's only surviving family member not attending her mom's memorial sounded unbelievable, but after everything Rosie had told her, she could believe anything. Shay was using it as inspiration; she wouldn't let her family go anywhere near the path Rosie had been forced to travel. Her momma wouldn't be happy if she did, and she'd probably find some way to tell her so too—like striking Shay with lightning for the second time.

She pushed the door open onto the third-floor hallway just as Aaron emerged from the doorway of their father's room. "Hey, little brother."

"Hey, big sis." Aaron gestured to Shay's face. "What's got you all grinny and happy?"

She touched her lips, unaware she'd been smiling. "Nothing."

He scoffed. "You've always been able to hide your feelings from the rest of our brothers, mainly because they're too wrapped up in their own crap, but you can't keep anything from me. Spill."

Shay shrugged. "I was just talking to a friend, that's all."

"The same friend you went to Tijuana with?" He narrowed his eyes when she nodded. "Just a friend?"

"A friend with benefits, if you must know."

"You lucky dog." He lightly punched her shoulder. "And clearly, one of those benefits is making you smile like a clown at a face paint sale."

"That's a weirdly emotive metaphor. Don't you hate clowns? I have a memory of you screaming like a coyote when Momma brought a clown to one of your birthdays."

"What can I tell you? The therapy is fixing more than my relationship with my whole family." Aaron nodded back toward their father's room. "Speaking of which, maybe now—"

"Stop." Shay put her hand up. "I've already had a real therapist suggest I talk to Daddy. I don't need second-hand therapy from you."

Aaron put his hand on her shoulder and squeezed hard. "I'm proud of you for having therapy."

She shrugged him off. "Don't be. I'm not. Rosie's a therapist." Although she wasn't one right now, Shay had a feeling Rosie would soon return to her calling.

"Rosie is the friend with benefits?" When she nodded, he grinned widely. "Great choice of *friend*. She'll save you a fortune in counseling sessions."

"Why are you saying friend in such a weird way? It's not like that."

"Not like what? Not like anything deeper than a friend? The Lord forbid you open your heart to anyone."

Shay frowned. "What're you talking about?"

"Come on, sis, you're not stupid. You were always such a loving kid. But it's like you shut down after Momma died. Isn't it about time you stopped being such a player and got serious with someone? Someone who makes you smile like Rose."

"Rosie," she said. "Look, Aaron, I love that therapy is making you re-evaluate yourself and your life, but you don't need to pay it forward. Not everyone gets to marry their high school sweetheart and live happily ever after, like you and Bisa." Not even their parents had managed it, and they were more in love than anyone she'd ever known. Although Gabe and Lori looked like they were heading that way.

"Okay, sis." He held his hands in the air. "You'll figure it out in your own time. But you're not getting any younger, so don't leave it too late."

She shoved his chest hard. "Asshole. I'm only thirty-eight."

"Exactly, you're nearing the end of your fourth decade, and you're still alone because you've spent all your post-Army time looking after your family."

"Someone had to after Momma died. That's what she would've wanted."

"No. She would've wanted you to be happy. Like she was." He glanced at his watch then tapped it. "I have to go. My happily ever after is waiting for me to have dinner and help the kids with their homework." He patted her shoulder on his way past. "Maybe you and Rosie could join us one weekend."

She couldn't help but smile thinking of Rosie with her at Aaron's house, but then she stopped herself. Would an invite to her brother's house overstep the boundaries of their situationship? Or would it be considered just a friendly gesture? After going with Rosie to pick up her mom's ashes, they'd definitely taken their friendship to a new level, and the intimacy between them had ramped up a hundred notches. Was she getting actual *feelings* for Rosie? She shook her head. Of course she had feelings, and they'd been getting stronger since she stepped on the plane to San Diego—she just needed to know what they meant.

"Shanae?" her daddy half-shouted, his voice echoing in the quiet hallway.

So he was getting his strength back then. She rounded the doorway and smiled, not sure what reception to expect. He gave her a small smile, but she couldn't interpret his expression. It certainly wasn't one she'd seen in a long time.

"Hey, Daddy." She dropped into the sleeper chair beside his bed. "How are you feeling?"

"Like Kelly Pierce cracked my head open with an ice pick and dug around in there for ancient artifacts," he said. "How do you think?"

And there he was again. Whatever they'd drained from his brain, it hadn't been his grumpiness. He groaned as if in pain. "Is something wrong? Do you need me to get a nurse?"

He shook his head and didn't make eye contact. "No nurse or doctor can fix this."

"Are you in pain? They can probably increase the morphine on the drip."

"Morphine can't make the pain in my heart go away, girl."

Was he delirious? They'd said to look out for signs of inconsistent behavior, and this didn't sound like him at all. She was half out of her chair, going to call for a nurse anyway.

He patted the bed. "Relax, Shanae. My head's fine, and I'm not confused." He opened his hand to her. "In fact, I haven't been this clear since your momma died. Seems like I needed a giant knock to the brain to wake me up."

Shay tentatively accepted the gesture, not wanting to speak in case she broke whatever spell this was. He hadn't held her hand since she was maybe ten years old on one of those rare family trips to the park for a community picnic.

"I was lost when your momma passed," he said quietly, "and I haven't been able to find my way back to any of you, but you especially."

The initial shock of whatever this was began to recede, and all the questions she harbored about the past six years pushed to be voiced. "Why? Why me? You've been so *angry* with me, so dismissive. I just don't know what I did wrong." She looked up at him and what she saw almost made her jump out of her chair like she'd received an electric shock. His dark brown eyes were edged with tears, and then one escaped and tracked along the deep lines of his face.

"You've done nothing wrong, girl. This is all on me. I was angry because you weren't there when your momma died. She wanted nothing more than to see her baby girl one more time before she passed, but by the time you got home, she was gone."

"That wasn't my fault," Shay said, finding her feet again. "My CO–"

"I know, I know. But I was already angry at your choice to join the Army. You got a math scholarship to Yale, Shanae. You were the first in our family to have a chance to do something more than blue-collar work, to be a Black professor. Hell, you could've been our first Black female president. But you chose the Army. Did you know that your grandpa spent three months in Long Binh jail—"

"The military prison in Vietnam?" She knew her grandpa had served, but this was new information.

He nodded. "For supposed insubordination. You know what your grandpa actually did?"

"No," Shay whispered.

"He refused to follow an order to beat a fellow soldier, another Black man, who was caught with marijuana." He pounded on the bed with his other hand.

"You need to calm down, Daddy, or the alarm's gonna go off." She gestured toward the monitor and his rising heart rate.

He glanced at it and nodded slowly. "Did you know it took the US government nearly sixty years to award his Black captain the Medal of Honor for his bravery in the Vietnam War?"

Shay shook her head. "I had no idea."

"The real fight for us was in America, not Vietnam. It was okay for us to put on a uniform and shoot Viet Cong, but back home, we couldn't even sit at a lunch counter."

"Things have changed, Daddy. That was nearly fifty years ago," she said with a conviction she had no right to feel and no evidence to support. She'd experienced it herself, especially from their old CO, Nelson. Her daddy's rejection started to come into focus; it was more about his dislike of her career choice than her as his daughter.

"Have they? Five percent of the most senior officers in the military are Black, Shanae. Five percent. It's not a glass ceiling; it's made of cement to stop us from getting to the top."

"We can only change that from the inside," she said. "Look, Daddy, thank you for sharing that part of your history with me, but it should be exactly that: *your* history. By taking that out on me, you've made it your present...and your future if we don't fix things."

He squeezed her hand gently. "This isn't a good apology, is it?"

She tilted her head slightly. It really wasn't, but it was progress, *and* it was the longest discussion they'd had in forever.

"I'm sorry. Your momma told me I should get better at admitting when I was wrong."

Fresh air caught in Shay's throat, and she coughed. A tear *and* an apology? She must've slipped into a multiverse. "Momma told you that a long time ago, and she's been gone six years. You're telling me that you've held onto your anger at me just because I joined the Army? Is that enough of an excuse to treat me the way you have? And none of this explains why you were never home when I was a child." She looked away, unable to hold his gaze following her outburst, and she had no idea where the last accusation had come from. She thought she'd accepted that part of her childhood. He took a few deep breaths and held his chest. Once again, she considered whether or not to call for a nurse. "Are you in pain?" Maybe she'd pushed him too far.

"No, no. I'm all right." He pushed up to a sitting position and tugged the sheet over his stomach. "You want to know why I was never home?" He mirrored her responding nod. "Because I had six kids and a wife to feed. I didn't finish school, Shanae. I was making less than seven dollars an hour working every shift I could get. When I wasn't bussing tables, I was cleaning up this hospital or driving bus routes. After all that, there wasn't a whole lot of time left to take you to the park or to watch one of your spelling bees." He ran his hand over his beard. "That's why raising you kids fell to your momma. That's why I couldn't read you a story and tuck you into bed at night. Don't you think I wanted all of those things? You think I didn't miss playing catch with you and my boys on the weekend?"

He clutched his hand to his chest again, and it hit her that he was stopping himself from sobbing. His version of an apology needed work, for sure, but he'd decided to finally talk to her, and she'd never thought about how much he'd had to work to keep their family off the streets. She'd never thought of it from his perspective at all. "But I've been here for six years, Daddy, and you haven't been working. You've had all this time to spend with me, and you haven't wanted it. You've been like Jekyll and Hyde, asking me to come and fix something, and then getting me out of your sight as soon as possible. Are you telling me that's all the result of you being angry at my career choice?"

"It wasn't just that." He sighed. "You remind me so much of your momma sometimes, it's painful. Like she's here but not here. It's emotional torture, and that's why I want you here, and then I act like I can't be anywhere near you." He pounded his chest with his fist. "It hurts so bad. Your momma was everything to me."

Shay inspected her nail polish, trying to focus on anything other than the spiky ball rolling around her stomach. Since Mexico, she'd been able to feel almost happy when she had thoughts of her momma. She'd been the antithesis of Rosie's mom, which had only served to increase the gratitude Shay had for being lucky enough to be her momma's daughter. But her daddy's grief bled from him and invaded her whole being, reminding her of what she'd lost too soon. "We *all* lost her, Daddy," she said quietly, wrung out from the conversation and just about done with it.

"I know," he said. "And I haven't been handling it." He touched the bandage wrapped around his head. "But this has knocked some sense into me. If the docs here hadn't caught this in time, I'd be with your momma right now, and as much as I want that in a way you probably don't understand, the Lord obviously saw fit to keep me here. And I'm figuring that gives me a second chance. A chance to put things right between us...if you'll let me try."

Shay didn't say anything. She twirled her finger curls and thought about the way her momma used to spend hours fixing her hair, telling her how pretty she was, and how she'd wanted to hear her daddy say the same thing. But almost every time, she'd ended up pulling on a silk sleep cap and going to bed without him ever seeing how beautiful her momma had made her hair.

Well, he was here now, saying he wanted to see her, but she hadn't anticipated where this conversation might lead. If she were totally honest with herself, she'd expected him to shut her down and refuse to talk at all.

But he hadn't.

And even better than that, he'd led the charge, owning up to his shortcomings in his own particular way and opening the door for them to embark on a new relationship. That was all she'd wanted since she'd left the Army, to relate to him as an adult instead of just his daughter. But she needed time to process everything he'd said, and he had to let go of a lot of anger. It wasn't going to be an easy path, and the perfect daddy-daughter relationship wouldn't happen for them overnight, but this was a start. This was more than she could ever have hoped for just a few short weeks ago.

Her daddy had been prepared to talk, but equally, she'd finally been prepared to listen. That willingness had a lot to do with Rosie and how she'd cracked open Shay's shell without even trying. She recalled Aaron's accusation that she'd closed herself off after their momma had died, and she was slowly realizing he might be right.

But where there'd only been darkness and shadow, light was now penetrating the cracks and illuminating the possibilities. She'd been lying to herself that intimate relationships weren't worth her time and energy, hiding from the vulnerability created from caring for someone...and allowing them to care for her. And then, possibly, losing them. And as that dawned her, she rocked from the recognition that Rosie had become that person for her, despite all of Shay's rules and boundaries.

Her friend with benefits had become the lover she craved time with. But Rosie was happy with their situationship, wasn't she? She'd said she was no longer searching for her Princess Charming, so Shay couldn't upset the delicate balance they'd found.

She looked up at her daddy, who was watching her with what looked like hope in his eyes. She nodded and squeezed his hand tightly. "Okay, Daddy, let's try."

His answering smile matched the one on his wedding photographs. It was so genuine and unguarded, so hopeful and full of anticipation of good things to come. She couldn't wait to tell Rosie how this had gone down...even if she couldn't tell her how she felt about their relationship.

Chapter Twenty-Five

FOUR MINUTES AND THIRTY-ONE seconds had never passed so slowly or been so incredibly painful. Rosie cringed when Axl Rose sang the thinly-veiled reference to his sexual organ, and Shay glanced at her, clearly trying to conceal a wry smile. Rosie shook her head. "Oh, God," she whispered.

Shay took her hand and squeezed it gently. "It's okay."

Rosie clenched her jaw to keep her mouth closed. Shay's intimate gesture moved her but surprised her too. Those feelings continued when Shay didn't pull away, and the warmth of her hand remained in Rosie's. They hadn't seen each other in the flesh since the photo shoot, and Rosie had missed Shay's touch and the feel of her skin, but mostly, she'd just missed *her*. "Thank you again for coming," she said quietly just before the song finally ended.

Shay ran her thumb over the back of Rosie's hand softly. "I made you a promise, and I never break my promises."

Rosie's heart raced. God, Shay was perfect for her. If only she was capable of making a promise to commit to them really being together. *That* would be a promise Rosie could treasure and hold onto for the rest of her life. She shook the ridiculous thought away. Rosie had known what she was getting into when they started their friends with benefits situation, and there was no changing the rules now. It wasn't forever. It was for right now. Their time together was still better than any of her relationships where there'd been some far-off vision of a future. Knowing there wasn't one on the horizon removed the pressure and allowed them to truly enjoy the present moment.

She made her way to the small stage where Alyssa had created a stunning floral arrangement of black roses and golden-sprayed foliage. Rosie's mom would've loved it, though she would've bitched about the gold being fake. But the memorial had cost enough already, and with a $50,000 debt still looming large, she'd have to lump it.

She turned and looked around at the small number of people gathered in the modest, exposed brick loft of Round Run Records. This place was the only one of sixteen stores she'd tried who were open to hosting a memorial, and they'd been her last hope to fulfill one of her mom's most adamant final wishes—she'd underlined it repeatedly and circled it so many times, the pen had almost gone through the paper. Rosie had always thought her mom loved music more than her. She lost count of the times her mom bought new vinyl instead of food, claiming music fed her soul. To a young Rosie, it was a claim that left her hungry and sucking on stolen sugar cubes from a nearby café.

She gripped the mic briefly before deciding she didn't need it to be heard and pushed it aside. "My mom used to love regaling me with fanciful adventures involving one friend or another, leading me to believe she was incredibly popular. When I called to tell all those friends about Mom's passing and this memorial, I expected them to rush to Chicago to say their final goodbyes." She gestured to the half-empty room. "But in the end, she wasn't even a little bit popular, because not a single person she actually knew wanted to be here. And the only people gathered here today have come for me, not Mom." She looked at Shay, whose presence meant so much, given what she was going through with her own family. Shay's answering smile brightened the room more than any of the unused spotlights could have, and her light chased away the darkness Rosie's mom cast in her heart. "It's sad for her, but I'm overwhelmed with gratitude to you. The friends and..." She thought of how to describe Shay and came up empty. What she'd give to call Shay her partner or girlfriend. "Well, I'm so grateful to Lori and my new friends who are my chosen family." Rosie blew a kiss in the direction of Shay, Gabe, and the rest of the gang.

Then she locked eyes with Alyssa and smiled. "And I'm grateful to old friends I've neglected, and I hope that now that we've reconnected, we'll stop wasting precious time." In her peripheral vision, she saw Shay glance over her shoulder, but her neutral expression gave nothing away.

"Memorials are supposed to be an opportunity to celebrate and remember the person who's passed. People are supposed to tell anecdotes and stories of special times. They read poems or passages from books that were important to the person. I'm told there can be dancing and singing too." She looked again at Shay, who smiled and nodded encouragement. "But there's none of that today, which I'm sort of ashamed about. But the great thing about being here with you is that I can say that without feeling judged. There's no one here who can share lovely stories about my mom that'll make you feel warm and cuddly inside. There are no heartwarming tales of her generosity or selflessness. There's no one here whose life was positively influenced by her. The most positive thing she did for me was give me life, so I'm thankful for that, at least."

Lori laughed lightly. "I'm thankful for that too."

"And me," Shay said.

Rosie heard similar sentiments from RB and Solo, which filled her heart with joy. Just a few months ago, she counted Lori and Ellery as her go-to friends, but now her circle had expanded to include all the people Lori had brought into her life via Gabe. Most importantly, Shay. It was another good reason never to declare she was in love with Shay and just to let their situationship run its natural course. "But hopefully I can learn from the absence of those things at this memorial and not make any of the same mistakes my mom made, like surrounding myself with fair weather friends who don't really care for me at all. I don't want to think about my own funeral for a long, long time," she smiled at the ripple of laughter, "but I hope to live the rest of my life truly connected in a meaningful way to my friends, my chosen family, so there damn well will be singing and dancing around my coffin!"

"In a good way," RB shouted.

"Yeah," Rosie said and pointed at RB, "definitely in a good way. So I'm going to stop jabbering at you now and say thank you again for being here. It means so much to me, you wouldn't believe it. And your reward for giving up your Saturday and putting up with this incredibly morose memorial is free food and an open bar at Bonnie's, where I hope we can celebrate each other and our connections." She nodded to the store guy at the sound system, and the opening guitar riffs of "Highway to Hell" boomed from the speakers.

Woody whooped and hollered and started playing air guitar. When the lyrics kicked in, Gabe, RB, and Solo joined in, and Rosie clasped her hand over her mouth as she laughed and shook her head. Her mom would've liked the rendition for their enthusiasm if not for their singing talent.

Shay held out her hand to help Rosie down from the stage and then gestured to Alyssa. "Who's your curly-haired friend?"

"That's Alyssa. She made the floral arrangements, but she's also a friend from college." She stopped herself from saying any more but didn't know why. Shay wasn't the jealous type. It was more likely she was interested in Alyssa for herself.

"Just a friend?"

Her question indicated that Shay had obviously picked up on the vibe Rosie was so eager to conceal. "Fine. I used to have a massive crush on her, and she wouldn't be pinned down into a monogamous relationship."

Shay grinned. "You've got a type: hard to get."

Rosie grasped the back of Shay's neck and pulled her in for a passionate kiss. "Hard to get *and* incredibly beautiful," she said, liking that Shay's eyes were half-lidded in drunken desire when she finally let her go.

Lori popped up beside them and pried them apart. "Put her

down. You don't know where she's been."

"Sure she does," Shay said and smiled. "I've been at the hospital or the garage."

"I don't need to know where she's been." Rosie glared at Lori, though she was just being overprotective. Lori knew Rosie's heart was on the line, but Shay was blissfully ignorant. "That's the beauty of a situationship: no jealousy or possessiveness."

Shay wrapped her hand around Rosie's wrist and tugged lightly. "I don't know about that."

Rosie looked at Shay, trying to figure out exactly which bit she was unsure of, but she just grinned.

Lori stroked Rosie's upper arm. "How are you doing?" she asked, tilting her head slightly.

"Surprisingly, I think I'm okay." She gestured back to the stage, where Alyssa was busy packing the roses into boxes. "I was nervous about that, but it went okay. I'm feeling her loss, but just not in a visceral way, you know?"

Lori nodded. "Nobody's expecting you to be a sobbing, grieving mess, Rosie. We only care about you and want to make sure you're okay, that's all."

"Thank you." She took Lori's hand and squeezed. "And I really am. I'm pretty sure I've done my grieving. And when I've dealt with the ashes per her final request, I'll get closure for good."

"Have you worked out when you're scattering them?" Lori asked.

Rosie rolled her eyes. "I don't know. Franklin wasn't happy about the five days in Mexico, especially considering where I was with the Unity Tools project. It might take a while before I can work up enough of his goodwill to secure a couple days' vacation."

Shay slipped her arm around Rosie's waist. "You could take a break between quitting that job and going back to your practice."

Lori's eyes widened, and she grasped Rosie's shoulders. "You're going back to being a therapist? That's so exciting!" She held Rosie at arm's length and narrowed her eyes. "But when were you going to tell me this yourself?"

Rosie shook her head and took Lori's hands. "I haven't told myself yet. Shay's just stirring the pot, aren't you, *darling*?"

Shay winked and kissed Rosie's cheek. "I just want you to follow your heart."

Rosie shared a look with Lori, who was clearly thinking the same thing: if Rosie followed her heart, it would lead only to Shay, and she'd run in the opposite direction. Rosie appreciated the support. Having Lori believe in her had taken some getting used to, but she had a feeling that it would be *too* easy to accept Shay's cheerleading.

"*Okay*," Lori said and arched her eyebrow at Rosie.

She shook her head almost imperceptibly so that Shay didn't see. Lori wouldn't try to play matchmaker the same way Rosie had after Lori's divorce because this was different. Trying to force them together would only split them wide apart.

"Well, when you figure out a date, will you let me know if you want my company? I can get Beth to look after the Sanctuary for a few days, and we can make it a road trip."

Rosie pulled Lori into a brief hug. "I'd love that. We'll take my car though—I wouldn't feel safe in your little Bolt thingy on the freeway."

"That's a good call," Gabe said as she came to stand beside Lori. "Where're you headed?"

"Memphis."

"The birthplace of rock and roll." Gabe looked impressed. "What's the occasion? Can I tag along, or is it BFF business only?"

Lori rolled her eyes and gestured back to the urn still on the stage. "It's where Rosie's mom wanted her ashes scattered."

"Oh, God. Sorry." Gabe hit herself upside the head. "Ignore me."

"We could all go...if you didn't mind?"

Rosie spun around to Shay, unable to decide if it was the offer or the way she'd made the offer which was the most startling. Hand-holding. Cheek-kissing. Emotional support at public gatherings.

And now double-date mini-breaks. It was as good as one of those fake romance tropes in those books Lori was always reading. Rosie wasn't inclined to turn down the opportunity to spend more time with Shay, even if it was at the expense of a BFF hangout. Lori would always be around, but Shay had made no such promise. "I don't mind at all." She turned back to Lori and Gabe. "And it'd be good to get to know you better, Gabe."

Rosie had given Gabe a hard time when she first came on the scene, but she'd since proven she was worthy of Lori. And it wouldn't hurt to score points with Shay's best friend; she never knew when she might need them.

Gabe grinned. "Oh yeah? So you can figure out my weaknesses and exploit them if I ever hurt Lori?"

Rosie tapped her nose. "Exactly."

Gabe jutted her chin toward Shay. "I should probably do the same then."

Lori frowned at Gabe, and the three of them exchanged looks as if they all knew something Rosie didn't.

"You don't have to worry about us hurting each other," Rosie said. "We both know what this is and what it isn't."

Gabe raised her eyebrows and tugged Lori close. "We should get to Bonnie's before...before Woody gets there and obliterates the buffet."

Lori frowned. "You can't be hungry already? You had two grilled chicken breasts in the truck on the way here."

"Got to keep these babies fed." Gabe flexed her arm and stretched the seams of her suit jacket.

Lori visibly swooned and when she clasped Gabe's giant bicep, her hand looked tiny.

"As much as I love these, you're being rude." Lori turned back to Rosie. "Do you need us to do anything?"

Rosie shook her head. "Nope. You're good to go. Alyssa's dealing with the flowers, and I just have to look after the urn." Which was an ordeal all by itself. Every time she picked it up, she had visions of dropping it and her mom spilling out all over the ground. Having to vacuum her mom up with a Dyson would surely result in a vengeful haunting.

Gabe put her hand on Shay's shoulder. "You should stay and help with that."

"I'm pretty sure I can handle holding an urn." Rosie frowned at Lori, hoping for an explanation, but she just shrugged. Gabe pulled Lori away gently and signaled for the rest of her little team to leave.

Ellery waved from the side of the room and then wandered over. "I've been waiting to see how you're doing."

"I'm good." Rosie looked around the room. "No Lenny today?"

Ellery rubbed her forehead and sighed. "I'm sorry, no. She was supposed to come, but..." She drifted off, clearly unable to find an acceptable excuse.

Don't ever be sorry for her absence. "That's a shame." Rosie wouldn't have been able to keep a straight face if Lori had still been there. "Work emergency?" she asked, though she had no idea what Lenny's current job of the month was. She and Lori couldn't keep up.

"Kind of. She says I've been obsessed with work since I moved into Lori's building at the Sanctuary. We're on a break until I come to my senses and prioritize her needs over the needs of other people's animals." Ellery shook her head. "Anyway, I don't want to talk about that. You're really okay?"

"I'm really okay." She noticed Ellery looking over her shoulder toward the stage. "Admiring the flowers?" she asked, knowing full well Ellery had zero interest in pretty things like floral arrangements, even though she was constantly sending them to Lenny. But Ellery did have a weakness for fiery femmes.

Ellery snapped her gaze back to Rosie. "Yeah, yeah. The flowers. They're...they're something else."

She suppressed a smile. "Something else is definitely right."

"Anyway, I'll get out of your hair," Ellery said. "I'll see you at

Bonnie's."

"Perfect." Rosie gave Ellery a quick hug.

"Not a fan of Lenny?" Shay asked when Ellery had gone.

Rosie grimaced. "Lenny is her own biggest fan. She doesn't need me or anyone else for that."

Shay chuckled. "So no." She thumbed toward the stage. "Does Red need help, or can we go too? I need to talk to you about something, and I don't want to do it here or at Bonnie's."

"Sure. Let me just check." *Shit.* Rosie's stomach dropped as she walked back to the stage. Shay had figured out that Rosie's feelings had gotten out of hand, and she was going to pull away. All the niceties today were just indicators of Shay's guilt that she was about to break Rosie's heart. God, she hoped Shay was still willing to be friends. She didn't want to think about not having Shay in her life at all, not now, not after everything they'd shared.

Maybe it was because of her family. Her dad's accident might mean that he needed extra care, and of course Shay had stepped up to fill that gap. God forbid any of her brothers did their share of the caring. Their relationship had become too demanding for her, and she had to cut it loose. *Fuck and damn it.*

Rosie had a quick chat with Alyssa, who said she'd be at Bonnie's as soon as she'd taken care of the flowers, which Rosie couldn't wait to see the back of. She picked up the urn and headed back toward Shay, who was waiting at the exit. "Where do you want to go?" she asked, hoping Shay wouldn't suggest somewhere Rosie really liked. Having her heart broken would be hard enough without having it associated with one of her favorite places.

"I thought we could walk along Navy Pier."

That worked. It was just across the street and would be busy on a Saturday afternoon, which was all the motivation Rosie needed to keep her ugly crying until she got home. She would've preferred Shay to wait until after the evening gathering, but Rosie figured she might be leaving early to get back to her dad. She *had* said that the weekends would be her time to look after him, and Rosie hadn't expected Shay to be here at all.

She clutched her mom's urn to her chest. Although Shay's car was only a short walk in the opposite direction, Rosie decided to keep it with her. She just wanted Shay to get this over with.

They took the short walk along East Grand to the pier in a strangely awkward silence, something they'd never had before, as they battled against the wind that her city was so famous for. It *was* an awkward silence Rosie was familiar with from other relationships. She'd come to think of it as the calm before the storm, but she hoped the tornado that was about to rip out her heart wouldn't take their friendship with it.

"I'm not sure how I'm supposed to say this," Shay said when they stopped at a relatively quiet spot on the pier.

Shay could barely make eye contact with her, and Rosie's heart ached at the conflict in her expression. It somehow made her feel a little better that this clearly wasn't easy. Perhaps it was because it showed that their time together had meant something to her, where countless other women had failed to make an impact. "It's okay." Rosie wanted to reach out and hold her close, but there was no way she could risk putting the urn on the uneven wooden planks of this part of the pier.

"It is?"

She nodded. "Of course." If Shay was struggling to put it into words, Rosie would help. Even though her heart was about to shatter into a thousand pieces, she would never begrudge the time they'd had together or forget Shay's support in Mexico. "We both knew what this was from the start, and you made it clear what you thought about long-term relationships. Even though it's something I never had, I understand the need to put your family first."

Shay frowned and shook her head slowly. "I don't think you understand."

Rosie tried for a smile and hoped she'd managed it. "I do. It's gotten complicated, your family needs you, and you want out of this. I *do* understand."

Shay continued to shake her head and laughed lightly. "Why would you think I want out of this," she gestured between the two of them, "when I've fallen in love with you?"

The world began to spin like the Centennial Wheel they'd just walked past. The wind whipped through her hair and whistled in her ears. Her body felt light and distant, and control of it slipped away slowly, as if her soul was becoming untethered from it, the same soul that yearned to hear those words coming softly from Shay's lips.

"Oh, shit!"

Wait, what? Not *those* words. And as Shay lunged toward her, Rosie became aware too late for the reason for Shay's reaction. *Something* shattered into a thousand pieces, but it wasn't her heart; it was the Mexican clay pot holding her mom's ashes. And the Windy City claimed its contents, gathering them up in a gray twister and carrying them out over Lake Michigan.

As the grainy remains of her mom floated up and away with the blustery breeze, it was as if Rosie's entire past was swept away on the currents of air. And in the unwritten future and infinite possibilities that awaited her, Shay stood front and center, offering Rosie her heart and the love she had stopped searching for, the love she thought she didn't deserve. "You'll be my Princess Charming?" she asked, hungry for confirmation of the words that had released her from the chains of her past.

"I will if you'll let me." Shay stepped closer and pulled Rosie into her arms. She gently tucked a wisp of Rosie's hair behind her ear and kissed her. "If maybe you could fall in love with me too..."

Rosie laughed and took Shay's face in her hands. She pressed her lips over Shay's, finally able to really claim Shay's kiss as her own, as just hers. Her soul reached out across the ether and deep in a place beyond physical representation, she felt Shay's soul wrap around hers, making her feel safe and loved and truly held for the very first time in her life.

She pulled away just enough to say, "I'm already in love with you."

Chapter Twenty-Six

IT HADN'T COME OUT exactly as Shay had planned it, and she definitely hadn't anticipated that her declaration of love would result in Lake Michigan being the final resting place for Rosie's mom. But now that it was out there, Shay felt damn near invincible, like nothing in the world could hurt her, and like she wouldn't let anything in the world hurt Rosie.

But none of that took care of the smashed urn at their feet. Shay looked at Rosie and then nodded at the lake before she put the toe of her pump against the ceramic carnage and nudged it toward the edge of the pier. Rosie pressed her lips together and clamped her hand over her mouth in a futile attempt to stop a giggle.

"Really?"

"We don't have a choice," Shay said. "Unless you have a bag hidden away in the folds of your dress?"

Rosie wrung her hands together. "I don't."

"And I left my purse in the car. Do you want a piece," Shay toed a substantial chunk of it closer to the gap beneath the fencing, "as a memento?"

Rosie wrinkled her nose as if the idea was abhorrent, then she widened her eyes. "I guess it'd remind me of the first time you told me you loved me... But it could also remind me of the day I dropped my mom in a lake."

Shay grinned. "Win-win?"

Rosie laughed then bit her bottom lip to stop. She knelt down, tucking her dress beneath her so it didn't drag in the remaining person-dust among the urn's shards. She selected a relatively small piece, popped it into her pocket and straightened. She nodded toward the pile. "I don't think I can do it. Will you do it for me?"

Shay caressed Rosie's cheek. "I'll do anything for you," she said before making short work of kicking the evidence of their transgression into the water, leaving only a smear of gray dust in the cracks of the old wooden planks. They moved away from the debris, further down the pier. No more declarations needed to be made over the not-corpse of a dead woman who hadn't deserved someone as amazing as Rosie in her life.

Shay took Rosie's hands and pulled her close, inhaling the scent of her sweet skin. She claimed another passionate kiss, her hunger for the taste of Rosie's lips overriding any other thought in her head. Rosie's sigh and the way her body softened against Shay fueled her desire further, and she tightened her embrace, simultaneously thrilled and overwhelmed by her own near-desperation to be as close to Rosie as physically possible.

When she pulled back only a little so that their lips were still touching, the look in Rosie's eyes seared into her memory. Shay wanted to capture her expression, so that she could bring it to mind any time they were apart, any time she needed to feel wanted and desired. The emotion held within Rosie's gaze was so incredibly pure and unguarded, so limitless and singularly focused that it was like Rosie was tapping directly into Shay's heart and asking for all of it to be mirrored and reciprocated.

"What now?"

"You're going to have to teach me how to be a girlfriend," Shay whispered.

Rosie slipped her hand under Shay's locs and kissed her hard. "I think you've been doing a pretty good impression of that for the past couple of weeks."

"Mm, you've been making me do a lot of things I've never done before."

Rosie pinched Shay's butt. "*Making* you?"

"Uh-huh. *Making* me, like you put me under a spell. I knew what I was doing, but I just couldn't stop myself." Shay cupped

Rosie's cheek and drew her in for another kiss. "I have a feeling it's just going to keep happening." She kissed her again, and Rosie responded with a tender intensity, a blend of softness and force that poured gasoline on the simmering fire between them.

Shay pulled away and let out a deep sigh. People around them came into focus, as if she'd forgotten where they were. "We should probably—"

"Go back to my place and make love until we fall asleep in each other's arms, exhausted and sated but still desperate for more?"

Shay laughed. "That sounds absolutely perfect but," she nodded to the lake, "you've got a memorial wake to host."

Rosie stepped away from Shay and looked out across the water, her expression contemplative. "Goodbye, Mom," she said quietly and then she took Shay's hand. "So I get to do this anytime I want now, right?"

Shay looked at their entwined hands, the contrast of their skin and the perfect way they fit together. "You tell me. You're the teacher."

Rosie wiggled her eyebrows. "I could totally abuse this power you're giving me."

Shay grasped Rosie's hand tighter. "I'm good with that."

They headed back down the pier, and Rosie settled into an unusual quietness.

"Are you thinking about your mom?" Shay asked when they got in the car.

Rosie nodded. "I was thinking that closure would come after I scattered her ashes, but I don't feel any different. And I don't think that has anything to do with not doing it in the right place or," she gave a wry smile, "with quite the right level of care and respect."

Shay turned in her seat to look at her. "I probably haven't helped with that. I was so desperate to tell you that I loved you. I should've waited until tomorrow, but I've got to go back to the hospital again tonight, and I just couldn't wait. I'm sorry."

Rosie squeezed Shay's thigh and shook her head. "Don't be.

There could never have been a wrong time for you to tell me how you feel. And today might even be the best day for it. I've been in love with you since Mexico, but I'd decided not to tell you because I didn't think you could ever feel the same."

"I get that," Shay said and wrinkled her nose. "I put up a lot of walls, and I was pretty specific about my rule."

Rosie laughed. "You really were. What changed your mind?"

"Mexico changed everything for me too. It just took me a while to accept it." Shay started the engine and headed out of the parking lot. "You wouldn't believe it, but it was a couple of conversations with Aaron and my daddy that made me realize that I'd found something precious without looking for it."

"Ah, see? You're already great girlfriend material shooting out lines like that."

"Yay for me." She pulled out into the city's traffic. The gray cloud had cleared, and the wind seemed to have died down. That thought took Shay back to Rosie's lack of closure on her mom. "If you don't feel any different, how *are* you feeling about everything?"

"Lighter, I guess. And there's still relief floating around too. Mostly, I'm sad that she never changed, and I'm fighting off the negative self-talk that I was never enough for her to want to be a better person or a good mom."

"You make me want to be a better person." Shay looked at Rosie as she stopped at a red light.

Rosie's smile brightened. "I do?"

Shay blew out a long breath and shook her head. "Like you wouldn't believe. I want to be everything you need."

Rosie gently fingered one of Shay's locs. "You already are. I don't need you to change a thing. What we've been sharing, what we've become together is more real than any relationship I've ever had."

"Do you miss her?" Shay asked.

"Not in any way to compare to how you miss your mom. And honestly, my mom was never really there *to* miss. I'm going to sit through the process and let it play out, but I won't let the ghost of her control my future like she controlled my past." Rosie caressed Shay's cheek. "And that future is you."

Shay pulled into the alley leading to their garage and turned to face Rosie. "I'm getting used to the sound of that. It wasn't so long ago that I couldn't comprehend a future that included someone walking that path alongside me." And now her heart ached with the potential of everything they could share.

They got out of the car and took the short walk to Bonnie's.

The establishment's namesake greeted them with a big wave. "Hi, honeys. Go on upstairs. Everything's set up for you."

"Thanks, Bonnie," Rosie said. "You're a superstar."

Lori waited for them with two glasses of wine on the mezzanine at the top of the stairs.

"Um," Lori scanned them both as she handed them the drinks, "you seem to be missing the guest of honor."

Rosie pulled the urn shard from her pocket and held it aloft for inspection. "I had a little accident. There was an argument between gravity and Mom's urn. Gravity won, and Mom went for one last swim."

Lori pressed her lips together briefly. "How did that happen?"

Rosie nodded toward Shay. "I lost my grip on reality, and the urn, when this one told me she loved me."

Shay grinned. The more she heard that said out loud, the more it seemed to grow in her heart.

Lori arched her eyebrow. "You're *in love* with my best friend?"

She'd been prepared for this. Rosie had given Gabe hell when she was quietly pining after Lori too. "Yes. Yes, I am."

Lori's expression grew even more incredulous. "Don't you believe relationships are a black hole for your time and emotion, and you get enough of that with your family?"

"Lori!" Rosie put her hand over her face, making it clear Lori had probably just quoted her verbatim.

And she'd been right. But things had changed. Shay simply

smiled. "It's okay, Rosie. Lori's just doing her job, like you did with Gabe," she said and winked. "Spending a lot of time with your best friend has made me see that I was wrong. And I'd been holding onto some other emotional baggage that I've managed to cut loose. Now that I've done that, I'm clear and free to love Rosie, and I promise I'll do that with all of my heart and soul." She wrapped her arm around Rosie's waist and stared into her eyes. "And if you ever think I'm not doing it right, you can kick my ass."

"What's that?" Gabe came up behind Lori and wrapped her arms around her. "Are you threatening to beat up my best friend, beautiful?"

Lori turned around in Gabe's embrace and kissed her. "I'm afraid it's more of a promise than a threat. Why? Are you thinking of standing in my way?"

Shay grinned at the size and height difference between Gabe and her firecracker girlfriend, even though Lori wore three-inch heels.

"I don't think you've got anything to worry about," Gabe said. "I've never seen Shay like this before, and I've seen her—"

"You can stop there," Shay said, fearing Gabe might put a number to the women Gabe had seen her with.

Rosie looked at Gabe. "You knew?"

"She knew before I did." Shay hugged Rosie tight to her hip. "Apparently, twenty years of friendship means she knows me better than I know myself."

Lori turned back around and smiled at Rosie. "Best friends are worth more than all the gold in the world."

Shay noticed RB and Woody hovering a few feet away and beckoned them over.

"Congratulations," Woody said. "Now that you're off the market, me and RB won't strike out as much."

Shay laughed. "I don't think the two are related, but if that's what you want to believe, go ahead." She looked around the room for the last member of their group. "Where's Solo?"

"This was her first real event without Janie by her side." RB shook her head. "She couldn't handle it, so we put her in an Uber and sent her home before she did anything stupid."

Shay looked at Gabe. "Do we need to do anything about this?"

"I don't think there's anything we can do yet," Gabe said. "They're still living together, and they're getting counseling, so they're trying to figure it out. All we can do is support her and make sure she doesn't go off the rails."

"Is Janie still seeing her co-worker?" Rosie asked.

Gabe shook her head. "Apparently, she was never seeing him. They had a few drinks together, but Janie swears up and down that nothing happened and there were no feelings on either side. When Janie told Solo they were talking, that's exactly what she meant. Just talking, like friends."

"I don't get it," Rosie said. "If Janie isn't cheating on her, what's the problem between them?"

Shay gave a humorless laugh. "That's what Solo is trying to figure out, and it's driving her to distraction."

"Forget that right now," Gabe said. "Let's celebrate you two lovebirds."

Lori nudged Gabe. "And pay our respects... It's a wake, remember?"

Rosie shook her head. "I think I've done everything I can for my mom."

"In that case," Lori said, "when are we going on our first double date?"

Rosie waved the question away. "No need to rush anything."

The group headed to the tables where the food was laid out, and Shay tugged Rosie back gently. "I'm here for it all, you know?"

Rosie frowned. "What do you mean?"

She motioned to Lori as she walked away. "The way you brushed Lori off about the double date. You sounded worried."

Rosie smiled and shook her head. "I'm not worried. I was just thinking that since I'm supposed to be teaching you how to be my girlfriend, maybe we should slow down and take a few steps back before we talk *double* dates."

Shay frowned and guided Rosie back against the wall and out of sight. "Isn't it a bit late for that?" She pulled Rosie in closer and nibbled the skin along her neck. "I thought you were all about moving into your new future?"

Rosie moaned lightly. "I am, but a girl likes to be properly wooed, you know? If you're going to be my *actual* Princess Charming, I'll need a first date."

Shay moved up and kissed Rosie's jawline. "I can do that. I'd love to take you out. Would you like me to choose what we do and when we go?"

Rosie sighed deeply. "Yes. I love surprises."

Shay had never been a big fan of them but falling in love with Rosie had been the biggest surprise of all *and* probably the best thing that had ever happened to her. She'd always been a good student; she'd take on board all of Rosie's teachings to become the very best partner Rosie deserved, *and* she'd deliver the most original first date of all time.

Chapter Twenty-Seven

ROSIE OPENED THE DOOR to a bouquet of red tulips so large that she couldn't see Shay holding them.

"They're from Red at the Flower Loft." Shay peeked around the side. "She said I should be bringing you red roses for a first date, but since I already know your favorite flower..." She offered them to Rosie.

"They're absolutely beautiful. Thank you." She turned from the door to put the bouquet in the kitchen, but Shay didn't follow. "Are you coming?"

"I was waiting to be invited inside."

Rosie wrinkled her nose before she realized Shay was doing as she'd suggested and treating this as a real first date. "Please come in." She pulled a vase from a cupboard and half filled it with water. When she placed the flowers inside, she noticed a single orange tulip nestled in the center of the red ones.

"That one's from my momma," Shay said. "She would've loved you, especially because you opened my heart again."

A bubble of emotion rose from her chest and emerged as a gasp.

"Are you okay?" Shay asked, reaching out.

Rosie nodded and pushed away the intrusive comparison to her own mom. She definitely didn't want to think about her right now. "It's just the way you talk about your mom; I wish I could've met her."

Shay placed her hand over Rosie's. "Me too."

"Do you think I'll get to meet your dad?"

"Hey now, that's at least fifteen to twenty dates down the road, princess. Don't rush this," Shay said and winked. "So are you ready to go?"

"Yeah. And this is really what you want me to wear?" Rosie motioned at her *very* casual outfit of jeans, sneakers, and sweater.

"You look perfect. Shall we?"

Rosie took Shay's hand, and they went downstairs to her car. "You're still not going to give me any clues about where we're going?" she asked when Shay had been driving a few minutes.

"I thought you liked surprises?"

"I usually do."

Shay glanced at her briefly. "Do you trust me?"

"Of course."

"Then relax and enjoy the ride."

Along the route, Shay updated Rosie on her dad's condition. He was back home after making a faster than expected recovery, and the rest of the family were pitching in with caring for him.

"Aaron's cracking the whip," Shay said. "Even Matthew's spending time with him, although that's ended up with Daddy being addicted to Candy Crush. Now they've both got their phones surgically attached to their hands. Has Janie made any progress with your mom's debt?"

Rosie huffed. "God, I hope so. She's getting the details of the whole application process so I can match the same times to my schedule and show I was nowhere near Lancaster. It looks like the ID used was fake too, and they've got CCTV in the bank. It shouldn't take long to prove I had nothing to do with it." That didn't stop the anchor of anxiety weighing heavy in her gut at the thought of all that money they were trying to get her to pay back.

"Yeah, but you don't need that extra worry, do you?"

"Definitely not." She squeezed Shay's arm, grateful for her understanding.

Shay took the freeway toward Chicago, which didn't give Rosie any clue as to where they were headed. They fell into general conversation, mostly about their mutual desire to see America's first Black female president elected in a couple of months. Time slipped past along with the miles until Shay pulled into a parking lot outside a small brick building Rosie thought she recognized but couldn't recall why. A giant freedom flag hung in the second-floor window.

"What is this place?" Rosie asked as she stepped onto the gravel, thankful she was in sneakers and not nice heels that would instantly be scratched up and ruined.

"You'll see." Shay took her hand and led her inside.

The double doors opened into a corridor, and while Shay signed them in at the reception desk, Rosie took the opportunity to investigate. A nearby table was filled with stacks of leaflets on every kind of neglect and abuse, all manner of STDs, and details of nearby health clinics offering free services. The rainbow theme continued, along with pamphlets on counseling and gender reassignment. It was all worthy work, but Rosie was struggling to see how it was first-date location material. A sign on the wall pointed to accommodation, and several signs pointing to the right indicated the canteen, break room, library, and offices. On the back wall, a brightly colored sign in graffiti-style said, "Homeless, not hopeless."

Shay put her hand on the small of Rosie's back. "This way."

"Kudos for originality," Rosie said. "I've never gone on a date to a homeless shelter before."

Shay smiled. "I hear the food at this restaurant is Michelin-worthy."

She opened a door that led into a large gymnasium-type room crammed full of tables, which in turn, were overflowing with kids who seemed to range from about thirteen to early twenties.

"Kitchen's open," someone yelled from the far end of the room.

The voice sounded familiar, but Rosie couldn't place it.

"Let's meet the chef." Shay guided her away from the melee the announcement had incited and headed toward the kitchen area.

"Jackie?" Rosie focused harder on the woman behind the counter, serving food to the huge line of kids gathering for dinner.

She looked at Shay. "What's going on?"

"Change," Shay said as if that explained everything.

Rosie stopped walking. "That's one of my ex-clients."

"I know."

Rosie frowned, trying not to jump to erroneous conclusions and panic. "How and *why* do you know that?"

"I asked Lori if she knew of any of your old clients that you felt hadn't made progress after working with you. She said you never mentioned names, and the only one of your clients she was aware of was someone whom she'd referred: one of her ex-wife's colleagues called Jackie." Shay nodded toward the kitchen. "I did a little digging with Woody, connected the dots, and that led us to Jackie Dunn, ex-lawyer and now Senior Director of Development here at Alphabet House." Shay pulled Rosie close. "You were worried your work wasn't making a difference...but it did. I've talked to Jackie, and she couldn't sing your praises enough. *You're* the one who put her on this path, Rosie. And now she's helping hundreds of LGBTQ homeless kids."

Rosie leaned heavily on Shay, overcome with the whole situation. "But—"

"Your ethics are safe," Shay said. "I did all of this, and it was Jackie who said that she'd love to see you again when I mentioned that I knew you." She placed her finger over her lips when Rosie opened her mouth to protest. "I know it's a bit of a gray area, but Jackie has no idea why I sought her out. She thinks it's all a cosmic coincidence. But I wanted you to see that what you were doing, the thing that you loved so much, was really helping people."

Rosie didn't know how to respond. All manner of emotions overwhelmed her and battled to be voiced, but beyond the questionable ethics was a beautifully thoughtful idea. She tugged at Shay's arm and began to back out of the room, hoping that Jackie would remain too busy to notice her. When they got back into reception, Rosie threw her arms around Shay and hugged her tight. "Thank you."

Shay looked confused. "You don't want to say hi?"

Rosie shook her head. "I don't need to. It's enough to know that she's on a different path and that she's attributed it to my intervention."

"Okay, I think I get it."

Rosie pressed her forehead to Shay's and exhaled deeply. "Thank you for understanding me. Thank you for this."

When Shay had signed them out again, she took Rosie's hand, and they headed back to the car. "I have a back-up plan."

"You do?" Rosie arched her eyebrow. "Impressive." She peered over Shay's shoulder as she opened the trunk of her car and smiled when she saw a picnic basket.

"We can head to Solo's boat and have dinner on the lake at sunset."

"That sounds wonderful." Rosie pressed her body to Shay's and pushed her against the car. She ran her finger along Shay's jaw and kissed her hard.

"I thought you wanted to take it slow," Shay said when Rosie allowed her to come up for air.

Rosie gave her a wicked smile. "What? You never kissed someone on a first date?"

"I've never *had* a first date."

"You're relying on me to teach you all about them, remember?" She captured Shay's bottom lip between hers and sucked it into her mouth before she kissed her deeper, a kiss that stripped away the last vestiges of her desire to take it slow.

"I remember," Shay said, breathless from their kiss. "But I'm getting the feeling that you're making it up as you go along."

"Isn't that what life's all about?" Rosie kissed the end of Shay's nose and smiled, her heart full of love and longing, of excitement and anticipation for all that lay ahead of them. What had started as friends with benefits had blossomed into a romance Rosie had never imagined possible. Shay was the Princess Charming she could never have dreamed of, scooping Rosie up onto her black horse and riding off into an unwritten future of passion and promise.

~ THE END ~

AUTHOR'S NOTE

Thank you for reading *Unwritten*. If you enjoyed Shay and Rosie's one night-to-forever romance, it would be amazing if you could pop a review on Amazon for me! And if you haven't read any of my other books, maybe you'd like to try my number one US bestseller, *Stunted Heart*?

Unwritten is the second in the Windy City Romance series. If you're eager to find out who might get their own happily ever after in book three, copy this link into your browser (BookFunnel will take you to a mini eBook of chapter one of book three):

https://bit.ly/WCR3

www.helenaharte.com
Follow me on Instagram, TikTok,
and Facebook at AuthorHelenaHarte

Other Great Butterworth Books

Sanctuary by Helena Harte
Passions ignite and possibilities unfold. Welcome to the Windy City Romance series.
Available from Amazon (ASIN B0D4B42RRW)

Heart of the Storm by Ally McGuire
Sometimes a storm is just what you need to clear the skies ahead.
Available on Amazon (ASIN B0CYTSQXWW)

The Promise by Addison M Conley
When the world keeps pulling you under, who do you reach for?
Available on Amazon (ASIN B0DDY9FH6Z)

Back to Back by Jo Fletcher
."When Fred and Ruby's worlds collide, can love rise from the rubble?"
Available on Amazon (ASIN B0D6M499K2)

Brave Enough to Love by Valden Bush
In a dance between truth and sacrifice, can they rewrite the rules of love?
Available on Amazon (ASIN B0CQP8PMVB)

Dead Ringer by Robyn Nyx
Three bodies. One killer. No motive?
Available on Amazon (ASIN B0CPQ8HFK7)

Medea by JJ Taylor
Who will Medea become in her battle for freedom?
Available from Amazon (ASIN B0CK2FB7GW)

Virgin Flight by E.V. Bancroft
In the battle between duty and desire, can love win?
Available from Amazon (ASIN B0CKJWQZ45)

Fragments of the Heart by Ally McGuire
Love can be the greatest expedition of all.
Available on Amazon (ASIN B0CHBPHR6M)

Stunted Heart by Helena Harte
A stunt rider who lives in the fast lane. An ER doctor who can't take chances. A passion that could turn their worlds upside down.
Available on Amazon (ASIN B0C78GSWBV)

Here You Are by Jo Fletcher
.Can they unlock their hearts to find the true happiness they both deserve?
Available on Amazon (ASIN B0CBN935ZB)

Dark Haven by Brey Willows
Even vampires get tired of playing with their food...
Available on Amazon (ASIN B0C5P1HJXC)

Green for Love by E.V. Bancroft
All's fair in love and eco-war.
Available from Amazon (ASIN B0C28F7PX5)

Call of Love by Lee Haven
Separated by fear. Reunited by fate. Will they get a second chance at life and love?
Available from Amazon (ASIN B0BYC83HZD)

Where the Heart Leads by Ally McGuire
A writer. A celebrity. And a secret that could break their hearts.
Available on Amazon (ASIN B0BWFX5W9L)

Stolen Ambition by Robyn Nyx
Daughters of two worlds collide in a dangerous game of ambition and love.
Available on Amazon (ASIN B0BS1PRSCN)

Cabin Fever by Addison M Conley
She goes for the money, but will she stay for something deeper?
Available on Amazon (ASIN B0BQWY45GH)

Breakout for Love by Valden Bush
They're both running from their pasts. Together, they might make a new future.
Available from Amazon (ASIN B0CWHZ4SXL)

Warm Pearls and Paper Cranes by E.V. Bancroft
A family torn apart by secrets. The only way forward is love.
Available from Amazon (ASIN B09DTBCQ92)

Judge Me, Judge Me Not by James Merrick
One man's battle against the world and himself to find it's never too late to find, and use, your voice.
Available from Amazon (ASIN B09CLK91N5)

Scripted Love by Helena Harte
What good is a romance writer who doesn't believe in happy ever after?
Available on Amazon (ASIN B0993QFLNN)

Call to Me by Helena Harte
Sometimes the call you least expect is the one you need the most.
Available on Amazon (ASIN B08D9SR15H)

What's Your Story?

Global Wordsmiths, CIC, provides an all-encompassing service for all writers, ranging from basic proofreading and cover design to development editing, typesetting, and eBook services. A major part of our work is charity and community focused, delivering writing projects to under-served and under-represented groups across Nottinghamshire, giving voice to the voiceless and visibility to the unseen.

To learn more about what we offer, visit: www.globalwords.co.uk

A selection of books by Global Words Press:
Desire, Love, Identity: with the National Justice Museum
Aventuras en México: Farmilo Primary School
Times Past: with The Workhouse, National Trust
Young at Heart with AGE UK
In Different Shoes: Stories of Trans Lives

Self-published authors working with Global Wordsmiths:
Steve Bailey
Ravenna Castle
Jackie D
CJ DeBarra
Dee Griffiths
Iona Kane
Maggie McIntyre
Emma Nichols
Dani Lovelady Ryan
Erin Zak